FESTIVAL IN PRIOR'S FORD

Evelyn Hood

This first world edition published 2013
in Great Britain and 2014 in the USA by
SEVERN HOUSE PUBLISHERS LTD of
19 Cedar Road, Sutton, Surrey, England, SM2 5DA.
Trade paperback edition first published
in Great Britain and the USA 2014 by
SEVERN HOUSE PUBLISHERS LTD.

British Library Cataloguing in Publication Data

Hood, Evelyn author.
  Festival in Prior's Ford. – (Prior's Ford series; 7)
  1. Prior's Ford (Scotland : Imaginary place)–Fiction.
  2. Villages–Scotland–Dumfries and Galloway–Fiction.
  I. Title II. Series
  823.9'14-dc23

ISBN-13: 978-0-7278-8352-0 (cased)
ISBN-13: 978-1-84751-500-1 (trade paper)

All Severn House titles are printed on acid-free paper.

Severn House Publishers support the Forest Stewardship Council™ [FSC™],
the leading international forest certification organisation. All our titles that
are printed on FSC certified paper carry the FSC logo.

Typeset by Palimpsest Book Production Ltd.,
Falkirk, Stirlingshire, Scotland.
Printed and bound in Great Britain by
TJ International, Padstow, Cornwall.

This book is dedicated to my dear friend
Aileen Cowie, who is always there for me, no matter
what the problem may be. With thanks,
gratitude, and as always, love.

Acknowledgements

My thanks to all those friends who shared their specialized knowledge during the writing of the Prior's Ford books, particularly Charlotte Peck, landscape architect, who has provided invaluable advice on the restoration of the Linn Hall gardens, and Pat Elliott of The Borders Design House, Auchencrow, Berkshire, who helped with the planned Linn Hall renovation.

My special thanks to my agent, Vivien Green, for her constant encouragement and her faith in me as a writer. I couldn't have done it without you, Vivien!

Main Character List
for *Festival in Prior's Ford*

Hector and Fliss Ralston-Kerr – live with their son **Lewis** in the kitchen quarters of the manor house, Linn Hall, and are struggling to restore the neglected house and estate. Lewis has a small daughter, **Rowena Chloe**, from his former engagement to **Molly Ewing**. **Molly** is now living in Portugal with her new partner, and **Lewis** is locked in a struggle to bring **Rowena Chloe** to live at Linn Hall.

Genevieve (Ginny) Whitelaw – came to Linn Hall as a gardener and is responsible for a lot of the estate's restoration. She is now engaged to **Lewis Ralston-Kerr.** Ginny's mother, well-known actress **Meredith Whitelaw**, looks on Ginny as a disappointment but still feels the need to meddle in Ginny's life.

Jinty McDonald – lives in the village with her husband **Tom** and their large family. She helps out at Linn Hall and also cleans the Village Hall and the local primary school to earn much-needed money as her husband spends most of his spare time in the local pub.

Naomi Hennessey – the local Church of Scotland minister, half Jamaican, half English.

Clarissa Ramsay – A retired schoolteacher living in Willow Cottage with her partner **Alastair Marshall**, an artist some twenty years younger than she is. Although Clarissa is very happy, she finds it difficult to cope with their age difference.

Jess and Ewan McNair of Tarbethill Farm – are working hard to bring the farm, which has been in the family for several generations, into the twenty-first century with the help of **Ewan**'s new wife **Alison**, daughter of **Joe and Gracie Fisher**, the landlord and landlady of the local pub, the Neurotic Cuckoo. **Alison**'s son **Jamie** by an earlier marriage loves living on the farm and intends to become a farmer when he grows up.

Helen Campbell – lives in the village with her husband **Duncan**, the head gardener for the Linn Hall estate, and their four children. She writes the village news column for the local paper, but only her close friends know that she also writes the paper's Agony Aunt page. Helen's ambition is to become a published fiction writer; in the meantime she earns some much-needed money by typing out work for other people.

Stella Hesslett – A librarian who lives in the village and drives the mobile library that visits the village regularly. Mid-forties, single, and shy.

Malcolm Finlay – an amiable academic who recently retired to Prior's Ford and lives in Thatcher's Cottage. A quiet man, he writes articles for academic publications.

Amy Rose – A friend of **Clarissa Ramsay**'s, Amy lives in America and frequently visits Prior's Ford. She has an inquisitive mind and loves solving problems.

The Almshouses – a row of six old cottages originally built to house impoverished elderly members of the village. Now renamed Jasmine Row, they are home to **Robert and Cissie Kavanagh, Dolly and Harold Cowan, Hannah Gibbs, Muriel Jacobsen, Charlie Crandall** and the latest residents, **Tricia and Derek Borland and their baby daughter**.

One

After more than a hundred years it had happened. The Prior's Ford almshouses, originally built for elderly, destitute villagers living on charity, had its very own baby.

To be exact, the infant belonged to Tricia Borland, daughter of the local garage owner, and her husband Derek, who worked in his father's butcher's shop in the village's main street, but as far as the other inhabitants of the old building, now modernized into six neat terraced houses and renamed Jasmine Row, were concerned, the baby, as the first infant ever to live in the row, was now its most important resident.

On the day Tricia and the new arrival were due to come home from the hospital every woman living in the row kept glancing from her living room window, and the moment Derek's little car drew up before the end house doors flew open and Cissie Kavanagh, Dolly Cowan, Hannah Gibbs and Muriel Jacobsen appeared just as the new father, his round, honest face wearing a watermelon grin, opened a rear passenger door and helped his wife from the car, handling her as though she were made of porcelain.

'Ooohh, it's good to be home,' Tricia said as the welcoming committee swooped down on her.

'So – where's the baby? We're dying to see her!' Dolly's blonde curls were bouncing with excitement.

'In her carrycot.' Derek went to the front passenger door.

'Glad it's all over, Tricia?' Cissie Kavanagh asked.

'You can say that again! I can't wait to get back into a pretty frock with a nice wide belt!' Although Tricia was quite a sturdy girl she loved to wear tight belts to emphasize her curves.

'Here we are.' Derek lifted the carrycot from the car and the women clustered around, cooing over the tiny sleeping face on the pillow.

'She's lovely!' Dolly drew the blanket back carefully to expose a minute curled fist by the baby's head. 'What are you going to call her?'

'We haven't decided yet. We never realized,' Tricia told her audience, 'what a responsibility it is, having to find a name that she's going to be stuck with all her life.'

'You've got a couple of weeks yet before you need to make a decision,' Cissie pointed out.

'I could just snatch her up and take her off home with me.' Dolly said yearningly.

'You can if you want to,' the new mother said at once. 'I'm dying for a sit-down and a decent cup of tea – that maternity hospital doesn't know how to make a proper cup of tea. We stopped off at my mum and dad's on the way back and Derek's folks were there too, so they all had a cuddle before she got fed and changed. She'll sleep for a while and I wouldn't mind a bit of peace and quiet.'

'Are you sure?' Hannah asked doubtfully.

'Yes, *are* you, love?' the new father wanted to know.

'Goodness, Derek, now she's arrived we're going to have her around until she's grown up. Right now I'd love a cup of tea and a nice quiet ten minutes to myself,' the new mother retorted. 'Surely that's not asking too much after what I've been through?'

'I tell you what –' Cissie took the carrycot from Derek – 'why don't we all take her into my house so that Tricia can have time to settle back home?'

'You'll let us know if she wakes?' Derek asked anxiously.

'Of course they will.' Tricia headed for her own front door. 'Come on, Derek, I'm parched!'

'I've never had children,' Hannah murmured to Muriel Jacobsen as the others followed Cissie, 'but I can't help feeling that if I had, I'd not be so keen to hand my newborn over to neighbours so quickly.'

'To be fair to Tricia, she's only been a mother for a week and she knows that the little one's safe with us. She'll settle down once she gets into the feeding and changing routine,' Muriel assured her neighbour. But as they followed the others into the Kavanagh's house she couldn't help recalling that Tricia was a bit of a social butterfly, and wondering how long it would take for the girl to realize just how demanding motherhood could be.

'These are being returned and these are coming out – and can I stamp that book out again?' Clarissa Ramsay wanted to know as she deposited an armful of books on the counter of the mobile library. 'It's taking a bit of reading but I think I could finish it if I had one more week.'

Stella Hesslett pushed her glasses further up her nose with one finger and consulted her computer. 'That's all right, Mrs Ramsay, nobody else is looking for it at the moment. I read it when it first came out and I enjoyed it very much.'

'I'm enjoying it too. It's the type of book that keeps you wanting to know what happens next, while at the same time you want to take it slowly and savour every scene.'

'Exactly.' Stella tapped busily at the computer keys before putting the pile of returned books below the counter and pushing the other pile towards Clarissa, who began to transfer them to her basket. 'Have you heard from Amy recently?'

'As it happens, she phoned yesterday – she sends her regards to you, and says that she hopes to visit us some time this year.'

Stella beamed. 'That would be lovely, something to look forward to.'

'You've gone very quiet.' Lewis Ralston-Kerr shot a swift sideways glance at his fiancée as his ancient van rattled noisily along the country road. 'I thought you were looking forward to showing off this terrific new project you've taken on for Fergus.'

'I've been looking forward to it for ages,' Ginny Whitelaw agreed, then added wistfully, 'and I still would be if it wasn't for my mother.'

'If I'd known what the postman was bringing you this morning I'd have robbed him on his way up the drive – or insisted on us leaving before he arrived.'

'I wish we had.' Ginny's voice was gloomy. 'I've been looking forward to this for weeks.'

'Me too – just the two of us, alone together for a whole day!'

Ginny nodded. 'And I've been longing to show you Fergus's lovely new house – and to get your input on the ideas I have for the garden. I wish we *had* left before the postman arrived – and I wish I'd been born an orphan!'

'I'm not sure that that's possible, my love. Even an orphan has to have a mother and father at some stage.'

'I wouldn't mind having an ordinary mother, the kind that

other people have. An easy-going mum who'd let me have the quiet wedding I want. Why did I get lumbered with a publicity-mad actress instead?'

Lewis took a hand from the steering wheel in order to give her a soothing pat on the knee. The two of them had been looking forward happily to their outing – until the postman delivered a parcel from Meredith Whitelaw, at present filming a popular television series in Spain. The parcel turned out to contain a bundle of bridal catalogues, together with a letter giving Ginny the name and telephone number of an upmarket wedding planner.

'A very successful woman, darling,' Meredith's swirling hand-writing had said – 'she's worked with some very well-known brides, including royalty. You have to phone her right away because she's in great demand.'

'Ginny, stop worrying. I give you my word that when we get around to planning our wedding we're going to do it our way, not your mother's.'

'You make it sound so easy, and it never is with her. Imagine me of all people having a wedding planner,' Ginny groaned.

'That was definitely a step too far. When we get back to Linn Hall we're going to return the catalogues, tell this wedding planner that her services aren't needed, and I'm going to phone Meredith and tell her that we'll have the wedding we both want when it suits us, not her.'

'Perhaps we should get married while she's still filming in Spain,' Ginny suggested, brightening slightly. 'She won't be free to come back to the UK until the end of June. We could get married before then, couldn't we?'

'If I'd my way we'd be married today, but sadly, it's just not possible because we've both got fairly hefty commitments to deal with this year. I want to try for a loan that'll enable us to start renovating Linn Hall's ground floor rooms – it would be great to be able to hold the wedding reception there. And we've already decided that the estate's going to be opened to the public from May this year instead of waiting until June. Duncan and I will have to take full responsibility for the preparations because this new job you've taken on will keep you busy from now until next year.'

Ginny peered through the windscreen. 'I think we take the

next turning on the left. You're absolutely right about not having time to get married soon, but knowing my mother, she'll not give up on the idea of a big social wedding when we finally get around to it. I've been a disappointment to her all my life and I know she'll expect me to make up for it now. I can see the headlines she's thinking up – "Actress Meredith Whitelaw attends her only daughter's wedding." She's probably offering the exclusive rights to *OK Magazine* as we speak.'

'You're not serious!'

'Unfortunately, I am.'

'What about your father? Couldn't he get her to stop interfering?'

Ginny gave a short, mirthless laugh. 'No chance! My father fled to Australia when I was small because he couldn't take any more of my mother's bossiness. To be truthful, he didn't exactly flee there because of her; he was offered a part in an Australian film and decided not to come back. He couldn't stand up to her then and I doubt if he can now.'

'Should we invite him to the wedding?'

'We can send an invitation, but he's well settled with his new family and since he's not set foot in the UK since I was six, I doubt if he'll accept.'

'Third turning on the left coming up.' Lewis turned the van into the side road. 'Are you sure this is the right way? It's more of a lane than a road.'

'It's a private road with a dead end, and the house Fergus bought is the only one on it.'

'There's Rowena Chloe to think of, too. I want to see her living in Linn Hall with us by August, in time for the new school year,' Lewis said, then added, 'I wish I hadn't just listed all the things that have to be done within the next seven months because it doesn't really seem possible, does it?'

'Of course it's possible – it has to be! Just think of how much has been done to the Linn Hall grounds in the last few years. If we can achieve that we can achieve anything!'

'Just keep on telling me that.'

'I intend to. Look, there's the house!' Ginny felt a thrill of excitement at the sight of the roof and chimney stacks rising above an unkempt hedge. 'It faces the Solway Firth and the only entrance is at the back. There it is – that break in the hedge. Slow down or you'll miss it.'

'It doesn't look all that special,' Lewis commented as he eased the van into a cobbled courtyard.

'That's what I love about it. This is the back of the house – the front overlooks the garden and the firth, and it's got quite a lot of potential inside. But the garden's very special – it takes up the whole length of the access road, though you don't realize that because of the high hedge. That's going to be lowered once the garden's been restored.' Ginny opened the passenger door. 'Come on – I'm longing to show it to you!'

She scrambled out and had disappeared round the side of the empty house before Lewis left the van.

'Good grief,' he said when he caught up with her. 'Now I can see what you're so excited about!'

The two-storey house was stone-built, with double glass-panelled interior doors opening into a generous porch which opened in turn on to a paved patio. From there, the garden sloped down towards the shore of the Solway Firth, permitting a magnificent clear view of the firth to anyone looking out of the house windows or sitting on the patio. Three wide steps led down to a half-moon-shaped, overgrown lawn edged with shrubbery badly in need of pruning.

'As I said, the garden stretches from one end of the private road to the other.' Ginny spread her arms wide. 'And the house sits approximately in the middle. Isn't that a breathtaking view?'

Lewis nodded. Even on this chilly February day the Solway Firth, spread before them, looked quite breathtaking.

'Imagine waking every morning to a view like that! I want the garden to be filled with colour throughout the four seasons, so that it always looks good to anyone sailing by.' Ginny dug into the rucksack she had brought from the van and pulled out a smaller bag. 'Tape recorder, camera, measuring tape, notebook and coloured pencils,' she told Lewis, dropping the rucksack on to the patio and starting down the steps and across the shaggy lawn. 'Apparently the previous owners preferred lots of greenery. I can envisage this garden divided into small sections, each leading into other areas. That way, anyone exploring it will be moving from one area to another – hopefully, a garden of hidden delights!'

As they were leaving the lawn, Lewis reached an arm to sweep some low branches out of their way and the two of them were showered with icy droplets from the previous night's rain. 'You've got a heck of a lot of pruning to do,' he observed.

Ginny pulled the hood of her anorak over her short dark hair. 'I know,' she said happily, 'what a magnificent challenge!'

An hour later, during which they took a lot of photographs and Ginny made a lot of notes, they returned to the house. Ginny had a key, and when they had explored the place they settled in the living room, with its view of the firth, to enjoy the sandwiches and coffee they had brought with them.

'There's going to be a massive amount of work ahead of you, Ginny.'

'I know, but as the designer I don't have to do it on my own. Fergus is putting together a team of experienced gardeners to work with me once I've planned the layout and decided exactly what will be happening during each of the four seasons. When he's approved of my ideas, they'll start work.'

'Lucky Fergus, with no money worries to get in his way,' Lewis said, and then wished he had had the sense to guard his tongue. He was pleased for Ginny, and proud that his fiancée had been asked to take on such a prestigious task, but he would have been happier if the television director she was going to work with was middle-aged, less attractive than Fergus, and happily married.

'I've only got a month at the most to plan the entire layout,' Ginny prattled on, 'I'm hoping that you'll help me because the work must start by March at the latest.'

'Of course I will, any way I can.'

'I'm really looking forward to being involved in some good hard work.'

'That goes without saying – remember when you were restoring the lake with only young Jimmy McDonald to help you? You spent most of your time covered with mud from head to toe.'

'I loved that job!'

'I know you did. You could never be the sort of television presenter that poses prettily with a spade and then steps aside to let someone else do the digging.'

'Oh, Lewis—' Ginny laid down her half-eaten sandwich and stared at him, her happiness suddenly disappearing.

'What's the matter?'

'Me, working in front of television cameras!' Her blue eyes, sparkling a moment before, were suddenly wide with fear. 'What if I make a mess of it?'

'You won't make a mess of it. We've already been through this, darling. You said yourself that when Fergus filmed you showing him round the Linn Hall estate you forgot all about the camera. The same thing will happen again – once you get into that garden with a spade or a trowel or a pair of secateurs in your hand you'll focus totally on work. You always do.'

'But what if—'

'No what ifs.' Lewis screwed the lid back on to the empty Thermos flask. 'Let's have one more look at the garden to make sure we haven't missed anything, then on the way back to Linn Hall we'll stop off at a decent restaurant. I'm still hungry!'

'We're not far from Prior's Ford,' Ginny said later when the waitress had taken their orders. 'We could easily have waited until we got back to Linn Hall.'

'I know, but I don't often get you to myself at home.' Lewis reached across the table to take her hand. 'It's been good today, just being us with nobody else around.'

'I've been thinking that too.' She curled her fingers around his, smiling at him.

'That house is going to look great when it's smartened up and properly furnished. Is Fergus planning to move in once the filming's over?'

'I don't know – he may have bought it just so that he could film the garden restoration.'

'If so he'll make a good profit when he sells. I really like it – it would make a perfect home for us, and Rowena Chloe would love the kind of garden you're planning.'

'We can never live here – you're forgetting that one day you'll inherit Linn Hall.'

'I know, but seeing that little place, just the right size for a family . . .' he said almost wistfully.

'We're going to turn Linn Hall into the lovely home it used to be and I'm looking forward to living in it.'

'So am I, now that I know you'll always be there with me.

You know that you don't have to wait until we're married before moving in, don't you?'

'I'm quite happy to stay in my camper van until after the wedding, thank you.'

'You're very old-fashioned!'

'I was born that way.' Ginny released his hand as the waitress arrived with their food.

Two

'It's going to be quite a year,' Lewis said as they left the restaurant and got into the van. 'You're nervous about appearing before the television cameras, and I'm worried in case Molly refuses to let Rowena Chloe come to live with us.'

Almost six years earlier he had fallen in love with red-headed Molly Ewing, one of the many young backpackers who helped out on the Linn Hall estate every summer in return for bed and board. For a while they were engaged to be married, but soon after giving birth to their daughter, Molly tired of the prospect of one day becoming the mistress of Linn Hall and returned to her real love – travelling and having fun.

She was currently living in Portugal with a former high school sweetheart, while Rowena Chloe lived with her maternal grandparents in Inverness and spent the summers at Linn Hall. Lewis adored his little daughter and his dearest wish was to see her living with him in Prior's Ford.

'It's not as though she lives with her mother – surely that gives you a good chance of winning your claim,' Ginny said now. 'And you're willing to agree to Rowena Chloe spending time with her grandparents, and with her mother.' Not that Molly had shown any sign of wanting her daughter to spend a lot of time with her, she thought, but was sensible enough to refrain from saying so.

'I know, but I daren't be too hopeful of getting what I want until it actually happens.'

'You can only do your best, Lewis, and everyone we know is sending good vibes your way – especially me.'

'I'm so lucky to have you in my life. Why didn't I realize years ago that you were the only woman for me?'

'To be honest,' Ginny said, 'I'd been trying to tell you that for ages.'

A lot of changes had been made at Tarbethill Farm. After Bert McNair's death his son Ewan had taken over the dairy farm, but found it impossible, in changing times, to make it profitable. Finally, acting reluctantly on the new business plan drawn up by Alison Greenlees, he sold the dairy herd and became a sheep farmer, renting out some of his fields to neighbouring farmers and turning two fields flanking the farm lane into allotments – a move popular with the villagers.

He and Alison were now married and Ewan was stepfather to her son Jamie. With the dairy herd gone, the large milking shed had lain empty until Naomi Hennessey, the Church of Scotland minister, heard of a Polish glass-blower in search of a workshop in a rural area.

'He's in Nottingham at the moment with his young daughter, but he'd like to move to a rural area, preferably one with the potential for sales. My friend thought that Dumfries and Galloway could be the ideal answer – villages, countryside and lots of summer visitors and shops like Anja's. I immediately thought of your milking shed – or have you already got plans for it?'

'Not so far, but we should do something with the building.'

'There's another thing,' Naomi ventured. 'This glass-blower needs accommodation, and apparently his daughter has her own horse. You have a cottage on the farm lane, and you could probably find a small field for the horse.'

'We could,' Ewan said thoughtfully. 'If this man's interested in Prior's Ford, he's certainly welcome to come and have a look at the farm.'

Stefan Krechevsky, a tall, broad-shouldered man with a warm smile and a shock of grey hair had arrived a few weeks later in an elderly jeep, and by the time he reached the farm he had fallen in love with Prior's Ford, having driven through the village first.

'You have such beautiful countryside,' he told Ewan and Alison. 'So peaceful. My daughter and I need to settle somewhere that makes us happy.' And when he saw the milking shed, his mind was made up. 'This would suit me very well, but I need only a quarter of the space. Would this be possible?'

'Ewan, we're planning to build a lambing shed in the spring, aren't we? Why don't we close off half of this shed for that purpose and divide the other half into two. That would give us a storage area and Mr Kor – Kre—'

'Stefan, please,' the man smiled at Alison. 'The area you mention would be ideal for me, if it is agreeable with yourselves.'

Ewan moved to the centre of the shed and looked around slowly, trying to imagine the size each quarter would be. 'I think that would work,' he nodded. 'It would provide plenty of space for lambing and another storage area would come in handy.'

'I will pay for the work on my area,' Stefan Krechevsky offered at once. 'I use furnaces and my workshop must be closed off properly to prevent accidents. I can send you a plan of what I need.'

'Ewan?' Alison looked at her husband.

'It sounds perfect all round.'

Stefan Krechevsky held out a big hand scarred by his work. 'Then we are agreed? I can rent from you part of this place, your empty cottage, and room for the horse that my daughter cannot live without?'

Ewan shook hands. 'Agreed. Come into the farmhouse and we'll sort things out.'

Jinty McDonald scurried up Linn Hall's long driveway, chin tucked down against her throat as she battled against the icy February wind lashing the shrubbery on either side. As she emerged from the drive to cross the open gravelled sweep before the big house the wind whirled around her and then eased slightly once she reached the side of the building. She lifted her chin and gulped in a breath of cold air before meeting another whirlwind once she got to the open courtyard at the back.

At last she reached the kitchen door, opened it with chilled fingers and gained the warmth of the big kitchen, shutting the door behind her with a huge sigh of relief.

'My, what a morning! That wind's comin' straight from the North Pole,' she said as soon as she had unwound the scarf wrapped about her mouth and nose. 'I'd to push against it all the way and once I got up the drive it did its best to stop me from reaching the door. Yes, Muffin, I know you're waiting for me to say hello,' she added as the big mongrel dog the Ralston-Kerrs had taken in after his elderly owner's death tugged gently at her skirt. She stooped down to hug him. 'You feel lovely and warm, you lucky dog.'

'Instead of staying out this morning for ages as he usually does, he bolted back indoors as quickly as he could. Jinty, you should have phoned us and stayed home.' Fliss Ralston-Kerr hurried to the big kettle that was always simmering on the stove. 'There's not all that much to do at this time of year, when the gardens are closed and there are no summer workers to see to. Cup of tea?'

'Och, I enjoy my mornings here – they get me out of the house.' Jinty shrugged her coat off. 'In any case, I wanted to share my good news with you. This is more of a cocoa day if you've got it, Mrs F.'

'Sit down by the fire while I'm making it. You must be frozen!'

'Actually, I'm not. It was worse on my face than on the rest of me. I was frozen through yesterday when I got home, and then I remembered last night that I'd bought a set of thermal undies at the sales after last winter and never needed them. So I dug them out this morning, still in the parcel. What a difference! I was warm from neck to boots on my way up the hill and I've got a lovely cosy glow around the Scilly Isles. You should get a set, Mrs F.'

'I did, the first winter after I got married, and I'm still using them. Here's your cocoa. What's this about good news?'

'I've been desperate to tell you – my Steph's gone and won a scholarship to RADA!'

'To where?'

'Wait a minute – I wrote it down.' Jinty dug into the pocket of her long cardigan and produced a piece of paper. 'It's the Royal Academy of Dramatic Art in Glasgow – and she's been accepted! She's going to be taught how to be an actress, Mrs F!'

'Oh my goodness. I'm so pleased for you, Jinty – and for Stephanie. How did that happen?'

'She's been working on it for ages without saying a word to

me or her dad until last night. She didn't want to tell us in case it didn't work. You know that she's been paying for acting lessons from someone in Kirkcudbright all the time she's been working as a nursery nurse, as well as being in the village drama club? Well,' she went on when Fliss nodded, 'her teacher said a while ago that she was ready to apply for auditions at RADA where *she'd* been a student years ago, and she wrote a letter recommending Steph. And when she heard that Steph had had lessons with Ginny's mum when she and Ginny came to the village, she got her to write to Mrs Whitelaw, with her being so well known. So she did, and she got a lovely letter back from her, saying how talented Steph is. That helped to get her the auditions – and she didn't even tell us, in case it all fell through. She's been to Glasgow three times, telling us she was visiting a girl she got to know when she was training to be a nursery nurse. Our Grant was the only one she told, and he said that with them being twins he should help, so he paid for her fares. And now she's in and she starts in August!' Jinty finally stopped to draw breath and drink her cocoa.

'Jinty, I'm so pleased for you, and for Stephanie. The twins have both done so well!' Fliss said warmly. Stephanie and Grant were the oldest of the large McDonald clan; Grant was now a star player with a professional football club, and Stephanie was a leading light in the local drama club. As her parents couldn't afford to send her to a drama college she had trained as a nursery nurse, her second ambition, in order to save enough money to follow her dream.

'Where's Ginny? I want her to thank her mother for that letter of support.'

'She'll be in later – she's working in the camper van on the plans for the garden she's going to create for that television man.'

'In that case –' Jinty drained her cup – 'let's you and me get started. I'm feeling so excited about Steph that I need to work some energy off.'

'I take it that we'll have our usual Scarecrow Week in the summer?' Muriel Jacobsen asked. The members of the Prior's Ford Progress Committee were gathered in the Church of Scotland manse, squeezed into the Reverend Naomi Hennessey's cluttered study.

'Is the festival worthwhile?' Pete McDermott wanted to know. 'The entries were down in number last year.'

'I'd hate to give up on it,' Naomi said. 'I love seeing all the different ideas people come up with. And it helps to bring in tourists.'

'That's why I'm asking if it's worthwhile. Fewer scarecrows mean fewer tourists.'

'If the number of entries is dropping, perhaps we should pep things up.' Lynn Stacey, the primary school's headmistress, had only recently joined the committee.

'Any ideas?'

'There must be lots of things we could do. My new teacher's keen on Scottish country dancing and she's offered to start an after-school class for the children. If they show enough enthusiasm and ability we could have a dance exhibition on the village green during Scarecrow Week. In fact,' Lynn swept on, warming to the new idea, 'now that the Linn Hall estate's been renovated and open to the public in the summer months, the children may be allowed to put on an exhibition of their dance skills there. That would leave the green available for other activities.'

'We could set up stalls on the green,' Muriel put in. 'The butcher could have one, and Colour Carousel – I'm sure that Anya would like to have a stall to show off the pretty things that she sells in the shop. And now that Alastair Marshall's come back to the village he could exhibit his paintings.'

'The local Women's Rural Institute would probably take a bakery stall as well as a craft stall,' Lynn added. 'And we could ask the Ralston-Kerrs if they'd agree to some sort of musical event. They've got such a lot of space on those lovely terraced lawns.'

'Are you getting all this, Helen?' Robert asked their secretary, who was scribbling frantically.

'I think so – musical event and school dance display in Linn Hall's gardens, stalls on the village green, scarecrows and food and craft stalls – it all sounds good. I'll start typing it up as soon as I get home. It might be an idea to pass copies to the Ralston-Kerrs and the WRI . . .'

'And the drama group and anyone else who may be able to help with suggestions,' Charlie put in. 'We've got a lot of enthu-siastic gardeners in the village and I've noticed visitors admiring their work – perhaps some of the locals would be interested in opening their gardens to the public.'

Naomi nodded. 'Gilbert MacBain for one; he's got the largest garden and he puts a lot of work into it.'

Helen glanced up from her notepad. 'He's got beehives too – I'm sure he'd be interested in selling honey on one of the stalls.'

'Well done, people – the ideas are coming thick and fast already. Don't you think that we should co-opt a representative from the WRI to help with the festival organization? They're a lively lot, and always so helpful, too.'

'If we're definitely going to have a summer festival merged with Scarecrow Week . . .?' Robert raised his brows at the group, and when everyone nodded, went on, 'Since we're unanimous, I agree that the WRI and drama group should be included. And the Ralston-Kerrs too, of course.'

'Could we make it a little later than usual?' Lynn asked. 'I noticed last year that quite a few local people missed Scarecrow Week because of July holidays – that may be the reason for fewer scarecrows.'

'When would you suggest?' Robert asked.

'The second week in August? That's not long before the schools' autumn term starts, so families may be back from holiday.'

'Agreed?' Robert glanced around the group. 'That's decided then – the second week in August, and let's hope for decent weather.'

'Do you want me to do an article about it for the local paper?' asked Helen, who wrote a weekly report on Prior's Ford activities for the *Dumfries News*.

'Wait until after our next meeting,' Robert advised. 'We want to make it as appealing as possible, and we need to contact the local people who could be involved first. We may have come up with more ideas by then in any case.'

'I agree to that.' Naomi glanced at her watch. 'I'm sure that lots of other ideas will come up now that we've started. But right now, who fancies a cup of tea?'

In Willow Cottage, overlooking the village green, the radio was playing music and Clarissa Ramsay was singing along loudly, something she only did when she was on her own. When a piece of particularly catchy music started she even began dancing, but stopped abruptly when she heard the front door open and a man's voice calling her name.

'In the living room,' she called back, snatching up the local newspaper. When Alastair Marshall arrived a moment later she was intent on reading it.

'Hi, you,' He leaned over the back of her chair and kissed the side of her neck. His mouth was icy cold and he had brought in a waft of chill fresh air with him.

'You're freezing!'

'I know – and you feel as though you're just out of the oven – you're a joy to come home to.'

'I don't know how you can spend so much time in that cold cottage on a day like this!'

'I lit the stove as soon as I went in.'

'Alastair, the windows don't fit, and neither does the door. That old stove can't make much difference!'

He knelt on the hearthrug, holding his hands out to the fire's warmth. 'When I'm working I don't notice the cold. In any case, knowing that when I finish I'm coming back to a warm house – and, even better, to you – helps me to ignore the cold.'

Alastair was an artist; when he and Clarissa first met he lived in a ramshackle old farm cottage on the edge of the village; now that they were living together in her cosy home he continued to rent the cottage for use as his studio.

Now he sat back on his heels and grinned up at her. 'Something in the kitchen smells great.'

'A casserole's in the oven. Was today worthwhile?'

He nodded. 'A very prolific session. I meant to be back earlier than this but when the work's going well I don't notice time passing.'

'I was thinking – couldn't we turn the tool shed in the back garden into a decent studio for you? We'd need to extend it a bit.'

He considered the idea for a moment, then said, 'Not sure about the light – and where would we put the gardening tools?'

'We could buy another tool shed.'

'Leave it until the summer, when I'll have a better idea as to the sort of light I'd get. How did your day go?'

'Well enough. The mobile library was here so I changed my books, and then met Cissie Kavanagh. She had the baby with her.'

'Good grief!' Alastair said. 'The Kavanaghs have a *baby*?'

'Of course not – they're pensioners.'

'That's what I thought.'

'She was babysitting for Tricia Borland – you know that the Borlands are living in one of the almshouses now?' Then, as he nodded, 'A lovely little girl, and so good. She smiles at everyone. Tricia had gone to Kirkcudbright to meet some friends. Cissie invited me back to hers for coffee. She told me that the Progress Committee are thinking of extending this year's Scarecrow Festival into something larger, with stalls on the green and various events incorporating the entire village and Linn Hall too. Something to bring in a lot of visitors. You'll find out more about it soon; she said that they're hoping you'll have some ideas about events.'

'Sounds good. Fancy some coffee?'

'Lovely. I'll make it while you get that paint off your hands.'

Alastair spread out his long artists' fingers. 'They are a bit colourful, aren't they?' he said in mild surprise. 'I'll not be long.'

'A letter arrived this morning, just after you went out. I put it on the hall table.'

'Thanks.'

When the coffee was ready Clarissa carried it into the living room, where she switched on the lamps. As she drew the curtains against the darkening afternoon she heard Alastair break into song upstairs. She glanced up at the ceiling, smiling. His voice was a pleasant tenor – much better than hers. He even managed to hit the right notes with ease, which was something she had never achieved.

Just before the two of them had finally given in and admitted their love for each other despite the fact that she was much older than he was, Alastair had committed himself to a two-year stint working in a Glasgow art gallery, but now he was back in the village and living with her in Willow Cottage. After the initial shock over a romance between a middle-aged woman and a much younger man, the villagers – or at least most of them – had come to accept the situation.

Clarissa had never been happier, but every now and again she still felt as though her new life was too good to be true, and feared that one day Alastair would tire of her, or fall in love with someone of his own age. The thought was quite unbearable, but no matter how hard she tried to ignore it, it continued to lurk in the back of her mind like toothache.

It crept into her mind now, and yet again she had to push it away firmly as she heard Alastair run down the stairs, taking two steps at once, as usual.

'Did you get your letter?' she asked as she poured the coffee.

'Yes – it wasn't anything important. Just a handout from the Glasgow art gallery, listing the exhibitions they're planning.'

'Anything you'd like to see?'

'Not really.'

'Are you quite sure? We're not joined at the hip – I'd be happy for you to go to Glasgow if there are ever any exhibitions you want to visit.'

'I know that, but I'm more of a country lover than a townie. I enjoy Prior's Ford – and being with you,' Alastair said.

Three

Ginny stabbed at her mobile phone, her heart sinking with each digit that appeared on the small screen. She hated having to speak to her mother because it was always difficult to pin her down to any subject other than herself, but she knew that if she left it to Lewis he would only end up being pushed into agreeing with some drastic idea of her mother's. He had not yet grasped the intricacy of Meredith-speak.

As she listened to the phone in Spain ringing, half of her hoped that Meredith wasn't there to answer it while the other half wanted to get the conversation over and done with.

There was a click, and then the perfectly trained, familiar voice said, 'Meredith Whitelaw's mobile telephone, Meredith Whitelaw speaking.'

'Mother, it's Ginny.'

'Darling, how lovely to hear from you! Give me a minute,

will you?' A hand was placed over the mouthpiece lightly enough for Ginny to hear her mother say, 'Sweetheart, it's my daughter, phoning to discuss her wedding. A mother always has to be on hand at a very special time like this, even a working mother!'

A man's voice said something, and Meredith purred, 'You are *such* a darling! *Hasta la vista!*' Then came the sound of something – a hand? – being kissed before a door closed and Meredith turned her attention back to her daughter.

'Did I interrupt something?'

'It was just Sam – our director. He came to tell me that our viewing figures for the last series have soared; isn't that wonderful?'

'Yes, it is. Is this a bad time to call?'

'No, I'm just having a siesta in my little caravan while they work on some of the less important scenes. It's so warm here that one needs plenty of rest. People don't realize that although it looks so easy on their television sets, filming is hard work. Did you get the bridal catalogues?'

'Yes I did. That's why I'm calling—'

'I haven't seen them myself because I ordered them by phone from the best bridal experts in the UK. I don't think I can manage even a brief trip to Scotland before the summer, which is such a pity, but I wanted to give you the opportunity to have a good look at them all. Don't buy *anything* until I get back, because you're sure to choose the wrong dress.'

'Mother—'

'Don't even try to deny it, darling, you're so absolutely hopeless when it comes to fashion – always have been – and I will not have my only child walking up the aisle dressed in those ghastly trousers and sweaters you always seem to be wearing.'

'I have no—'

'As you know, Genevieve, I'm not an interfering type of mother – even if I wanted to be, which I don't because I'm far too busy with my career to find the time, but I have a certain social standing to uphold and I'm determined to make sure that you have a perfect wedding. It's not just for me; it's for you as well. After all, you're going to marry the future lord of Linn Hall!'

'There isn't a title, Mother.'

'Are you sure? You'll be living in the largest house in the area, and the villagers look on Lewis and his parents as their lords, don't they?'

'The word is "laird", Mother – it's a term of endearment, a Scottish thing. It doesn't mean Lord with a capital.'

'I know that,' Meredith said swiftly. 'I took the part of Flora MacDonald in a play about Bonny Prince Charlie when you were a baby. What I'm saying is that you're marrying into a locally important family and so I have to ensure that you have a *proper* wedding. We need to book a good church and hotel in Edinburgh. Perhaps you could look into that before I get back, to save time.'

'Lewis and I are too busy to think about a wedding at the moment.'

'Don't be silly, I'm only going to be back in Britain for a few months in the summer. The wedding will have to be held then, and bookings must be made as soon as possible. That will leave you and me time to organize outfits for ourselves and the brides-maids – do you know how many you're going to have? – and you must invite Fliss to join us when we go shopping. She's certainly going to need a good wedding outfit. There are caterers to book as well.'

Ginny resisted the temptation to throw her phone at the wall of the camper van, settling instead for a loud and firm voice. 'I actually phoned to tell you that I don't need the catalogues or the wedding planner. Lewis and I have decided on a small, quiet wedding.' Then, as her mother said nothing, for once, she couldn't resist adding, 'possibly quite soon.'

The silence was broken by a gasp of horror. 'Oh my God, you're pregnant! How could you do that to me? How am I going to hold my head up before my friends and my fans? It's going to be in all the papers – don't you realize that British newspapers are sold in Spain? I'll be a laughing stock!'

'I'm not pregnant, Mother!' It took several attempts to be heard over Meredith's hysteria, but finally Ginny managed it.

'You're not? Are you sure? You're not just trying to calm me down, are you?'

'I'm not pregnant and I'm not lying to you.'

'How could you give me such a fright? I'm supposed to be resting before my next scene, and now you've got me all hot and bothered!'

Ginny stifled a sigh. 'I was just trying to explain that both Lewis and I have got too much work on at the moment. We don't plan to get married this year – and when we do find the time we're going to have the wedding we both want, in the local church so that all our friends can share the day with us.'

'You can't—'

'And the reception will be held at Linn Hall. Lewis is hoping to get the ground floor rooms refurbished by then, and in the meantime I've taken on the job of designing a garden for a friend. It's going to take all of this year and quite a bit of next year too.'

'I didn't know about this.'

'I wrote to you about it. Didn't you get my letter inside your Christmas card?'

'I remember something about someone's garden but you didn't say you were going to take so long over it. What size of garden is it?'

'Large enough. The owner wants it to be completely reorganized and at the moment I'm busy designing it. He's a television director, and he wants to do a series next year, showing the work being done on the garden. Gardening programmes are very popular on television at the moment, Mother.'

'Oh yes, you did mention that and I wondered – who's going to present these programmes?'

'Well – he wants me to do it.'

'You?' Meredith's voice rose an octave. 'Don't be silly, Genevieve, you can't appear before a television camera!'

'Fergus seems to think that I can.'

'Who's Fergus?'

'The television director who owns the garden I'm designing,' Ginny said patiently. 'It was all in the letter.'

'But you're not photogenic – I don't understand why, because I'm very photogenic, and so's your father. We took lots of photographs when you were a baby and you look terrible in every one of them – crying, scowling, screwing your eyes up – we finally stopped trying. You were a great disappointment to us both.'

'I know,' Ginny said.

'I have to go, I'm on in fifteen minutes and you've got me so upset that I'm going to have to do some calming meditation or I'll ruin the filming. Think about what I've said, darling – please have a proper wedding for me! And try to keep on not getting pregnant; I don't think I could bear the shame,' Meredith said, and hung up.

Jamie Greenlees buried his face in the glass of milk that Jess McNair had just set down in front of him and gulped noisily until half of the milk had gone.

'I quite liked living in the Neurotic Cuckoo, but I *love* living here on the farm,' he told Jess happily when he came up for air.

'And we love having you and your mum here.' She pulled a handkerchief from her apron pocket and leaned down to wipe the milky moustache from his small face.

'It's going to make learning to be a farmer much easier.' He took a biscuit from the plate she had put down beside the glass and bit into it.

'It's certainly the best way to learn.' Jess mopped up the crumbs he had sprayed over the table.

'M'hmm.' He crunched up the last part of the biscuit, finished the milk and jumped down from the chair. 'Where's Mum?'

'In the milking shed with Ewan and Wilf and the workmen – and you know that you're not allowed in there while work's going on.'

'But I'll be able to go in when it's all finished and the man's blowing his glass, won't I?'

'Only if he says you can. It won't be the milking shed any more then, it'll be his workplace. And workplaces can be quite dangerous.'

'How can you blow glass? Is it like blowing bubbles?'

'I don't know, love. We'll have to wait and see.'

'P'raps it's more like blowing your nose,' Jamie suggested and gave himself a fit of the giggles, which swiftly turned into an attack of hiccups.

'That's what happens when you gulp cold milk down too quickly,' Jess told him. 'Try holding your breath as long as you can – that might stop them.'

Jamie shook his head. 'I – like them,' he said. 'I'm going to let – Tommy hear them. Rabbits can't – catch hiccups, can the–they?'

'No they can't and you're not going out until you've changed into your play clothes. You know your mum likes your school uniform to be kept clean.'

'Oh b–bother!' He made for the inner door and could soon be heard thundering upstairs to his room.

Jess was smiling as she took his used glass and plate to the sink. The happiest time of her life had been when she and her husband Bert had run the farm together and when their three children, Victor, Alice, and Ewan, were of school age. In those days they were making quite a good living and the house was filled with noise. She had foolishly assumed then that life would always be perfect, but had learned the hard way that happiness isn't guaranteed for ever.

Alice was the first to leave; now she and her husband, Jack Pate, were raising their own three children on their Lake District farm, and too busy to visit Tarbethill often. Victor, more interested in mechanics than farming, had fallen for Jeanette Askew, a town girl, and had been disowned by Bert when he decided to give up farming in favour of working for his future father-in-law, who owned two garages.

By the time Victor left, Tarbethill, like so many small farms in Britain, had begun to struggle for survival. Bert, beset by problems, had given way to despair and killed himself, leaving Jess and Ewan, who, like his father, loved Tarbethill and never wanted to leave it, facing ruin. At that stage Jess began to fear that she would never know happiness again, but had found new hope in the form of Alison Greenlees, who had come from Glasgow with her parents, Joe and Gracie Fisher, the new landlord and landlady of the Neurotic Cuckoo.

Alison and Ewan were instantly attracted to each other, but when his father died, Ewan, having inherited Bert's stubborn streak, decided that Alison and young Jamie deserved better than life on a crumbling farm.

Fortunately Alison was also stubborn, and had a good head for business. She drew up a plan for reforming Tarbethill Farm that Ewan reluctantly agreed to after pressure from Jess, Naomi Hennessey, and Victor, now married and living in Clover Place, a small housing estate near to the farm.

Once given a chance, Alison's business plan had worked and now she and Ewan were married. Jamie's presence on the farm where she had longed for years to see her grandchildren play had brought joy back to Jess's heart. One day, she was certain, there would be babies to cuddle and the farmhouse would again be filled with noise and laughter.

She didn't even realize that she was beaming until Ewan, coming in from the yard with Alison, asked, 'What's so funny, Mum?'

'What d'you mean?'

'You're wearing a Cheshire cat grin.'

'Really?'

'Really.'

'Och, it's nothing – just that Jamie drank his milk too fast and gave himself hiccups. He's just gone upstairs to get changed, and then he wants his rabbit to hear what hiccups sound like.'

Both Alison and Ewan laughed. Laughter and smiles, Jess realized, came so easily to them all now.

'How's the work goin' on in the milking shed?' She nodded at the big kettle on the stove, now puffing steam. 'I've made up sandwiches for the men and I was just goin' to see to the tea.'

'I'll do it.' Alison poured boiling water into the teapot, also large, swilled it round and emptied it into the sink, then reached for the tea caddy.

'Where's Wilf?' Jess had expected the elderly farmhand to arrive with them for his afternoon break.

'Maisie's arthritis is bad, so I told him to go home early.'

Jess shook her head. 'Poor Maisie – it can cause her terrible bother when it flares up. I'll try to drop in tomorrow to see how she's doing.'

'The work on the milking shed's coming along well, isn't it, Ewan?' Alison put in.

'Aye,' Ewan agreed. 'I reckon that Stefan and his lass can move in soon.'

'They'd be better to wait until the snow's been and gone,' Jess said. 'It's on the way – Wilf said the other day that he can smell it in the air.'

'I've never heard of anyone smelling snow!'

'If Wilf says he can smell it, you can be sure that it's on the way,' Jess told her daughter-in-law. 'He's worked for us since he was a lad and he's never been wrong about the weather yet. You and I had better make sure that the cottage is kept well aired and warmed for Stefan and his daughter, just in case they decide to come soon.'

'You take the sandwiches out to the workmen, Ewan, and I'll take the tea,' Alison was saying when Jamie burst into the kitchen with the tragic news that his hiccups had suddenly disappeared.

'Good,' Ewan said, but the little boy shook his head.

'I wanted Tommy to *hear* them. He's never heard hiccups before and it was going to be a special treat.'

'There's always another time, chicken.' Alison ruffled her son's blond hair.

'P'raps I should have another glass of milk. That might bring them back.'

'And p'raps you should help us to take some tea and sandwiches to the men working in the milking shed,' Ewan suggested. 'The glass-blowing workshop's almost finished – come and see it.'

'Cool!' Jamie's small face immediately broke into a broad grin.

Ginny found Lewis on his own in one of the polytunnels where the more fragile plants were being overwintered.

'Can I please have a hug?'

'Gladly.' He pulled her into his arms and kissed the top of her head. 'What's wrong?'

'I've just been on the phone to my mother.'

'Ah. How is she?'

'Confused, and so am I, now. To be honest, I think she's going bonkers.'

'I've always suspected that.'

'She just wouldn't listen to what I was trying to tell her.'

'That's not going bonkers, that's just the way your mother is. I noticed it from the first minute I met her.'

'That's reassuring because I was wondering, coming through the garden, if I might inherit it from her – bonkerism, I'm talking about.'

'Not a hope. I won't ever allow it.'

'She actually said, just before she rushed off to do some meditation exercises, that I was to try not to get pregnant.'

'After our wedding or before it?'

'I think she meant before. Possibly after as well. I can't see my mother as a grandmother.'

'Why this sudden interest in pregnancy?' Lewis wondered. 'Did you tell her you were, or that you were planning to be? Because I'm all for it if you are.'

'I didn't mention it – it was all her idea. And it's not going to happen before the wedding because we've both got too much to do before we can even *start* to think about the wedding, let alone becoming parents.'

'True. Was she thrilled about you designing Fergus's garden, and being filmed working on it?'

'More horrified than thrilled. Apparently I'm not photogenic.'

'Fergus doesn't seem to think that, and he should know. Don't let her get you down, Ginny. You're going to do a brilliant job.'

'I hope so.'

'I *know* so.' He released her, tipped her face up to his, and kissed her. 'How far have you got with the plans?'

'Not very far, and now I'm beginning to wonder if . . .'

'None of that, now. Forget Meredith and listen to me. You've done a fantastic job here and you're going to do a fantastic job for Fergus. I know it and you know it, and if your ditzy mother doesn't know it she's a fool.' He turned her around and slapped the seat of her jeans. 'Get back to work, woman. We need the money.'

Four

By the beginning of March the temperature had dropped and a bitter east wind kept most of the villagers indoors as much as possible.

'The snow's not far away, Ewan.' Wilf glanced up at the low clouds driving across the sky as he and Ewan left the farmhouse after their midday meal. The working dogs, Angus, Cleo and young Bess, pregnant with her first litter, were at their heels, but the hens that normally clucked around the yard clustered together in a sheltered corner and the farm cats had retired inside one of the sheds. The washing that Jess had hung out that morning was doing its best to pull free of the line.

'With any luck it'll come soon and be on its way out before the lambs start to arrive.'

'I'd no' count on that, Ewan,' the older man said. 'In all my time at Tarbethill I've never seen the snow doin' as we hoped. It's got a mind of its own – always had an' always will. Not a winter's gone by without us havin' tae flounder about in snow-drifts, tryin' tae save some poor buried animal.'

Ewan pulled his cap firmly down over his ears and nodded. In Dumfries and Galloway lambing usually began at the end of March, and as Wilf said, the snow and the lambing season always seemed to coincide.

'We'd best get the pregnant ewes closer to the lambing shed and make certain that everythin's ready, just in case,' he said.

A week later most of the ewes had been brought down from the higher ground to fields near the farmhouse and the new lambing shed made ready for any complicated births. In the house, Jess and Alison were delving into what Jess called her 'lamb cupboard' where, over the years, she had collected blankets, cardboard boxes and feeding bottles.

'You've got enough here to look after an army!' Alison marvelled.

'If we're lucky, most of the ewes'll be able to give birth on their own and take care of their lambs without help, but there are always one or two who can't, or won't. And since we've given up the dairy herd and bought more ewes than ever before, we may well need this lot. I'm glad that you're going to be here to help – you and Jamie both.'

'He'll certainly want to be involved – it's all part of learning to be a farmer.'

'Victor and Ewan were both helping their father by the time they were Jamie's age – with the calving and lambing as well as everything else. It's all part of nature's cycle.'

'I'm not so sure about that side of it,' Alison said doubtfully.

'Let Jamie decide for himself,' Jess advised. Privately, she was certain that her new grandson, who was afraid of nothing and already seemed to her to have the makings of a good farmer, would want to be fully involved in the coming events.

As it turned out, her faith in Jamie was soon to be justified.

Just over a week later Ewan and Alison, taking advantage of the
dark nights and short days, came back from a rare evening with
friends at the Neurotic Cuckoo to find Jess anxiously waiting for
them at the open farmhouse door.

'Something's up.' Ewan stopped the car at once and Jess,
clutching a heavy woollen cardigan over her shoulders against the
cold wind, came to meet them.

'Thank goodness you're back!'

'Jamie . . .?'

'He's fine, Alison, fast asleep these past two hours. It's Bess, I
think she's in labour. She's been uneasy since just after you left
and I tried to get her into the kitchen, but she panicked and went
to ground under the deep-litter house. I cannae coax her out.'

Alison glanced at Ewan and saw in the light from the open
door that his face was grim. Bess, the youngest of their three
sheepdogs, had been easy to train and promised to be as good
one day as Old Saul, her grandsire, known in his day as one of
the best working dogs in the area. This was her first litter. The
new deep-litter henhouse was raised on supports, making it a
handy hiding place for the frightened bitch.

'If she starts to whelp under there on her own and in this
weather, we'll be lucky if any of the pups survive.' Ewan began
to pull his jacket off. 'I'll have to get to her.'

'I doubt you'll manage it,' his mother said. 'She's right in the
middle and the shed's not very high from the ground.'

'I'll have to give it a damned good try. We can't afford to lose
her or her litter. Where are the other dogs?'

'I've shut them into their shed out of the way, and I've brought
the whelping box into the kitchen and made everythin' ready. I
was just about to phone for you to come home when I heard
the car.'

The three of them hurried over to the deep-litter house, where
Ewan crouched down and tried to coax the young bitch to come
to him, but with no luck. 'I'm going to have to go in there to
bring her out,' he said at last, but after a few valiant attempts he
had to admit that the space wasn't high enough.

'I'm only goin' to get stuck, and that's not goin' to help Bess.'

'Let me try.' Alison started to unbutton her coat, but Ewan put
a hand on her arm.

'I'll not let you take the chance; Bess doesn't know you well enough yet. I'm goin' to have to phone Wilf.'

'If you can't get under the shed,' Alison pointed out, 'he's got no chance.'

'She knows him well – he might be able to talk her out.'

'She knows you just as well. We'll need to bring the vet out. He's thin as a stick. If you ask me,' Jess said, 'that wife of his doesnae feed him properly.'

Ewan shook his head. 'Apart from havin' to pay the man more than usual for a late night call-out in this weather, I don't think we've got the time to wait for him to get here. I'd best phone Wilf.' He started towards the farmhouse, the two women close on his heels.

He was picking up the kitchen telephone when the door leading to the rest of the house opened to reveal Jamie, pyjama-clad and tousle-haired, blinking at them. 'What's happening?'

'Go back to bed, pet, it's nothing for you to worry your wee head over,' Jess told him.

'What is it, Mum?' he insisted.

'It's Bess, darling. She's going to have her pups, but she's hiding under the deep-litter house, and we can't get to her. Ewan's going to ask Wilf if he can come over because it's a cold night and we need to get her into the kitchen where the puppies can be kept warm.' Alison went to her son. 'I'll take you back upstairs and tuck you in.'

'I can't go to bed while Bess is out in the cold. Can I not go and talk to her? She likes me.'

Ewan's hand was on the phone; now he drew it back. 'D'you think she'd come out for you, Jamie?'

'Ewan—'

Jamie nodded. 'Of course she would – I tell her stories. She likes that – I could go out and tell her a story now.'

'You most certainly could not, young man!'

'Wait a minute, Alison, it might be worth a try. Jamie's right – Bess does like him and he'd be able to get closer to her than anyone else can.'

'Ewan . . .'

'Mum, I'm not going back to bed until I know that she's safe and warm,' Jamie said swiftly. 'I'm going to get dressed.'

'Jamie . . .!' Alison almost shrieked, but he was already running up the stairs.

'I'll make sure that he puts on plenty of warm clothes,' Jess said, and followed.

'I will *not* allow you to put my son in danger, Ewan!'

'He's the only one of us who can get near Bess. I can't afford to lose her or her pups. I've decided to keep one to train up, and sell the others. A good sheepdog's valuable, and the farmers around here have always been willing to pay well for a Tarbethill pup.'

'You don't think that my son's valuable?' Her voice shook.

'Listen to me.' He took hold of both her wrists, refusing her when she tried to pull free. 'Jamie's desperate to learn farming and I think he's already showing promise. This – what's happening tonight – is part of his learning. I've got complete confidence in him, and what's more important is that I think Bess has confidence in him too.'

'But she's terrified! What if she attacks him and we can't get in to save him?'

'Bess would never harm the boy. I trained her – I know her well.'

'But right now she's not herself. If anything happens to my baby I'll never forgive you!'

Again she tried to pull free from his grip and again he refused to let her.

'And if you stop him from trying to help Bess I doubt if he'll find it easy to forgive you. The bitch is looking for reassurance, and she'll get it from him. She trusts Jamie and he knows that she wouldn't hurt him. And if anything bad happens to that bitch and her pups because you refused to let him try to save them – well, I'll find it difficult to forgive you myself.'

Tears of fear and frustration filled her eyes. 'If he gets hurt, even slightly, then you and I are finished, Ewan!'

He released her wrists. 'I know that, Alison, but farming's a tough life, and Jamie's a tough lad. Let him prove it to you. I trust him, and tonight you're going to have to trust us both.'

They stepped back from each other as Jess and Jamie arrived back in the kitchen, the boy dressed in his warmest trousers and jersey with a long woollen scarf wound around his neck several times and fastened with a large safety pin. He was loudly protesting against Jess's attempts to pull a knitted hat over his head.

'I'm not a baby – I won't die without a hat!'

'Nevertheless,' his mother took the hat from Jess and pulled it down firmly over his head to cover his ears, 'you're not going outside without it.'

When they reached the deep-litter house Jamie squatted down to peer into the pitch-dark beneath it. 'Bess? Come on, lass. I can see her eyes glittering, Ewan, she's right in the middle.' He dropped to his hands and knees, pushing his head under the shed.

'Jamie, be careful!'

'I *am* being careful, Mum, don't fuss! It's all right, Bess, it's only me. Want to hear a story? It's nice and warm in the kitchen, we should go there. It's cold under here. I'm going to take you into the kitchen.'

The dog whined, and then, to Alison's horror, her son suddenly disappeared beneath the shed.

'Jamie!'

Ewan's arm held her back when she tried to follow Jamie. 'He knows what he's doing. You have to trust him.'

For a few stifling seconds Jamie felt lost in the darkness. Panic gripped his stomach like a large hand, and then the hand turned into a wooden spoon, stirring his insides vigorously, the way Gran Jess stirred her cake mix. He hesitated as the churning moved up into his throat, choking him. All he wanted was to be outside in the night air, on his feet and with his arms tight around his mother. He closed his eyes as sudden panic seized him, then when Bess gave a frightened whimper he opened them again. After a moment his eyes adjusted and he could make out Bess's eyes, fixed on him.

'Hello, Bess.' He heard her shift slightly. As he began to concentrate on her the unpleasant churning sensation faded away and he started to crawl slowly towards her, talking all the while.

'C'mon, girl – it's not nice under here. I think there are probably spiders and all sorts of nasty things watching us. Let's go into the house instead.' He inched forward until he was close enough to the bitch to reach a hand towards her. When he felt her nose brush against the tips of his fingers and then her tongue come out to lick his hand it was almost as reassuring as having his face pressed against the warm security of his mother's body.

'Good girl! Come on now, follow me,' he coaxed, and began to edge backwards. 'We don't have far to go.' To his relief, Bess began to shuffle after him and in no time at all he was outside and able to stand up.

'She's just coming,' he said. 'It was a doddle.'

'Good lad!' Ewan praised him. 'I knew that you could do it!'

'So did I,' Jamie said and then as his mother tried to lead him towards the house, 'Mu-um! I need to make sure that Bess gets out!'

Just then the young bitch crept into view and needed no persuading to follow them into the kitchen, where she settled into the warm blankets by the fire with obvious relief.

'What happens now?' Jamie asked.

'Now we leave her to have her puppies,' Ewan told him.

'Will she manage on her own?'

'Probably, but I'll stay with her just in case she needs any help.'

'I'm staying too.'

'You're not,' Alison told her son, 'you're going up to bed and I'm going to bring you a hot drink.'

He dragged the woollen hat off and shook his head vigorously. 'I'm staying with Bess! It was me who got her out from under the big shed and I know she'll want me to stay with her in case she needs my help again.'

'I agree with him, Alison. He's earned the right to see the pups safely delivered.'

'He's only a little boy!'

'I am *not* little!' Jamie was outraged.

'I was helping my dad during the lambing and calving when I was Jamie's age.'

'Ewan's right, Alison,' Jess put in as she set mugs on the table. 'That's what life on a farm's all about. Tea all round now, and hot chocolate for you, Jamie. What d'you think?'

'Great,' he said, unwinding his scarf, his eyes blazing with excitement. Just then Bess decided to produce her first pup, and the matter was settled.

The birthing was swift and without any problems; little more than an hour later Bess was fully occupied in caring for five healthy pups, and the rest of the household were free to go to bed.

'Can we keep them all?' Jamie begged.

'We can't afford to, love,' Jess told him. 'We'll keep one to train up when they're old enough, and sell the rest to other farmers. This lot are descended from Old Saul, and he was the best working sheepdog in the area. We never have trouble selling our pups.'

'I tell you what,' Ewan said, 'I was going to keep one and sell four, but if it hadn't been for the terrific job Jamie did tonight we might have lost Bess and all her pups. So now I'm going to sell four as planned, and the one we're keeping is going to belong to Jamie. How does that suit you, kid?'

'You mean it?' Jamie's voice was a high squeak.

'I mean it. It'll be a working dog, mind, not a pet, but you get to name it, and I'll help you to train it and turn it into a good working dog.'

'Can I, Mum?' Jamie's eyes were sparkling, 'can I have my own dog?'

'As long as you remember that it's a working farm dog and not a pet.'

'Magic! Wait till I tell them at school to—' Jamie was halted by a huge yawn, then finished when he was free: 'Tomorrow!'

'I think you deserve to take tomorrow morning off,' his mother said. 'You'll need a decent sleep after all this excitement.'

'No way! You've got to promise to wake me at the proper time because tomorrow's Show and Tell at school and I'm going to have the best story ever!'

'I'm a very lucky man,' Ewan said when he and Alison finally got to bed.

'You certainly are. If anything – anything at all – had happened to my Jamie tonight you'd either be dead by now, or at the very least trying to get to sleep underneath the deep-litter house without as much as a blanket.'

'Fair enough. We'll never be money-rich, but thanks to you we're going to be able to keep Tarbethill.' He raised himself on one elbow and looked down at the pale oval of her face on the pillow. 'It would never have happened without you, Alison. I wanted to keep running the place the way my dad did but you managed to show me that I was heading for disaster. Now I know that farming's like life – it's all about moving forward, not trying to hold on to the past. I think that even Dad would agree that nothing can stay the same for ever.'

Alison reached up to stroke one hand down the side of his face. 'It means a lot to hear you say that.'

'There's more – I wasn't just blessed by you coming into my life. You brought Jamie with you, and that was another blessing. He's not only a great kid, but now Mum and I don't need to worry about what's going to happen to the place when we've gone because your lad's going to look after it. And I'm hoping that we'll be able to help by giving him brothers and sisters to share the work.'

'I'm certain we will, my love,' Alison said. 'But not tonight – I'm desperate to get some sleep!'

Five

The amount of papers and books needed to plan out Fergus Matheson's new garden had become too prolific for Ginny's small camper van, and she was now forced to make use of Linn Hall's big dining-room table. As the unused room was too expensive to heat, all that could be provided was a small electric fire, so she was wearing every warm piece of clothing she had, including gloves, a scarf, and a woolly hat pulled well down over her ears.

She was so intent on her work that she didn't hear Lewis arrive. When he said, 'Good grief, it's colder in here than it is in the garden,' she jumped and knocked a pile of papers on to the floor.

'I'll get them – I brought you some hot chocolate and scones; drink the chocolate before it gets cold.' He set the food and drink down and began to collect the papers while Ginny stripped her gloves off so that she could wrap both hands around the large mug, dipping her head over it to let the steam warm her face.

'Oh, that feels wonderful!'

'Stop worshipping it and get it down you – it won't stay warm for long in this room.'

By the time the papers were tapped into a neat pile she had

finished the drink and put the mug aside. He bent to kiss her. 'Mmm – your mouth tastes of chocolate and your nose is as cold as a small iceberg.'

'I know – poor little thing!' Ginny tried to rub some warmth into the feature under discussion. 'I'm fully expecting it to drop off and smash into pieces at any moment. If only I had more space to work in my nice cosy camper van!'

'It's bitterly cold outside, but at least the sun's shining and the thick layer of snow's turning the garden into a winter wonderland.' Lewis cast a glance round the large dining room. Ginny had drawn the long heavy curtains back from the window behind her to let the light in but the rest of the room was shadowed and depressing. 'This place looks so forbidding!' He began to uncover all the windows.

Ginny took a scone and sank her teeth into it. 'Mmm – I love strawberry jam!'

'We're really going to have to do something about this entire floor before it's too late – this chill can't be good for the furnishings.'

'It's not too good for your intended either.' Ginny pointed out, licking a drop of jam from an index finger.

Once Lewis had brought more daylight into the room he helped himself to a scone. 'I wonder how soon I could try for another loan.'

'There's no harm in trying now because you don't know how long you're going to have to wait for a decision from the powers that be. I'm just about ready to ask Fergus to come and see the first rough plan for his garden – there's no sense in going too far with it until he approves of my ideas. He might hate them.'

'I expect he'll be pleased.'

'If he is, he might draw up a contract. Once that happens I could perhaps persuade him to give me an advance. The money could help with starting work on this place.'

'But the advance would be *yours*.'

'*Ours*,' Ginny corrected him, tapping the small ring on her left hand; then as he frowned and opened his month to protest, 'Lewis, if you hadn't given me a job here I wouldn't have started to study garden design, and if you hadn't allowed me to try out my ideas on the estate, Fergus wouldn't have offered me the chance to work on his new garden. Which means that if it wasn't for you

I'd still be working in a garden centre.' She sucked air into her lungs and then said, 'Does that make any sense? What I'm saying is, we're a team, which means that what Fergus pays me for this work is ours.'

'I don't deserve you!'

'Yes you do. Have you got a minute? I'd like your thoughts on what I've done so far.'

'Of course.'

Ginny pushed aside a pile of books and started to search through several rough sketches. 'The garden's wide but fairly shallow, broadening as it slopes down to the firth. The house is above it, sitting roughly in the middle. I'm thinking of a new stone patio stretching the width of the house where the owners can sit in the summer and look down to the river. Large pots of flowers along the front of the house, and as it makes sense to have vege-tables near to the kitchen I thought that I could put a small raised vegetable bed at each end of the patio. What d'you think?'

'It makes sense so far.'

'I'd like to have wide shallow steps leading from the patio to the water – it's a bonny house, and that would allow passers-by on the water to catch a glimpse of it. Two small lawns, one each side of the steps, then fairly low floral shrubbery edging the lower part of the grass. From there until the water's edge I think that the people using the rest of the garden, which is going to be divided up into small separate areas, should have some privacy.'

She selected one of the sketches. 'A rose garden with a curving stone pathway, a garden seat and as many low rose bushes as possible, in as many colours as possible, each bed edged with white perennial flowers. And I think it would be good to have a tranquil garden, where people can just sit and unwind, with a small fountain – the sound of running water is so soothing. And pots of scented flowers; a mixture of day-scented and night-scented. And down by the firth –' she picked up another sketch – 'the barbecue with circular paving, seating, small tables and a view of the water. And here, tucked into a corner, is a green-house. That's as far as I've got.'

Lewis took so long to study the rough designs that she began to feel nervous. 'I can make any changes you want to suggest. I need your approval before I show the overall designs to Fergus.'

'No you don't.'

'I do!'

'You don't,' he said, 'because it's perfect. I could never think up such good ideas. I'm a gardener because I have to be, and the work that Duncan and I have done on this place is more a matter of getting rid of the rubbish that hides what's been there for years, but you—' He paused, shaking his head in admiration. 'You're more of a designer than I could ever be.'

'You're not just saying that?'

'Of course not, you muffin. It's great, and if Fergus doesn't think the same he doesn't deserve to have you on his programme.'

Her face lit up. 'Honestly?'

'Honestly.'

'That's a relief! I've still to draw it all out properly and start deciding which plants are best for each area . . .'

'But first we're going to the kitchen to thaw out,' Lewis said, and she nodded, and then said as she gathered the papers together, 'I need a favour, Lewis – can I take over the small greenhouse in the kitchen garden? I need to start sowing seeds for the new place.'

'Of course. What's mine is yours, be it greenhouses or problems,' he assured her cheerfully.

'Hi, Clarissa!'

'Hello Amy.'

'How did you know it was me?'

Clarissa Ramsay smiled at herself in the hall mirror as she said into the phone, 'It may have something to do with your American accent.'

'I suppose. So what's goin' on in that lovely little village of yours?'

'It seems to be fairly quiet at the moment.'

'Come on!' Amy Rose said. 'You can't kid me – I've been in Prior's Ford more than once and there's always somethin' happenin'.'

'Well, there's talk of a special summer festival to be linked with the usual Scarecrow Festival. Something that involves the whole village – stalls on the village green and things like that.'

'Sounds interestin'.'

'And I've heard that there's going to be a programme on television about the Linn Hall estate. Remember Ginny Whitelaw, that nice girl who helped to restore the gardens?'

'The one who's goin' to marry her boss?'

'That's her. It seems she showed a television director around the place last year and he took a liking to it. Apparently he's planning to do a documentary about it. The whole village is buzzing with the news. It would certainly help to publicize the gardens and bring more visitors to Linn Hall and into the village in general.'

'Sounds good, but I'm callin' to ask about you and Alastair. How does it feel now that he's finished with that job in Glasgow?' I bet you just love havin' him around again.'

'I do.' Clarissa hesitated, and then said, 'I still can't believe that we're actually living together.'

A sigh floated along the line. 'Don't tell me that you're still feelin' guilty about it. Anyone listenin' to you would think that you'd kidnapped him and now you're keepin' him bound an' gagged in your bedroom!'

'It's just that sometimes I think back to my time as a teacher in England and wonder what my colleagues and my pupils would say if they knew that I'd ended up living with a toy boy.'

'They'd be jealous, same as I am. Listen, Clarissa, Alastair's crazy about you – I've seen the way he looks at you. You've got to stop worryin' and start tellin' yourself that as far as he's concerned age doesn't come into it.'

'I'll try.'

'Do that, and then try even harder. There was a reason why I called – what was it? Oh yes – how was the visit to your stepchildren?'

'It went surprisingly well, thank goodness.' When Clarissa, in her fifties and recently widowed, met and fell in love with Alastair Marshall, an artist in his thirties, her stepson Steven had accepted the situation, but stepdaughter Alexandra, who had idolized her late father, made no secret of her disgust and fury. 'I was dreading it, but the change in Alexandra has been quite astonishing. She's turned into a human being, mainly thanks to her friend Gerald.'

'So you met him?'

'Indeed we did, and he's just right for Alexandra. In his fifties, which makes him considerably older than she is, but as Steven said, that seems to have made it easier for her to bond with him.'

'A replacement father? That sounds strange.'

'Anything *but* a replacement father. He's kind and understanding, and clearly devoted to Alexandra, whereas Keith was unloving and domineering. When Steven set up house with Christopher, Keith more or less rejected him and concentrated on turning Alexandra into the sort of offspring he could be proud of. Looking back, I can't understand why I ever married him – it's as though he cast a spell over me.'

'But fortunately, when your stuffy husband died Alastair broke the spell, and this Gerald seems to have done the same for Alexandra. So – happy endings all round.'

'Certainly for me.'

'Not Alexandra?'

'There's no engagement ring as yet, but Gerald's sensibly taking things slowly.'

'Wise man. And what about Stella?' After meeting Clarissa on holiday in America, Amy had visited Prior's Ford twice. She had come to look on the village as a second home, and had become a good friend to the quiet librarian.

'She's fine. Still walking on cloud nine after that wonderful Christmas the three of us had with you and your cousin Patsy in Florida.'

'That was a blast, wasn't it? Patsy's still talkin' about it too. We'll do it again some time. If Alastair's there, tell him to come to the phone and say hi.'

'Right now he's over at the old farm cottage where he used to live. He's using it as a studio since there's not enough room here.'

'That boy's somethin' special and don't you forget it. I tell you, Clarissa, if he'd been a billionaire Patsy would've tried to make him become her fourth husband. Count yourself lucky that she seems to have this rule that every man she marries has to be richer than the last one. I've just been thinkin' – I wouldn't mind visitin' while that festival's on.' Amy, as always, bounced from one subject to the next. 'When did you say it was to be held?'

'Around the middle of August.'

'I'll see what I can do. Mebbe Patsy'll come with me this time.'

'There's nowhere very grand for her to stay – just the local pub.'

'She can bunk up with me in your spare room. You're forgettin' that she used to live like us – until she got a taste for marryin' money. Better go – kiss Alastair for me, an' tell Stella I said hi, an' I'm lookin' forward to seein' her in the summer.'

Half an hour later the phone rang again. This time the voice at the other end of the line was female, with a lilting Irish accent. It was vaguely familiar, but Clarissa couldn't think why.

'Hello, could you tell me – is Alastair there at all?'

'He's out at the moment.'

'Will he be back soon?'

'He's gone to his studio, and when he's there I never know when he'll be back. Not for a few hours at least. Can I help you? I'm Clarissa Ramsay, his partner.'

'Of course – Clarissa!' Recognition warmed the soft voice. 'I was trying to recall your name. I kept thinking Cassandra, but I knew that was wrong. I'm Nuala Brennan; we met before when I had an exhibition in the art gallery where Alastair worked last year.'

'Oh yes, I remember.' The lovely young Irish artist with high cheekbones, wide green eyes tilted up at the corners and a tumbled mane of wavy auburn hair falling almost to her waist. 'As I said, Alastair's gone to his studio – an old farm cottage on the outskirts of the village where we live.'

'Would he have a phone there?'

'I'm afraid not. He hates being interrupted when he's painting. I could take a message, if that helps.'

'That's very kind of you. I really need to speak to him as soon as possible. The gallery owner has invited me to do another exhibition, and I'd love it if Alastair could set it up the way he did last year.' A soft laugh floated into Clarissa's ear. 'Last time was my first, and I was scared out of my wits. I couldn't have got through it without him. As soon as I was offered another showing my stomach began to flutter at the thought. I would love it if Alastair could help me again, but apparently he doesn't work there now.'

'It was a two-year contract.'

'Yes, they told me. I asked could he not come back to help

me and they did write to him, but it seems he's got quite a lot on just now.'

'He's working on a summer project at the moment, and spending most of his time in the studio.'

'My show's at the end of April and I'd really like to talk to him about it.'

'Yes, of course. Hold on for a moment.' Clarissa took paper and a pen from the telephone table drawer. 'How do spell your name?'

'N-u-a-l-a,' pronounced Noola. 'It's Irish. And the surname's Brennan. D'you want me to spell that too?'

'No, I can manage that one. What's the number?' She noted it down carefully and promised to tell Alastair about the call as soon as he came home.

Malcolm Finlay was in a cheerful mood. It was a sunny, blowy March morning, the dark evenings were disappearing, spring bulbs were beginning to splash colour all over his garden and this was the day of the mobile library's weekly visit to Prior's Ford.

Spurning his woollen scarf and the winter cap with ear flaps, he took his Panama hat from the hat-rack in the hall, picked up his stick and the two library books due back, opened the front door and stepped out into the sunshine. For a long moment he paused to take in the sight of his neat garden before drawing a deep breath of clear fresh air and setting out.

There were a lot of people about, most of them, like Malcolm, cheered by the arrival of better weather at last. As he made his way along River Lane, which ran between Slaemuir, a small council house estate, and Mill Walk, a private housing estate, he lifted his hat to passers-by, exchanging greetings and comments on the pleasure of being out and about on such a pleasant day.

A shy man by nature, he had moved to Prior's Ford some nine months earlier in the belief that life in a village would suit his need for anonymity; instead, he had found the villagers friendly and welcoming without seeking to find out all about him, which suited him perfectly.

Reaching the main road, he saw the library van parked in Kilmartin Crescent, near the Neurotic Cuckoo pub. Most locals crossed the village green to reach it, but Malcolm preferred to walk along the main street and then cross the road to the Crescent's opening, thus helping the grass while at the same time spinning out the pleasant anticipation of reaching the van.

It was almost midday, which meant that lunchtime beckoned, so only a few people browsed along the shelves when Malcolm went in, and another two waited to have their books stamped out. Malcolm joined them, and when his turn came he raised his hat to the librarian.

'Isn't it a beautiful day, Miss Hesslett?'

'It is indeed – and those books you ordered have finally arrived.' Stella Hesslett collected three tomes from the shelf below the counter.

'That's excellent! Now I can complete the current series of articles.'

'I'm sorry you've had to wait for so long, but apparently it took some time to locate them,' Stella Hesslett apologized.

'It's understandable. Not many people are likely to ask for academic reading like this. I greatly appreciate your hard work on my behalf.'

'It's what I'm here for.' Her slight blush, he thought, was both becoming and attractive. She produced a plastic bag and began to pack the books into it. 'This will make them easier to carry.'

'Thank you.' He was about to leave when to his astonishment he heard himself say, 'When do you stop for lunch?'

Stella was already gathering up the returned books. 'In about fifteen minutes.'

'I was thinking of going to the Neurotic Cuckoo. Would you care to join me?'

Stella almost dropped the armful of books. 'Me? Have lunch with you?' she blurted out.

'I just wondered – a bit of company . . .'

'I usually bring sandwiches,' she faltered.

'They do a nice lunch,' he said hopefully.

For a moment they looked at each other, and then Stella said, 'Well – yes, it *would* make a pleasant change. Thank you.'

'I'll just take these books home and then I'll meet you in the pub.' Malcolm tipped his hat to her again and turned away, apologizing profusely as he almost bumped into the first of the two women waiting to have their books stamped out. As she and her friend left the library van five minutes later she said, 'What d'you think of that, then?'

'I've never seen Stella Hesslett blushing before,' the other woman agreed.

'And so was he. A wee romance startin', d'you think?'

'If so, good luck to them. I wouldn't mind a bit of romance myself.'

'With him?'

'With anyone,' her friend said as they began to cross the green, 'It's been a while, to tell the truth.'

Six

When he had put his library books in his study Malcolm returned to the front door and opened it to find Helen Campbell on her way up the garden path.

'Good morning, I've brought your latest chapters back.'

Helen's husband Duncan was head gardener at the Linn Hall estate and as the impoverished Ralston-Kerrs couldn't afford to pay high salaries she 'took in' typing to help feed their four growing children. Since arriving in the village Malcolm had become her most lucrative client as well as her most interesting.

'Thank you, my dear. I appreciate all you're doing for me.'

Helen beamed at him. 'I'm the lucky one – getting paid to be the first to see your work. These particular chapters were gripping, as always. I wish I could write as well as you do.'

'You're very kind, but also flattering. I'm looking forward to reading your serial when it's published in May.' He took the envelope from her. 'I've got some more work for you – it's all ready if you have a moment.'

He took the envelope inside, reappearing almost at once with an identical envelope. 'This is material for an academic magazine; they've asked me to post it next Monday at the latest – is that asking too much?'

'I can do that,' Helen assured him cheerfully. 'Bye!' and she hurried off.

*   *   *

When Malcolm passed the mobile library on his way to the Neurotic Cuckoo he saw that there was still one reader browsing the shelves inside. He paused at the door, caught Stella's eye, and waved to her before moving on.

A couple of men at the bar were being served by Joe Fisher and a third customer sitting at a table gave the newcomer a friendly nod. Malcolm nodded in reply as he headed for a table by the window. He vaguely recognized the man as one of the people from the row of terraced houses locally known as the almshouses, but couldn't recall his name.

'Afternoon, Dr Finlay.' Gracie Fisher arrived at his table. 'Lunch? Or are you in for a drink?'

'Lunch, and I've invited Miss Hesslett to join me when she's free.'

Gracie's eyebrows shot up. 'Oh, that's nice!'

'At the moment she's still occupied in the library van.'

A mobile phone rang and the man at the other table took it from his pocket.

'I'll bring two menus,' Gracie offered, 'and when Stella arrives I'll give you both time to choose what you want. Would you like a drink while you're waiting?'

'I'll wait until Miss Hesslett arrives, thank you!'

'No problem,' Gracie said, and went over to the other occupied table. 'Still on your own, Charlie?'

Charlie, Malcolm thought. *Charlie – Charlie – Crandall, of course!* The old brain was still working.

'Afraid so. It's not like Hannah, she's usually punctual but this morning she said she'd look after Tricia Borland's baby, and apparently Tricia's not back yet.'

'That lassie,' Gracie said indulgently, 'has plenty of willing babysitters in the almshouses and she certainly knows how to make the most of them.'

'All women love babies.'

'Indeed they do,' Gracie was agreeing when the door opened. Malcolm looked up eagerly, but the woman who hurried in went straight to the other table. 'Sorry to keep you waiting, Charlie.'

'Not at all. So Tricia's arrived back?'

'Actually, no, but Dolly's going to be home for the rest of the day and she offered to take wee Layla until Tricia arrives.'

'From what I gather, Tricia never seems to keep to the promised timetable,' Gracie, still at their table, commented.

'She's still young, and new to motherhood. She'll settle down.'

'Let's hope so,' Gracie said somewhat drily just as Stella arrived.

It was after five o'clock and beginning to get dark before Clarissa
saw Alastair pass the kitchen window. As always, she felt a thrill
of pleasure go through her at the thought of being with him
again.

'You've had a long session today,' she said when he arrived in
the kitchen.

'One thing led to another – I got an amazing amount of work
done.' He hugged her tightly. 'It's getting chilly out there, but
you're as warm as a hot water bottle.'

'I took a phone call for you,' she said, then, when he raised
his eyebrows, 'from Nuala Brennan.'

'What did she want?' He released her and began to take off his
heavy winter jacket.

'You. Apparently she's having another exhibition in that gallery
where you worked, and she wants you to organize it because you
organized the last one so well. She told me that the gallery owner
wrote to you about it, but you said you had a lot of work on at
the moment.'

'Yes they did and yes I have.' He shrugged the jacket off and
hung it up on the back of the door leading to the porch. 'You
know that I've been co-opted on to the Progress Committee to
help with the August Festival – now they want me to help set up
a local exhibition of art and photography in the Village Hall and
Lynn Stacey's keen to include paintings done by the schoolchildren.
She's going to make time for me to run a weekly art class with
the kids. My hands will be full from now until the Festival.'

'But Nuala's exhibition's at the end of April, ages before the
Festival.'

'The local school closes late in June, which, if I try to fit in
Nuala's exhibition, gives me just under two months to work with
the local kids. It's not long enough, given that I've only just
started on my own collection for the Festival.'

'Did the Glasgow gallery offer to pay you to set up her
exhibition?'

'Yes, but thanks to the two years I recently spent there I've got enough money to let me stay here and concentrate on my own work – and on you – for quite a while.'

'You're right,' Clarissa said. 'You've got a lot on your plate at the moment.'

'But—'

'But what?'

'I can read your voice as well as your expressions, Clarissa. You think that I should help Nuala.'

'I should mind my own business and let you mind yours.'

'We're a couple – my business is yours and vice versa,' he said, then, sniffing the air, 'Other than cooking, which you do so well.'

'And art, which is your special talent.'

'But let me guess – you're feeling sorry for poor little Nuala. OK, I'll give her a ring and see what I can do for her.'

'Thanks, Alastair, you're a good man!'

'Are you sure about that?' he said as he headed for the door. 'I've never been bullied by a woman before, but I'm beginning to wonder if this is what it feels like.'

He turned to grin at her, and the cushion she had just thrown smacked into his face. 'Ouch!'

'Actually,' Clarissa said, 'I was using gentle persuasion. Dinner will be on the table in fifteen minutes.'

Dinner had been set on the table and then returned to the oven before Alastair arrived to eat it.

Clarissa was reheating the pot of home-made soup when he came into the kitchen, which they both preferred to the small dining room unless they had guests.

He dropped a kiss on her head, 'That smells good – I'm starving. Sorry I took so long, but it was you who insisted I had to phone that girl right away. If there were such things as talk-marathons she'd be a world-class star.'

'No harm done; everything's re-heatable.' She began to ladle soup into the bowls on the counter. 'I thought Nuala was quite a shy girl when I met her.'

'She was like that with me at first, but once she gets to know you it's a different story.' He carried the bowls to the table.

'So what's going to happen?'

'I've told her that the best I can do is spend the three days before her exhibition helping to work out what hangs where, then I'll attend the first evening to see her started before I leave.'

'Will that be enough?' she asked as they settled at the table.

'It'll have to be.' Alastair helped himself to bread. 'This is her second exhibition; the last one went well, and if she wants to become known and successful she's going to have to develop confidence and faith in herself. My life's here now, with you and with the village. I can't keep rushing off to hold her hand. I'll phone the gallery tomorrow to see if they're agreeable to me paying a swift visit.'

'Will you still be paid for your help?'

'I'd better be. And I want you to come to the opening with me. We'll book into a decent hotel and pamper ourselves. No arguments,' he added as she opened her mouth to speak. 'If *you* don't attend the opening then I'm not going either.'

'I think it looks good,' Fergus Matheson said. 'In fact, I'm delighted with it.'

'It's a very rough layout. I'm not good at sketching, and I've not got around to thinking of actual plants.'

'Even so, I think it's close to my own ideas – not that I could have put them down on paper the way you have.'

Fergus and Ginny were in the Linn Hall dining room, studying the garden layouts she had created for him. 'I could pick you up tomorrow around eleven. We'd get there by noon and spend the afternoon matching the plans to the actual garden.'

'I'm not sure I can manage tomorrow . . .'

'Manage what tomorrow?' Lewis asked from the doorway.

'I want the two of us to take these plans along to my new house. The sooner we can make sure that the layout fits the garden the better. I imagine that you've already seen them,' Fergus said, and when Lewis nodded, 'What d'you think?'

'They're excellent.'

'That makes two of us. Why don't you come along?'

Lewis shook his head. 'Duncan and I are planning to start getting the overwintered plants ready to move back outside.'

'And I'm going to help.'

'Ginny, you and Fergus have a lot of decisions to make if you're

going to lick that neglected garden into shape for next year. You'll
have to prioritize. You can't be in two places at once, and now
that we've got young Jimmy McDonald on our gardening team
Duncan and I can cope on our own.'

'Lewis is right, Ginny. That's something I wanted to talk to
you about today. The overgrowth has to be removed or pruned
back before you can begin to make changes and I'm hoping we
can start filming that part within the next two weeks.'

'Two weeks!'

'I need to film the whole process from beginning to end,'
Fergus told her. 'And the sooner the better. I've got your gardening
team standing by.'

'My team?' Ginny was beginning to feel dizzy.

'She's the kind of gardener who likes to get at the soil and do
most of the work by herself,' Lewis said, grinning.

'Not this time, Ginny. For this project you're the designer and
presenter, which means that you design the garden and make all
the decisions, and the team follows your instructions.'

'But I'm a gardener! I do the heavy work.'

'According to those –' Fergus tapped the sketches on the table –
'you're an excellent designer. Once we get going you can work
along with the team as well, but everything has to be done swiftly
in order to keep to the film schedule – this year, starting from
now, the ground has to be cleared and the separate areas laid out
as you've planned. As soon as we get that done, you start planting.
I'll be filming and editing as we go along so that the series can
go on screen this time next year. I know that it all sounds confusing
but it's my job to make it come together. And trust me, it will.'
He looked at his watch. 'Got to go. See you tomorrow morning
at half-past eight.'

'What have I done?' Ginny wailed as they watched Fergus's
blue sports car disappear down the drive.

'You're seeing the benefit of all the hard work you've done
here.'

'But I can't possibly present a gardening series! Couldn't we
ask Fergus to find a professional presenter so that I can concentrate
on the gardening?'

'Good idea – your mother would jump at the chance of
presenting the series and keeping you well out of sight. Come

on, darling,' Lewis coaxed as Ginny clutched at her short black hair and groaned, 'you've worked hard on those plans and done a magnificent job. You deserve to get the credit. And the money.'

'I wish *you* could be co-presenter!'

'It's a nice idea, but we've all worked so hard on the estate and I'm hoping that this year we'll start reaping the rewards. I've got to be here to see it through. Thanks to the way you've trained Jimmy the lad's worth his weight in gold. With him to help us, Duncan and I can keep the place going until your project's over. And I know you'll see it through and emerge with flying colours.'

'You've got Rowena Chloe to think about as well.'

A shadow moved across Lewis's face. 'I know. We've both got a lot ahead of us. But let's look on the bright side – we'll be able to tell your mother that there's really no question of us getting married this year with so much to do.'

'We could, if we married quietly on our own,' Ginny suggested, but he shook his head.

'That would disappoint everyone – your mother, my parents and the villagers. They love a good local wedding.'

'So do I, as long as I'm not the bride. I'd really like a secret ceremony,' Ginny coaxed, but Lewis would have none of it.

'We'll do it properly when we've got time to plan it. There's another thing for me to tackle – trying to raise another bank loan in the hope of bringing Angela Steele in to start work on this ground floor. I'll start on that one by the end of this week, but for now – let's get back to the kitchen for some hot coffee.'

The first lambing season at Tarbethill Farm, a dairy farm until the previous year, was going remarkably smoothly despite a sudden bad snowfall towards the end of March. Ewan, anxious to look after his first flock of pregnant ewes, fitted as many as possible into the lambing shed and left the overflow in the field nearest to the farmhouse. When the lambing began he and Wilf, with assistance from Victor and Alison, dealt with the ewes.

Jess had set up a nursery in the farm kitchen, with boxes, blankets, a heat lamp and feeding bottles. Jamie, still bursting with pride over the way he had rescued Bess from beneath the deep-litter house, spent as much time as possible helping her to care for the orphaned lambs – twins whose mother had died, and another eight rejected by their mothers. Sadly, his suggestion that he should be allowed to care for them full-time was firmly turned down by his mother.

'But there are too many for Gran Jess to look after. She needs my help,' he protested.

'She can manage fine by herself while you're at school,' Alison said firmly.

'She's not getting any younger, you know. You don't want her to tire herself out, do you?' he was saying when Jess came in from the yard, a bowl of eggs in her hand.

'Here, you,' she protested. 'I'm not in my dotage yet.'

'What's a dotage?'

'You'll never live to find out if you don't keep up with your learning,' Alison told him.

'How can I grow up to be a farmer if you keep sending me to school? They don't teach farming there, just dull things like sums and spelling. I need to stay here where Ewan can teach me all the things I should know!'

'Ewan and Victor both went to school and they've turned into good farmers,' Jess chimed in. 'Farmers need to know a lot that can only be taught in school, like how to write so that they can keep records of their work, and how to do sums so that they can buy and sell their animals.'

'And it'll soon be the Easter holidays. You'll be home for two weeks and you can help with the lambs then. But you've got to remember that they're outdoor animals, Jamie. As soon as they're strong enough they'll be going into the fields with the rest of the flock, so we don't want to spoil them.'

'And you've already got a lot of work ahead of you,' Jess pointed out. 'Bess's puppies will be old enough to leave her in a few weeks' time, and Ewan promised that you can have one.'

'I'd nearly forgotten about that.' Jamie suddenly brightened up at the prospect.

Seven

'Life with Jamie,' Alison said as she and Jess walked along the lane together to check that the farm cottage was ready for the Krechevskys, 'seems to be one small battle after another. Was it the same for you with your sons?'

'Not exactly, because Bert had them both down as farmers as soon as they were born. He was the one who made all the decisions about them, and it was more my job to keep a tight rein on him rather than on them. There were times when I wondered if he should give them a chance to make their own decisions – when Victor finally decided to give up farmin' it destroyed Bert, rest his soul.'

'None of us can look into the future,' Alison said as they reached the cottage. 'And there's no sense in looking back either, because what's done is done. We can only look to the future and hope for the best.'

As they walked up the path to the door Jess patted her coat pocket. 'I took the cottage key from the drawer, didn't I?'

'You put into your left pocket.'

'So I did. Jamie reminds me so much of Ewan when he was that age – he never wanted anythin' as much as he wanted Tarbethill to stay in the family. It's as if that wee lad of yours is my Ewan's own flesh and blood instead of his stepson.'

'They certainly share a stubborn streak,' Alison acknowledged. 'It took a long time for me to persuade Ewan that we belonged together, didn't it?'

'There you are then, lass. You managed to get Ewan to do as you and me both wanted, and you'll manage the same with Jamie,' Jess said contentedly, putting the key into the lock and opening the door. 'Good, Ewan remembered to switch the heating on this mornin' – just low for now, to start the place warming up slowly after lyin' empty all winter.'

'I like this wee house – it's got a welcoming feeling about it,' Alison said as she followed her mother-in-law inside.

'I always thought that – it's where me and Bert lived after we married. Our three were born here. We'll have a quick look round to make sure that everythin's ready for the man and his daughter, then get back to work. The furniture's awful old,' Jess added anxiously as they went into the small living room. 'D'you think they'll be all right about it?'

'It's very comfortable, and he did say that he wanted the cottage furnished since they've been living in rented accommodation. I think it looks very nice.'

Together they went through every room to make sure that all was ready for the new inhabitants.

'We'll fill the larder just before they arrive,' Jess said as they went back downstairs after checking the two bedrooms. Then, as a sudden thought struck her, 'What sort of food do Polish folk eat?'

'I don't know, but since Naomi said they've been living in England for a good few years I think we'll be safe buying the sort of food we eat ourselves.'

'And I could add some of my own baking as a wee bit of a welcome.'

'That,' Alison said, 'is the best welcome anyone could get!'

Easter, as Naomi Hennessey reminded a large congregation on Easter Sunday, was a time of regeneration. The final winter snowfall was being firmly nudged aside by spring, and gardens were radiant with colour – first the shy snowdrops, quickly followed by yellow and purple crocuses and bright daffodils. Buds began to appear on trees and bushes and were being coaxed by the sun to unfurl their soft green leaves.

Not long after Easter, Tarbethill's first-born lambs were beginning to move from the lambing shed to a field, staying close to their mothers as they emerged into daylight and then, once they realized what fun the new green world was, starting to venture out on their own. Soon they were chasing each other around and giving the ewes a much-needed chance to graze in peace.

Both Ginny and Lewis were hard at work, but for the first time since they had met they were spending their days apart – Lewis preparing the Linn Hall grounds for their opening to the public at the beginning of May, Ginny some fifteen miles away working on Fergus Matheson's garden and returning in the late afternoon, tired after a day of clearing years of tangled overgrowth and pruning back the shrubbery that was to remain and become part of the new garden.

By the time she got home at the end of each day both of them were too tired to do much more than eat and fall into bed – Lewis in the Hall, and Ginny, to his frustration, in her camper van, parked in the stable yard.

'You'll thank me one day,' she insisted one evening when they found time to go to the Neurotic Cuckoo for a drink. The bar was quiet, giving them the chance to catch up with each other's news.

'I'd rather thank you now.'

'Lewis, we're both working hard. I want us to wait until things ease up and we have time to get married without having to fit the ceremony in-between other activities.'

'You're such a prude!'

'I've always been a prude,' she acknowledged cheerfully. 'I suspect that it comes from my weird life as my parents' daughter. All I've ever wanted is to have a normal life, doing normal things. And that includes falling in love, getting engaged and then getting married – in that order. You know as well as I do that right now we're both exhausted by the end of each day and more interested in a good night's sleep than thoughts of romance.'

He opened his mouth to argue, shut it again, and then admitted, 'I suppose you're right. I'm just feeling sorry for myself.'

'I know why that is – you're missing Rowena Chloe; we all are.' The little girl often spent Easter as well as the summer holidays at Linn Hall, but this year her maternal grandparents had taken her to Portugal, where Molly now lived with her partner Bob Craig.

'I've not heard a word from Molly or her parents since I started trying in earnest to get them to agree to let Rowena Chloe live here with us.'

'What about your lawyer?'

'I must have forgotten to tell you – I phoned him yesterday but he hasn't heard anything either. I think he's getting tired of hearing from me.'

'I'm sure he understands, love.'

'I'm beginning to wonder if Molly's keeping us waiting out of spite.' Lewis ran his fingers through his already tousled brown hair. 'Perhaps I've done the wrong thing – shown myself to be too eager. I might end up not seeing her at all.'

'If that happens you can fight Molly in the courts. She's been living in Portugal for almost two years now and she's not shown any sign of wanting to have her daughter with her. All the indications are that she's quite happy to let her parents look after Rowena Chloe – that fact alone should surely count in your favour. And you've made it clear that you're willing to agree to her having parental access. We just have to be patient, and hope for the best. If you push too hard she could make it difficult for you.'

Lewis summoned up a smile. 'You're right; I should cope with the silence and prepare to meet trouble if it comes instead of expecting it. At least I know that whatever happens I'll always have you.'

'That I can promise you.' She reached across the table to take his hand.

'Another drink?'

'The thought's tempting but if I said yes I'd probably be slumped on the table, snoring, before it was finished.'

'Me too. On the other hand . . .' A massive yawn stopped Lewis, and when it was over he said, 'On the other hand, it would be one way of spending the night together, if Joe didn't throw us out at closing time.'

'I'm hoping that our first night together will be more exciting than that when it finally happens,' Ginny told him as she got to her feet.

They said goodnight to Joe Fisher and walked back to Linn Hall hand in hand. Reaching the stable courtyard at the rear of the Hall, Lewis took Ginny into his arms and kissed her. When they finally moved apart he said, 'Are you absolutely sure that you . . .'

'Absolutely sure. Go to bed; you're tired out and so am I.'

Alone in her camper van, Ginny climbed into bed and tried to read herself to sleep with a novel borrowed from the mobile library, but her eyes skimmed unseeingly over the first page because her mind was recalling the time she had come into the kitchen and overheard part of a conversation between Jinty and Fliss, who were in the pantry used by the Ralston-Kerrs as a living room.

It had happened about two years earlier, while Lewis was still besotted with Molly Ewing and Ginny was beginning to fall in love with him and had to keep reminding herself that he was already spoken for, and that every time he looked at her he only saw a gardener, never a woman.

Jinty was speaking as Ginny stepped into the empty kitchen. 'What I'm saying, Mrs F, is – does he know for sure that that wee girl's his flesh and blood?'

'She must be, unless Molly's lying – and why should she do that?'

'You've heard her mother goin' on about how one day Molly will be the mistress of Linn Hall. The woman's thrilled about the very idea.'

'I don't know why – the dear old place is close to falling down about our ears through lack of money.'

'I know that, but it still looks good to folk like me and the Ewings, and the three of you are looked up to by the whole village. I'm just wonderin' if Molly's using that bonny wee soul to get what she wants. Someone should get Lewis to make sure that Rowena Chloe's his legitimate heir before he walks Molly down the aisle.'

'I couldn't talk to Lewis about a thing like that!' Fliss said, shocked. 'Nor could Hector – you know what a shy man he is!'

'I wasnae goin' to say a word, but when Molly's folk were here the last time her sister Stella was in the garden with me – I can't remember why – and she told me that Molly had had an abortion when she was just a schoolgirl. It makes me wonder what sort of life she's led since then.'

There was a gasp, and then Ginny heard Fliss say, 'I wish you hadn't told me that, Jinty. Lewis adores Rowena Chloe and he'd be devastated if he discovered that she wasn't his daughter.'

'I know, but I've wondered since then if, when Molly fell pregnant with Rowena Chloe, she decided to have the baby just to strengthen her grip on Lewis. If she was a proper carin' mother, that wee lass would be livin' in Portugal with her now.'

At that stage Ginny had crept back outside to the courtyard, counted to twenty and then gone inside again and stamped over to the sink to wash her dirty hands as noisily as she could.

She, like Fliss, now wished that she had never heard Jinty's revelation. But she agreed with Fliss that if what Jinty had said about an earlier abortion was true, Lewis must never find out.

'They're here – they're here!' Jamie shrieked, bursting into the farmhouse kitchen. 'I've just seen them coming up the lane!'

Alison and Jess, who had been enjoying a chat over a cup of tea, both jumped to their feet. 'Where's Ewan?' Jess wanted to know.

'He knows already – he's in the lambing shed and I told him – come on quick!' Jamie was jumping up and down in his excitement.

'There's no hurry,' Alison pointed out, 'They're coming to stay. We're probably going to see them every day from now on.'

'Honestly!' Jamie said in exasperation before disappearing out of the door.

'Is there enough water in the kettle?' Jess wanted to know as she reached for her coat.

'It's full, and everything's ready,' Alison responded, snatching up her jacket. They hurried out into the farmyard just as Stefan's Jeep arrived, pulling an enclosed trailer, and Ewan and Wilf appeared from the lambing shed.

'Good afternoon!' Stefan Krechevsky emerged from the Jeep to greet them with open arms and a wide smile. 'It is so good to be here in your beautiful country at last!'

'It's good to see you, Stefan.' Ewan shook the man's hand. 'Where's your daughter?'

'She couldn't wait to see her new home, so I left her there with the key you sent to us and came to let you know that we'd arrived. This,' Stefan gestured to the trailer, 'is the equipment for my workshop.'

'Wilf and I will help you to unload it.'

'Later,' Jess said firmly. 'You'll be hungry after your journey and we've got food ready for you. Jamie, run to the cottage and bring Berta back here.'

★   ★   ★

When Jamie reached the cottage the door was open. He knocked, and as there was no answer he went inside and called tentatively, 'Hello?'

'Hello – I'm coming,' a voice called from upstairs and a moment later a girl came running lightly down to where he stood. Jamie's mouth dropped open as she reached him.

She was taller than he was, with wide brown eyes and a long plait, so blonde that it was almost white, over one shoulder and nearly reaching to her waist. Her slender figure was clad in tight-fitting jeans and a scarlet gilet over a cream sweater. She was the most beautiful girl Jamie had ever seen.

'Hello,' she said, 'I'm Berta. Who are you?'

He opened his mouth, closed it again, gulped noisily, and then managed to say, 'J–Jamie. I live at the farm. They've sent me to take you there for something to eat.'

'That's great, let's go.' She led the way out of the cottage, saying over her shoulder as they went down the path, 'I'm really looking forward to living here. Are you the farmer's son?'

'Yes – no,' Jamie stammered. 'I mean, sort of. My mum married him last year. I'm going to be a farmer. I've got a rabbit called Tommy.'

'I like rabbits. Can I see him?'

'You can play with him if you like. And we've got some puppies too. Their mum was scared when they started coming and she hid underneath the hen house in the middle of the night and I had to crawl underneath to rescue her. She had five pups – you can see them too – and I'm getting one but I haven't chosen it yet. It's going to be mine but it's to be a working sheepdog like its mum, and Ewan's going to show me how to train it.'

'I've got a horse called Titan.'

'Is he here?'

'He's in England. He's arriving next week.' She turned to smile at him, flicking the long plait over one shoulder. 'Can you ride?' Then when he shook his head, 'I'll teach you, if you like.'

'Honestly?'

Berta smiled down at him. Her teeth were white, even and perfect, just like the teeth he had seen in television advertisements. 'Honestly.'

'Cool!' Suddenly, Jamie's life had become a world of sunshine and magic.

Eight

Naomi Hennessey's small car drove into the farmyard and Naomi eased herself out and on to her feet.

Jess, who was scattering food for the hens who still roamed around the yard, greeted her friend with a beaming smile. 'It's lovely to see you, Naomi! Have you come to visit our new tenants?'

'I have indeed. How are they settling in?'

'Och, they've only been here a few days, but they're like part of the family already. Stefan's in his workshop – d'you want to go in and say hello?'

'I will, and then I'll come to the kitchen for a cup of tea with you, if you've got the time.'

'You know that I always have time for you! I'll be taking a few scones from the oven when I've finished with the hens,' Jess assured her friend.

'I couldn't have arrived at a better time then.' Naomi headed for Stefan's workshop while Jess scattered the rest of the hen food before bustling into the kitchen.

The new workshop's double doors were open wide and when Naomi stepped inside the heat from the furnace made her reel back for a moment. The workshop interior seemed dark compared to the sun outside, lit as it was only by the blazing furnace.

'Miss Hennessey!' Stefan greeted her warmly, shaking her by the hand. 'I am so glad to see you and to be able to thank you for finding us this beautiful place with such charming people.'

'So you and your daughter have settled in well?'

'Very well. We now have a lovely little home, Berta and I, and I'm very pleased with my workshop.'

'I hope that you're going to be able to sell your work; Prior's Ford is very quiet at the moment, but during the summer we have a lot of visitors and you should do well with your glassware. I must introduce you to Anya Jacobsen, who runs a shop called Colour Carousel. It's full of beautiful things and I'm sure that she'll be delighted to display your work.'

'Alison already took me to see the young lady you mention, and she has kindly agreed to exhibit my glassware. At the moment I'm still setting up and getting used to my work surroundings.'

'And Berta is settling in?'

He nodded. 'Like me, she is happy to be here. Her beloved horse will arrive next week, and Alison has also arranged for me to meet the local head teacher, who will kindly assist me in making arrangements for Berta to start attending the correct school for her age group.'

'Kirkcudbright Academy – it's a very good school and I'm sure Berta will be happy there.'

'She is already making friends with young people from the village who attend the same school.'

'So everything is going well for you both – that's grand. I'm going to the farmhouse now to have a cup of tea with my friend Jess. Would you like to join us?'

Stefan shook his head. 'I must prepare my workshop so that I can get started.' He took her hand and, to her surprise, kissed it. 'Once again I thank you, Miss Hennessey!'

'Naomi.'

The glass-blower bowed acknowledgement. 'Naomi, he said, then, putting a hand to his chest, 'and Stefan.'

'Stefan,' she echoed, and went back out into the sunshine.

'I've never in my life had my hand kissed,' she told Jess a few minutes later. 'I almost started to giggle like a silly girl.'

'You and me both.' Jess set two cups of tea down on the table. 'I could just imagine the look on my Bert's face if he'd been here. But I have to say that it felt really nice to have my hand kissed. Try some of this raspberry jam with your scone – Wilf's son grew the raspberries on his allotment last year and his wife gave me a couple of jars.'

'The newcomers seem to have settled in well.' Naomi split a scone, taking a moment to inhale the delicious scent of baking fresh from the oven. She buttered the scone briskly and began to add raspberry jam.

'They're lovely people and I'm glad we were able to help them. Their English is really good.'

'Apparently they've been living in England for quite a few

years now. I understand that they came over here not long after Stefan's wife died.' Naomi bit into her scone. 'I wish I could bake like you, Jess!'

'And I wish I could write sermons like yours. Berta's a lovely girl, in looks as well as manner. Our Jamie's got a real crush on her, especially since she's offered to teach him to ride when her horse arrives.'

'I hope things go well with Stefan's business.'

'Me too, and it's not just for the rent – although that's very useful.'

Naomi finished her scone and reached for another. 'You're right about the raspberry jam, it's delicious. It's so good to see this farm overcoming all the problems you've been through in the past few years.'

Jess beamed at her friend. 'I can't believe it. There was a time when I thought nothing was ever going to be right for us again. First Victor giving up the farm, then Bert's death and Ewan decidin' against marryin' Alison and tryin' to keep things goin' on his own. Then suddenly everythin' started to work out – now Alison and Jamie are here and I've never seen Ewan happier.'

'It's good to see you happy too.'

'How could I not be, with Jamie for my grandson? That wee lad's the light of my life, Naomi.'

'And no doubt there will be other grandchildren eventually.'

'I certainly hope so. It's lovely that Jamie's so determined to follow in Ewan's footsteps and become a farmer. He's been a great help already with the lambs, and I told you about him getting Bess out from under the hen shed when her pups were comin', didn't I?'

'You did.' Naomi took a third scone. 'At this moment I should be in my study working on Sunday's sermon, but instead – to tell the truth, I wouldn't mind another cup of tea.'

Now that Ginny and her team of three gardeners had started to clear the garden by the Solway Firth Fergus was there with a cameraman almost every day. Once again Ginny had to get used to working before the camera, often having to explain exactly what they were doing. As before, she hated being filmed and having to do a running commentary from time to time, but once again she very quickly forgot that she was being filmed, and with Fergus there to ask questions she began to relax and concentrate on what she was doing. It had been his idea that when he was going to be on the scene, he would pick her up each morning and take her back to Linn Hall at the end of the day, to save her having to drive.

'You're a natural,' he said as he was taking her back home one day. Then, as she said nothing, 'You still don't believe that, do you?'

'No, I don't. I love gardening and that's all. I'm not an expert.'

'I've almost finished editing the filming I did last year when you were showing me around the Linn estate gardens, and once you see it you'll understand what I'm talking about. I'm hoping to get a television slot within the next month.'

'Do you have to?'

'Of course. It's going to publicize the coming series on the work you're undertaking for my garden and it will also be a great advert for Lewis and his parents.' He glanced across at her. 'You're not going to deny your beloved the opportunity to get a bit of free advertising, are you? The Linn Estate is well worth seeing and I want everybody to know that. When does it open this year?'

'The middle of May; Lewis and Duncan and Jimmy have been working flat out to get everything ready for then. That's why I've been pushing the gardeners at your place so hard – I want to free up some time then so that I can help Lewis and the others.'

'I've noticed that you're quite a slave driver.'

'The sooner all the unnecessary shrubbery's cleared the better. Then I can start on the planting programme.' They had reached the village and were passing the Neurotic Cuckoo. 'Just drop me here – I can walk the rest of the way.'

'Don't be silly.' He kept going, ignoring her protests. As he swung the car through Linn Hall's gates and started up the drive a young couple sauntering down from the house waved, and Ginny waved back. Glancing into the mirror as they continued up the drive Fergus asked, 'Who are they?'

'The first of the summer workers. Linn Hall couldn't do without them, and fortunately they keep coming. They live in the two gatehouses, boys in one, girls in the other; Angie and Jonathan are regulars. I should be ready to start buying plants next week.' Ginny returned to the subject of Fergus's garden.

'That's good news. I'd like to visit the garden centre with you.'

'Of course – give me two more days to finish clearing the ground. Would Wednesday suit you?'

Fergus took the car into the stable courtyard and stopped. 'Great – half past eight tomorrow morning as usual?'

'I'll be ready. Thanks for the lift.'

'My pleasure.' As she started to open her door he tapped her on the shoulder, then when she turned towards him he leaned over and kissed her on the cheek.

Ginny reared back in embarrassment, almost bumping her head against the door frame 'What was that for?'

'Oh, just to say thanks for everything,' Fergus said easily.

Face burning, she got out of the car quickly and was relieved to hear it start to move off. As it turned in a tight half-circle she saw him wave from his open window, his head turned away from where she was standing, and looked over to see Lewis emerging from the stable shop.

'Everything all right?' he asked as he crossed over towards her. 'You look a bit flustered.'

'It's been a really busy day. We're finally ready to start buying the plants. Fergus and I are going to the garden centre on Wednesday.'

'That's good.' He pulled her into his arms and kissed her soundly. 'Perhaps we'll be able to see more of each other from now on.'

'I hope so,' Ginny said fervently.

After living in a village for several years Clarissa found Glasgow quite intimidating. She and Alastair had booked into a hotel and as he had to make the most of the time available they headed for the Art Gallery almost as soon as they had checked in.

Watching as Alastair was warmly welcomed by everyone, Clarissa began to suspect that she had made a mistake in agreeing to accompany him to the city. The feeling got stronger when Nuala arrived, and rushed to throw her arms around him.

'Thank you, thank you, and thank you again!' she said fervently.

'I know I'm being an absolute nuisance but I simply can't do this without you. You must think that I'm a dreadful coward!'

'Yes, you are,' he told her, disentangling himself. 'Poor Clarissa practically had to be dragged here – she's not really interested in cities or in art galleries.'

'I'm so sorry, Clarissa.' Nuala took both of Clarissa's hands in hers. 'I didn't realize that you were coming as well. What a pest I am, dragging you all the way here!'

'I don't mind, really.'

'She's just being polite. I refuse to go anywhere without Clarissa,' Alastair said. 'Right, let's get on with it. We don't have much time.'

'You were quite rude to that poor girl!' Clarissa protested two hours later, when Alastair whisked her off for lunch.

'Firm, not rude. Nuala's like a spoiled child at times – I'd forgotten that. I wish I hadn't agreed to do this,' he said. 'I can't have you hanging around feeling miserable, even though it's just for a few days. Maybe we should go back home.'

'Of course not! I wasn't miserable, just a bit bored; I have to admit that art isn't really my thing. I'd really rather wander around Glasgow than go back to the gallery this afternoon.'

'Are you sure?'

She smiled across the table at him. 'Absolutely,' she lied. 'There are lots of places to go and things to see here. I'll enjoy exploring, and it would leave you free to get on with your work.'

'In that case, buy yourself something really nice to wear to the opening and I'll pay for it.'

'I've already brought something to wear. I don't need anything else.'

'I insist.' He offered her his credit card, but she shook her head. 'It's a complete waste of money!'

'No it's not. I'm already looking forward to seeing you in something gorgeous and expensive – make sure it's expensive. I'm being well paid for this job and it would give me a lot of pleasure to spend it on you.' He pushed the card into her hand and then opened his menu. 'We'll start right now. Let's both choose something disgustingly expensive, and this evening we'll go to see a show, if you can find one that you'd enjoy. We're in the big city, so let's make the most of it and do whatever the Glaswegians do.'

Clarissa followed Alastair's advice and found that wandering around Glasgow, stopping off for coffee whenever she felt like it, could be surprisingly pleasant.

During the two days she spent on her own she concentrated on hairdressers and dress shops, so that on the day of the exhibition's opening, while Alastair was busy putting finishing touches to the exhibition, she knew exactly where she was going.

Her first stop was an upmarket hair salon close to the hotel. 'I'm attending a very special occasion,' she said to the male hairdresser, 'and I want my hair to look perfect, but at the same time I don't want it to be too elaborate.'

He ran his fingers lightly through her short hair before smiling at her in the mirror. 'You have very good hair, madam,' he said, 'and I quite agree with what you say.' Then he started work.

Two hours later she was on the way to the chosen dress department in a large and well-known emporium. There, she spent almost an hour trying on various outfits and, sadly, losing heart as the saleswoman studied her critically each time she emerged from the fitting room before saying, 'I think I can find something more suitable.'

Clarissa was almost about to give up and look for another dress shop when the woman said, 'I've just remembered an outfit that came in yesterday and hasn't yet been put on the rails.' She then disappeared, returning ten minutes later with a dress and matching three-quarter-length jacket.

The silk dress was classical, sleeveless, in Royal blue with a cream belt, cream trimming round the plain neckline and a flared skirt. The three-quarter-length jacket, worn open, was cream with Royal blue trimming and three-quarter length sleeves.

Clarissa looked at it doubtfully. 'Isn't that a little – young for me?'

The woman smiled at her. 'There's something about you that makes me disagree. And you won't know if it's the right dress for you until you try it on.'

The dress fitted perfectly, and felt just right. When Clarissa drew the curtain back and walked out of the fitting room the saleswoman gave her a delighted smile. 'As I thought, madam, this is the right dress. How does it feel?'

Clarissa moved to the nearest mirror and studied herself. 'It feels perfect.'

'All it needs now are shoes, a bag and the right make-up. Why don't I take you to our shoe and accessories departments? And we have some excellent staff in our cosmetic department as well.'

Nine

'Your hair looks wonderful,' Alastair said as soon as he returned from the gallery. 'What have you done with it?'

'I found a very good hairdresser who suggested that I should try highlights.'

'I hope you took my advice and bought something new to wear as well.'

'I did, but unfortunately I've given your credit card quite a shock.'

He grinned at her. 'Good for you. What's the point in having money if you don't spend it? I can't wait to see your new outfit. But let's go and have something to eat before we get ready for the exhibition.'

'Is it all set up?'

'All set up – and I think she's going to do quite well from it. Let's head for the dining room.'

Butterflies fluttered in Clarissa's stomach as she dressed for the exhibition. Perhaps the new outfit wouldn't look as good as it had under the shop's lights. But to her relief the dress and jacket still looked and felt perfect, as did the new shoes and the clutch bag. She opened the box of cosmetics and drew several deep breaths to calm her nerves before starting to apply them in the way that the expert in the department store had shown her.

It took some time, but when she was finally ready and looked in the mirror she was astonished to see a totally different woman calmly looking back at her. Suddenly, the Clarissa who had first arrived in Prior's Ford as Keith Ramsay's middle-aged wife had been replaced by a confident and elegant woman. A woman who had undergone a total change, not only because of the stylish outfit and smart hairstyle, but by the love of the right man. All her doubts about the age difference between herself and Alastair had disappeared – and it felt wonderful.

'Almost time to go, Clarissa,' Alastair called just then from the next room.

He had raided the drinks cabinet and was pouring out two glasses of wine. 'I thought we'd drink to the exhibition before we leave,' he said over his shoulder, then as he turned to hand her a glass his hazel eyes widened. 'Wow!'

'Will I do?'

'Do? You look – absolutely fantastic!'

'To be honest,' Clarissa said more honestly than he would ever know, 'I feel absolutely fantastic. And you look wonderful too.'

He shook his head, his eyes still drinking her in. 'I feel inadequate compared to you.'

'No need; I never knew that you could look so dashing in a suit.'

'I have been known to scrub up well when the occasion demanded.'

Clarissa laughed as she took the offered glass of wine. 'Here's to the exhibition.'

'Oh no,' Alastair still looked dazed. 'Here's to you, for ever and always. You never stop amazing me, Clarissa. I'm so lucky to have found you.'

'We're both lucky,' she said, and raised her glass. 'Here's to us – for ever and always.'

Clarissa half expected to lose her new-found self-assurance once the two of them arrived at the art gallery, but it stayed with her, even when Alastair had to mingle with the crowd, leaving her on her own. Champagne glass in hand, she wandered around the gallery, studying Nuala's paintings.

'She's a very talented young artist, isn't she?' Two women around her own age joined her in front of one of the paintings.

'Yes indeed,' Clarissa agreed.

'Do you own any of her work?'

Clarissa shook her head. 'My cottage is full of my partner's artwork, with no room for anything else.'

'Really? Are you an artist yourself?' the second woman enquired with interest.

'Sadly, I'm not at all creative.'

'Nor am I. To tell the truth, my sister insisted on dragging me along – under protest, as I know absolutely nothing about art.'

'She's a total novice when it comes to art,' the other woman agreed. 'I started attending a night-school course a few years ago and loved it so much that I've been attending courses and visiting art galleries ever since. I acquired one of Nuala Brennan's paintings at her last exhibition, and it's been greatly admired. I was hoping to buy another this year but the prices have gone up significantly, so I'm not sure that I'll be able to afford it. My loss, but on the other hand it means that she's doing very well, so I'm delighted for her. Such a very pretty girl, isn't she?' She nodded to where Nuala, her green eyes sparkling, was in deep discussion with Alastair. 'Don't she and that young man she's with make a perfect couple? I wonder if he's an artist too.'

'Yes, he is,' Clarissa said. 'He's a very good artist; in fact, he organized her first exhibition, and this one.'

'You know him?' one sister said, while the other followed with: 'You're not his mother, are you?'

'I know him very well, but I'm not his mother – he's my partner.'

A few days earlier Clarissa wouldn't have had the courage to say that to anyone, let alone complete strangers. But now, at last, it was said with confidence.

And the look of mingled surprise and envy on the faces of the two women made her so glad that she had suddenly developed the courage to say it out loud – and to know that it was true beyond any doubt.

The friendship between Malcolm Finlay and Stella Hesslett had slowly but steadily developed and had now reached the stage where Malcolm invited the librarian to have lunch with him in the Neurotic Cuckoo each time the mobile library van was in the village.

Stella had become aware that their regular meetings were beginning to cause a certain amount of comment, and had to force herself to suggest one day over lunch that they should stop meeting in public. The effort made her blush, and the blush deepened when Malcolm misunderstood her.

'My dear lady, please accept my apologies. I had no intention of f–forcing my company upon you,' he stammered. 'I thought – I mean, I find you a most interesting companion to talk to – I didn't realize that I was forcing you into being polite. Please accept my assurance that you will not be troubled again—'

Stella was as upset as he was, especially when she noticed the surprised glances from the others in the lounge bar. 'Please don't, Dr Finlay!' She reached out a hand towards him and then hurriedly drew it back. When he tried to speak again, she hissed at him, 'We're attracting attention!'

'Are we?' Malcolm glanced about the room and then snatched up his napkin, clapped it over his lower features and muttered out of one corner of his mouth, 'Good heavens, so we are!'

Stella picked up her glass of water and sipped at it. 'Drink some water,' she murmured as she set the glass down, 'then we'll both finish eating in silence and talk later.'

'Is everything all right?' Gracie Fisher had approached their table. 'Is something wrong with the food?'

Stella smiled at her. 'No, Gracie, it's delicious. Isn't it, Dr Finlay?'

Malcolm, who was now gulping water, emptied the glass, wiped his mouth with the napkin and cleared his throat. 'Delicious,' he agreed. 'A mouthful went down the wrong way – my fault entirely. All put right now – may I have some more water?'

They finished their meal in silence as Stella had suggested. Once they were outside the pub and away from listening ears he burst into more apologies. 'My dear lady, I do apologize for whatever error I made. What was it?'

They were approaching the mobile van, and Stella took out her keys. 'Dr Finlay, the error was mine and I apologize for confusing you. It's just that—' She found herself blushing again. 'You may not have realized it because you're new to the village, but you and I are beginning to be noticed.'

'Noticed? In what way?'

'It's because we're lunching together so often.'

Malcolm was astonished. 'Often? I would say — occasionally.'

'It's become a weekly occasion.'

'Has it? Weekly?'

She smiled at him. 'Weekly, and I enjoy our meetings very much—'

'So do I — very much. I find you a most interesting companion, Miss Hesslett.'

'The problem is that Prior's Ford is a typical village, and in a typical village everybody notices what everyone else is doing. You and I having lunch together regularly in the local pub is the sort of thing they like to gossip about.'

'Really? How strange,' he marvelled. 'But I think it most unfair that two people who enjoy each other's company have to stop seeing each other just because people gossip.'

'We don't have to stop enjoying each other's company. I was going to suggest,' Stella said, 'that one evening next week you come to my house for dinner. I've been meaning to invite you in any case, as a way of returning your kindness.'

'I can assure you, Miss Hesslett, that it's not a matter of kindness. I really do enjoy and appreciate the chance to talk about books — my favourite subject.'

'Mine too. Shall we say next Tuesday evening at seven o'clock?'

The arrival of the new Polish residents caused quite a stir in Prior's Ford, especially when they were seen in the village. Stefan, although he didn't realize it, set a few female hearts aflutter with his looks and his friendliness, while Berta raised a lot of interest, especially among the young lads, and had no trouble at all in making friends of both sexes.

A few residents found it harder to come to terms with what they saw as a foreign invasion. One of them was Cynthia McBain, who had been born in the house she now shared with her husband Gilbert and was of the opinion that 'her' village was in danger of being taken over by incomers.

'We're talking about one man and his daughter, Cynthia,' said Hannah Gibbs when Cynthia voiced her views at a meeting of the local drama group, held to discuss their next production, a winter pantomime, 'and they seem to be very pleasant people.

Jess McNair tells me that they're both settling in very well at Tarbethill Farm.'

'According to the newspapers,' Cynthia retorted, 'Britain's being flooded by foreigners these days.'

'Mainly the towns and cities,' Cam Gordon pointed out. 'There's not a lot of work in villages like this for a flood of outsiders, is there?'

Cynthia glared at him. She disapproved of Cam, who, in her opinion, never took anything seriously and was far too interested in having fun, particularly with pretty girls.

'*We* have our share of foreigners,' she snapped. 'Ingrid Mackenzie for one, and her niece who runs the gift shop.'

'Really, Cynthia! Ingrid is married to a Scot, her daughters were both born here and she's a very popular inhabitant of this village.' Lynn Stacey couldn't help sounding irritated. 'And as for Anya, she came here to take over the gift shop when Ingrid had to return to Norway to look after her parents.'

'Perhaps they're just the start of something ominous!' Cynthia said, and then, as nobody answered and even her husband Gilbert, normally so loyal, remained silent and was beginning to look very uncomfortable, she muttered, 'I'm simply saying what others think.'

'Name the others,' Cam challenged. Fortunately, the door opened at that moment to admit Anya Jacobsen. 'I am so sorry, everyone, to be late,' she said in her attractive lilting accent. 'I was rearranging the shop window and I forgot the time.'

The atmosphere in the hall changed at once. Cam, as always, went to hug his girlfriend. 'You've arrived just in time, sweetheart,' he said loudly. 'And we're all *delighted* to see you – aren't we, fellow thespians?'

There was a general chorus of agreement from all but Cynthia, who summoned up a thin smile.

'You've arrived just in time, Anya,' Lynn told the girl, and then, briskly clapping her hands, 'Right, everyone, pull your seats into a circle and let's get down to the business of choosing our next pantomime.'

Once Stefan had set up his workshop to his satisfaction the local newspaper ran a full-page feature article on him and interested villagers began to find their way up the farm lane to watch him at work. They were all made welcome and Stefan was more than happy to explain and demonstrate the process of glass-blowing.

'His workshop isn't getting in the way of the farm work, is it?' Naomi wanted to know when she came into the farm kitchen after a visit to Stefan, and found Ewan and Wilf taking their break.

'It's not bothering us,' Ewan assured her. 'Since we opened up the allotments and tarred and widened the lane we've got used to people coming up and down. Stefan doesn't mind visitors – he says he's used to them, and as long as nobody goes farther than the farmhouse there are no problems with our work or with the animals. And letting people watch Stefan making his ornaments might well help with his sales now that Anya's agreed to display his glassware. After all, the more he sells the more sure we are of having his rent paid regularly.'

'Having the two of them here gives us no trouble at all, Naomi,' Jess added. 'Stefan won't even come in here for a cup of tea – he has bottles of water in his workshop because of the heat. The two of them are very happy in the cottage, and Jamie and Berta are great friends already. Her horse is coming up from England soon, and she's promised to teach Jamie to ride.'

'He's been in heaven ever since that lassie arrived,' Ewan said with a grin.

'So have half the boys in the village from what I hear,' Naomi said drily. 'She'll certainly not be without friends.'

Ten

It took several visits to the chosen nursery gardens before Ginny and Fergus had collected all the plants necessary for the new garden. By that time all the undergrowth had either been removed or pruned back hard, and the various parts of the garden had been marked off.

It was the beginning of May, and to her delight Ginny had managed to reach the stage where her excellent team of gardeners could be relied on to work on their own at times, freeing her to spend some time at Linn Hall, helping Lewis to prepare for the official opening in the middle of the month.

To her surprise, when she pointed this out to Fergus he didn't receive it well.

'I don't see why you need to be at Linn Hall so often,' he protested; 'surely Lewis knows exactly what to do by now.'

'So do your gardeners; they're all professionals and I don't need to be with them every single day. I haven't missed an opening of the Linn estate before and I don't want to miss this one.'

'You mean you want to be with Lewis.'

'Of course I do. If it wasn't for Lewis giving me the chance to become a proper gardener I'd still be working in a garden centre.'

'I doubt that, especially if I'd found you first.'

'That,' Ginny said, 'is an extremely large "if". I'll spend at least two full days a week in your garden just to make sure that everything's going well – which it will be – until the Linn estate's up and running. It's a very important part of my life now that Lewis and I are going to be married. One day we'll be completely responsible for the place.'

They were in Fergus's sports car, on their way back to Linn Hall after a busy day. To Ginny's surprise, he turned the steering wheel, guiding the car into a lay-by, where he stopped and switched off the engine.

'Listen to me, Ginny –' he turned to face her – 'you don't seem to realize this, but you're facing a really good future. You're a gifted gardener – a natural with a good eye for design. You've done a great job at Linn Hall and you're doing a great job at my place. You're also photogenic, which makes you the perfect television presenter.'

'I am not interested in—' She started to protest, but he silenced her by putting a finger against her lips.

'Just shut up and listen to me for a minute. With my help you could do very well for yourself. Think about it.' The tip of his finger moved across her lips before curving down her cheek and coming to rest on her chin.

Ginny pulled back. 'Stop flattering me!'

'I will – when you stop being in denial. It's nothing to do with flattery; you come across very well on television – you'll see that for yourself soon. I've got a slot for the Linn Hall programme.'

'What?'

Fergus grinned at her. 'I've pulled a lot of strings and managed to arrange for it to be aired two days before the Linn Hall opening, which should make you and Lewis very happy. That's what you call great timing; with any luck it's going to bring in quite a lot of extra people.'

'That's wonderful!'

'Look on it as my gift to you – and to your fiancé and his parents.'

Suddenly the documentary that had been talked about several times had become reality. 'I–I don't know if I'll be able to watch it,' Ginny said feebly.

'You'd better – I went to a lot of trouble to get the timing right. Watch very carefully, and you'll see what I mean by your natural gift for presentation.' He switched on the engine and turned the car back on to the road.

The *Dumfries News* that weekend had as its front-page story 'Local Lass Becomes Television Star', followed by a lengthy article about Ginny, including a photograph of her working in the Linn Hall gardens. The story also made the most of the fact that she was the daughter of famous actress Meredith Whitelaw.

Jinty bought several copies of the paper on her way to work at Linn Hall and handed them out to everyone when she arrived. Ginny groaned when she saw it. 'I wish I'd never met Fergus and agreed to do his garden. I wish *you'd* shown him round the estate instead of me that day, Lewis!'

'Don't be daft,' Jinty said. 'It's wonderful for Linn Hall, and for the village. You'll need to send a copy of the paper to your mum. She'll be so proud of you – we bought ten copies when they did that nice story about our Steph getting into the Drama College. I met Gracie Fisher on my way here and she says that the pub's going to run the programme on the public bar television set when it comes on. Everyone will want to see it.'

'I certainly won't watch it!'

'Oh, but you must, dear,' Fliss protested. We're all going to watch it. I'm so glad that we finally managed to buy a television set of our own!'

Lewis gave Ginny a hug. 'Yes we are, you as well,' he said firmly. 'Think of the publicity it's going to give us.'

As soon as she could, Ginny escaped from the kitchen and went to her favourite refuge – the walled kitchen garden she had retrieved from dereliction and remodelled when she first started to work at Linn Hall. The walled area always managed to soothe her when she was upset, but today she was in such turmoil that it didn't seem to be able to work its magic for her.

She had left the area's gate ajar and had settled herself on a large upturned plant pot, arms wrapped around her knees, staring at the ground when Muffin arrived and nudged at her elbow. She looked up to see him peering anxiously into her face.

'Hello, you big lump of tangled wool,' she said, giving him a hug, then when he started licking her face, 'You know I'm feeling down, don't you? You're a lot smarter than you look, dog.'

The two of them were sitting together, Ginny's arm around the dog and Muffin leaning happily against her, when Jimmy McDonald found them.

'Is it bein' on the telly that's botherin' you?'

'Go away!'

He ignored the order, turning over another empty pot and folding his lanky frame on to it section by section, something that only Jimmy seemed to be able to do. 'I wouldn't like it either if it was me. Life can be a right bitch sometimes, can't it?' He reached out to scratch Muffin under the chin.

Ginny nodded, then said, 'D'you know something, Jimmy? You're the only person who really understands me.'

'That's because *you're* the only person who really understands *me*. Nob'dy ever understood how much I wanted to be a gardener like my grandad until you came and made it happen for me. You gave me the chance to try it, and you taught me and never once lost your temper with me,' said Jimmy, who had grown up in a large family and had never known what it was like to be treated as an individual. 'That's why I know how you feel about bein' seen on the telly.'

The two of them sat together in silence for several minutes before he unfolded himself joint by joint until he was back on his feet. 'But you'll get through it, Ginny, because you're that kind of person.'

'I'm not so sure.'

'I am. I think you're blo—bloomin' fantastic,' said Jimmy, then, blushing furiously, he hurried off. Muffin, apparently deciding that Ginny could now safely be left on her own, followed him in search of new adventure.

Now that it was May the people who lived in the almshouses had returned to their usual summer habit of meeting once a week in the open garden behind the terraced houses. As always, the women supplied tea, coffee and refreshments; today Muriel Jacobsen provided the tea, Dolly and Harold Cowan brought a large pot of coffee and Cissie Kavanagh and Hannah Gibbs offered scones and sandwiches.

Hannah also brought Layla, the Borlands' baby daughter, who was lying on a rug contentedly gurgling and kicking her fat dimpled legs.

'And where's your mummy today?' Cissie asked her, and was blown a bubble in reply.

'Shopping in Kirkcudbright,' Hannah said. 'I thought she'd be back by now.'

'Tricia doesn't seem to spend much time with her baby, does she?' Robert Kavanagh commented.

'She's young yet,' Dolly said. 'Not used to being a mother.'

'Difficult to get used to being a mother when your baby's always being looked after by someone else.'

Cissie frowned at her husband. 'I've said to you before, Robert – it's early days yet for Tricia.'

'I don't remember you farming our kids out among other people when they were that age,' he said around a mouthful of scone. Then, swallowing, 'In those days mothers were expected to look after their own children.'

'I'm inclined to agree with you, Robert,' Hannah nodded. 'But it's a difficult subject to raise with Tricia. She's very young – perhaps we should give her a little more time.'

Dolly scooped Layla up into her arms and kissed the blonde fluff on the little head. 'I have to admit, though, that I do love looking after her. You're a sweetie-pie, aren't you?'

'Gangah,' Layla agreed. She beamed round the circle of adults, and then, spotting Harold's long, lugubrious face, gurgled and held out her arms to him.

'I don't know why, Harold, but I really do think that you're this little girl's favourite person!' Dolly marvelled.

Ginny revelled in being able to spend more time at Linn Hall helping to prepare the estate for the summer opening. 'It's like taking off a uniform and putting on a comfortable old coat,' she told Lewis as the two of them toured the grounds in a final check to make sure that everything had been attended to.

'That doesn't sound very flattering.'

'Believe me, it *is* flattering. Working on Fergus's garden is more of a duty than a pleasure.'

'I can't believe that. You've loved planning it all out, I know you have.'

'You're right about the planning – it's been really exciting and a lot of fun, and the fact that he likes what I've decided on is a bonus. But doing the actual work with a team, nice people though they are, and especially being filmed while I'm working, isn't my idea of a good time. I miss you and Jimmy, and I even miss Duncan. That's what I mean by the uniform and the old coat – working for Fergus I'm on show, wearing the uniform, but being here –' she put her arm through his as they wandered round the lake – 'I feel so relaxed in the nice comfortable old coat. I miss being with the usual gang and I especially miss being with you.'

'Not as much as I miss being with you. I really envy Fergus, spending so much time with you. But it won't be for ever.'

'It only feels like for ever, I suppose. I wonder where we'll be this time next year?'

'Married!' Lewis said firmly.

'Having done it our way, I hope – not my mother's. And with Rowena Chloe living here as a proper permanent member of the family.'

'If Molly ever gets around to letting me know what's happening.'

'She will, my love, even if we have to go to Portugal to confront her. Come to think of it, I quite fancy us going to Portugal – just you and me.'

'When would we ever find the time to do that?' Lewis asked, and they sighed wistfully in unison.

'That,' Malcolm Finlay said happily, 'was one of the best meals I've ever had. Thank you so much for inviting me, dear lady.'

'I should thank you for accepting the invitation.' Stella Hesslett smiled across the table at her guest. 'I love cooking, and it's such a pleasure to cook for someone who enjoys food.'

Malcolm patted his generous stomach. 'I can't deny that; it's one of my great weaknesses.'

'Would you care for a glass of port?'

'My goodness, this is turning out to be an exceptionally pleasant evening. I often enjoy a glass of port in the privacy of my own home, but it's rarely offered when I dine out!'

Stella folded her napkin and got to her feet. 'My father always insisted on port after the evening meal, so I keep a bottle just in case I have a guest with similar tastes – though I never have until now.' She collected a tray from the sideboard, waving Malcolm away when he went to help her load it. 'Why don't you take a comfortable seat while I fetch your drink?'

'I hope you're going to join me in a glass of port.'

'I'll have wine instead.' She loaded the tray deftly and carried it into the kitchen, saying over her shoulder, 'Won't be a moment.'

Malcolm settled into an armchair that seemed to open its arms to enfold him. The small room was quite sparsely furnished, but each piece in it – the table and its four chairs, the sideboard, the generous bookcase and the armchairs on either side of the fireplace had all been well chosen, giving the room an air of ease and serenity. Comfortable though he was, he couldn't resist the temptation to get back on to his feet in order to explore the bookcase.

Every book had the air of being loved and well read. Most were classics written by authors dear to his own heart. One, a library book, lay on top of the bookcase, a bookmark showing that it was almost finished. He picked it up and saw somewhat to his surprise that it was a Lilias Drew novel.

He was still holding it when Stella returned to the room carrying a small silver tray with a full bottle of port and two glasses, one holding red wine.

'Forgive me,' Malcolm said, 'I can never resist looking at book-cases. You and I seem to share the same reading interests.'

She flushed a soft becoming pink, her eyes on the book in his large hands. 'I love writers like Dickens and George Eliot, but I have to keep up with today's trends as well – it's part of my job. At the moment, Lilias Drew is very popular with the people who use the mobile library.'

'Ah – of course,' Malcolm said, 'What do you think of her?' The moment the words were out of his mouth he wished that he had had the sense to keep quiet.

'I can understand why she's so popular because she writes an easy-to-read, interesting story, but I still prefer my old friends.' Stella put the tray down on the small table by the chair he had used. 'I can read their books over and over again and still find something new each time. I have cheese and biscuits in the kitchen if you would like some?'

'That sounds wonderful.' He put the book down and returned to the armchair.

'Pour yourself a drink while I fetch them, together with the coffee.'

The port was excellent and Malcolm sipped it slowly, savouring every drop. He heard a car coming down the road and then to his surprise it stopped outside Stella's gate. He set his glass down on the small table by his chair and eased himself to his feet so that he could see out of the window.

It was a taxi, and as he watched, the driver got out and opened a rear door. A woman emerged and started wrestling impatiently with Stella's gate while the taxi driver opened the boot and began to bring out suitcases.

Malcolm hurried into the hallway. 'Miss Hesslett, you seem to have a visitor,' he called out, and then, realizing that his hostess hadn't heard him, he headed for the door at the end of the hall. 'Miss Hesslett – Stella,' he tried again, and then turned back as somebody began banging on the door while at the same time ringing the doorbell. It sounded like an attack rather than a mere visit.

He was just wondering whether he should open the door himself or have another shot at alerting Stella when she hurried from the kitchen. 'What on earth—?' She squeezed past his considerable bulk to reach the front door.

As soon as she began to open it, it was pushed wide from outside, almost sending her reeling against the wall.

'For goodness sake, Stella, what's taken you so long?' The woman from the taxi pushed her way into the hall. 'I've had the most terrible time – the only person I could come to was you!' she said, and then, to Malcolm's consternation, she threw herself at Stella and burst into tears.

'Elma? For goodness' sake, what's happened?'

'Everything! He's left me!'

'Douglas?'

'Of course Douglas! Who else d'you think I'm talking about? That conniving, cheating husband of mine – how *dare* he walk out on me!'

'Could somebody allow me to get this luggage inside?' the taxi driver asked plaintively from the doorstep. 'And pay my fare? I've got work to do.'

'Of course – sorry. I'll just—' Stella tried to free herself from the sobbing visitor, who clung on like a drowning swimmer clutching at a lifebelt.

'Let me – if you would just like to take your friend in there –' Malcolm gestured to the living room – 'I'll see to the luggage.'

'Thank you,' Stella said gratefully.

Once she and her sobbing burden disappeared, out of sight but not earshot, Malcolm helped the taxi driver to bring two large suitcases into the hall and paid the man, adding a generous tip.

'Thanks, mate – she's howled like that all the way from the station,' the man said. 'It's been murder! Good luck to you is all I can say.' And he departed.

Malcolm hovered for a moment in the hall, wondering whether he should just go, or whether Stella needed more help with the new arrival. Eventually, when the sobbing seemed to be abating slightly, he tapped on the closed living room door. It opened after a moment and Stella came into the hall.

'I'm so very sorry,' she said. 'Elma's my half-sister and apparently her marriage has broken down – I expect you've realized that.'

'Is there anything I can do to help?'

She shook her head. 'I don't think there's anything anyone can do to help her at the moment. I'll just have to try to calm her down.' Then, noticing the cases, 'Has the taxi gone away? But what about his fare?'

'It's all been taken care of.'

'I must repay you—'

'My dear lady, you have enough to do at the moment. I'll leave you and your sister to talk, unless there's something else that I can do. Shall I take the suitcases upstairs for you?'

She shook her head. 'We can manage all that later. I'm so sorry about the coffee, and the cheese and biscuits—'

'Stella,' the newcomer shouted from the living room, 'this is port! Haven't you got any whisky?'

'No, sorry—'

'Oh God! Gin then? Don't bother with any tonic. Or vodka? You must have *something* drinkable!'

'I should go,' Malcolm said hurriedly. 'But if I can help in any way — any way at all, please contact me.'

'Thank you — I'm so very sorry!' he heard Stella say wretchedly as he escaped.

Eleven

On the evening when Fergus Matheson's one-hour documentary on the Linn Hall estate ran on television the village streets were silent and empty. Everyone was indoors watching the programme, and the Neurotic Cuckoo's bar was crammed.

Up at Linn Hall itself, Fliss and Hector Ralston-Kerr were alone in the butler's pantry as they watched the programme. After agonizing all day, Ginny had decided that she couldn't watch it and it had taken Lewis some time to persuade her to change her mind. She eventually agreed to view it on the small, normally unused television set in her camper van, and Lewis insisted on joining her there to make sure that she didn't go back on her word.

He had the foresight to bring a bottle of wine with him, hoping that it would help her to relax, and made sure she had a couple of glasses before the programme actually began.

At first, when she herself appeared on the screen clad in her usual shirt and jeans, her short hair ruffled by a breeze, Ginny scrunched up her eyes and grabbed one of his hands tightly; but once the camera was focused on the lake she had lovingly restored he felt her begin to relax. From then on she only winced when she herself appeared on camera, relaxing notably during the long periods when Fergus concentrated on the actual grounds, with Ginny's voice animatedly describing how, bit by bit, each area was restored.

The hour passed very quickly and as the credits ran, Ginny let out a long sigh of relief and let go of Lewis's hand. 'And there you are,' he said, rubbing his hand tenderly and stretching his cramped fingers, 'it wasn't such a terrible ordeal, was it?'

'It wasn't an easy one either, but the shots of the garden were wonderful. You're right, Lewis, it's going to do a lot of good for Linn Hall.'

'And for Fergus's series on his own garden when it's completed. And for you as well.'

Ginny screwed her nose up and shook her head. 'I'm committed to doing Fergus's garden, but once that's over with, Linn Hall is going to be my only interest.'

'I wouldn't be so sure. You're very photogenic, Ginny.'

'Me – photogenic? I don't think so! When I was little my mother took me around every photographic studio she could find. And I remember her crying over the results.'

'She was wrong.' He took her face between his two hands and studied it. 'You've got good bone structure, obviously inherited from your parents. Fergus had the ability to see that. And once you forgot about his camera you were so natural and interesting to listen to. If Fergus or anyone else asks you to do more television you could make a lot of money. Gardening programmes are very popular.'

'Let other people do them, then, because they're definitely not for me.'

Lewis shrugged. 'It's up to you, my love.'

'My future's here with you and your parents and hopefully with Rowena Chloe. I promise you that. End of discussion,' Ginny told him.

⋆　⋆　⋆

To her astonishment and embarrassment, however, she was over-whelmed by the compliments she received as she went about the village during the next few days. And when the Linn Hall estate was officially opened to the public for the summer she found herself being recognized by people who had seen the programme and insisted on seeking her advice on their own gardening problems.

'Grin and bear it,' her friend Lynn Stacey advised her calmly. 'Your fifteen minutes of fame will soon fade from their minds.'

Lynn was right, but until the memory of the television programme faded, Ginny found herself ducking behind trees and shrubbery every time she saw a group of visitors approaching.

Following her sister's sudden arrival, Malcolm Finlay didn't see Stella again until the mobile library's next visit, when he went to collect some books he had ordered.

'How are you?'

'Very well, thank you.' She smiled at him. 'I have your books here.' She brought two scholarly tomes from beneath the counter.

'Thank you, that's very kind of you. And how is your sister – half-sister? Is she still staying with you?'

'Yes, she is.'

'You look tired.'

'I'm fine, really. Just not used to having someone else in the house.' She stamped his books.

'I can understand that. When you're used to living alone, company can be quite tiring. Could we perhaps meet for lunch in the pub later?'

Stella shook her head. 'I'm afraid not. Elma doesn't like to be alone too much. I've arranged to meet her there for lunch.'

'Ah. Well, perhaps another time.'

'Perhaps. Thank you again for your kindness the other day, when Elma arrived.'

'It is I who should thank you for an excellent dinner and for your companionship.' He picked up the books. 'I look forward to our next meeting.'

'So do I,' Stella said almost wistfully.

After leaving the library van Malcolm took the books home, where he spent an hour working on an academic article. After completing and checking it he delivered it to Helen Campbell, who typed all his handwritten work for him, then as it was almost lunchtime he headed for the Neurotic Cuckoo, looking forward to a drink and a well-cooked meal.

He had walked as far as Main Street when he suddenly remembered that Stella had planned to meet her sister in the pub for lunch.

Regretfully, he turned and went back home to make a sandwich and open a bottle of beer.

Berta Krechevsky's horse, Titan, arrived in Tarbethill Farm one afternoon at the beginning of May. Jamie was at school at the time, but as soon as he arrived home and was told by Jess that the horse was in a small field near to the farmhouse, he headed towards the back door.

'And just where do you think you're going?' Jess asked.

He spun round. 'To see the horse!'

'I don't think so, young man. Not in your school clothes.'

'But—'

'You know how your mother likes it – out of your school uniform and into your home clothes, and when you come back downstairs I'll have your milk and biscuits ready for you.'

Jamie jiggled up and down on the spot. '*Pleeeease,* Granny Jess! I can't wait till afterwards!'

'But the horse can. He's going to be living here from now on. And in any case, you have to remember that he belongs to Berta and he's never met you before. You should really wait until she comes home from school and introduces you and the horse to each other properly.'

Jamie stopped jiggling and stood considering Jess carefully, clearly trying to decide if there was any point in further argument. She gazed back at him calmly and after a moment his shoulders drooped.

'Sometimes,' he said sadly, 'there are too many grown-ups around here.' Then he trudged towards the door leading to the hall and the stairs.

By the time Berta finally arrived back from school he was waiting for her at the end of the lane.

'He's here,' Jamie shouted as soon as she got within earshot.
'Titan?'

'Yes,' he yelled, and she broke into a run.

'He's in his field and Gran Jess says I'm not allowed to go to
see him until you take me there so that you can introduce us. I
didn't know people had to be introduced to hor—'

The sentence was abruptly halted as Berta grabbed his hand
on her way past, pulling him up the lane after her. She was
running so fast by then that he almost fell over his own feet and
only just managed to keep up.

'Where's the fire?' a man working on one of the allotments
called out, and was ignored.

'Aren't you going to change out of your school uniform?' Jamie
panted as they whizzed past the cottage.

'Later – I've got to see Titan!' Berta said, and ran on.

'Hey, Berta,' Stefan shouted as the two of them rushed past his
workshop's open doors.

'Going to see Titan,' his daughter yelled back, and they kept
running. Hens scattered as they shot through the farmyard and
then at last they were at the field, where a handsome chestnut
horse with a white blaze on his forehead and three white ankle
socks was grazing on the fresh green grass.

'Titan!' Berta called, and the horse's head came up at once.
He whinnied a delighted welcome and cantered immediately to
the fence.

Berta finally released Jamie and threw her arms around her
horse's neck, rubbing her face against his and murmuring to him
in a language new to Jamie. After a while she stepped back slightly
so that she could kiss the animal's soft nose. The affection between
horse and girl was so clear and so close that Jamie felt quite
jealous, and wondered if there was any way of teaching Tommy
to rush to him and nuzzle his neck the way Titan was now
nuzzling Berta's, instead of just raising his head and then slowly
lolloping over to say a brief 'hello' before returning to the task
of eating more grass.

When the two finally drew apart Berta reached into her blazer
pocket and produced some sugar lumps, which she fed to the
horse. Then she dipped into her pocket again and handed two
lumps to Jamie.

'Open your hand out flat and put the lumps on your palm so that he can lift them off,' she told him. 'He's very careful, and as long as you keep your hand flat to let him get at the treat you'll be fine.'

Jamie did as she instructed and laughed with delight when Titan's velvety-soft lips tickled his hand as the sugar lumps were removed.

'He's terrific! I wish I had a horse.'

'Perhaps you will, one day. In the meantime Titan and I are going to teach you to ride.'

'You really mean it?'

'I already said I would, didn't I? And I always do what I say I will.'

'When?'

'We'll start on Saturday if your mother agrees. But now,' Berta said, stroking Titan's neck, 'I'm going to get changed and then I'll bring the saddle and bridle from the cottage. I can't wait to ride him again!'

It was a beautiful morning, and Ginny was in the stable shop helping Lewis to stock the shelves before the arrival of that day's visitors to the gardens, when her mobile phone rang.

'Drat!' she said as she pulled it from the pocket of her shabby jeans. 'I hope it isn't Fergus asking if I can go over there today. I was really looking forward to showing the kitchen garden to that group of women who've booked in.' Her first task when she began to work at Linn Hall was renovating the walled kitchen garden and since then it had become very popular with visitors.

'Don't answer it,' Lewis advised.

'I'd better, just in case. If it is him he'll only keep ringing.' She switched the phone on. 'Hello?'

'Oh good, I've managed to get hold of you, Ginny.'

'Mother? What are you phoning about? I'm actually quite busy at the moment.'

Lewis, who was halfway up a ladder filling a high shelf, stopped what he was doing at once to listen.

'Not as busy as I am – Ginny, I'm in Kirkcudbright at the moment—'

'Did you say Kirkcudbright?' Ginny asked, and Lewis slid down the ladder, landing with a thump.

'Don't interrupt, I haven't got much time and I need you to come to my hotel immediately.'

'I can't! We've opened the estate to the public early this year and the first visitors will be arriving within the next half hour.'

'Genevieve —' Meredith only used her daughter's full name when she was irritated — 'I flew here yesterday for the sole purpose of talking to you and I'm flying back to Spain tomorrow. The director has had to rearrange filming to give me those three days and I simply cannot believe that your time is as important as mine.'

'Can't whatever you want to talk about wait until you come over in the summer?'

An exasperated sigh could be heard, and then Meredith snapped, 'I'm not *coming* to Britain in the summer; I'm going to be in France, staying in someone's chateau. That's one of the things I want to talk to you about as it means that you can't get married in the summer.'

'But—'

'I can't stay talking on the phone all morning,' Meredith said impatiently, and went on to give the name of the hotel, announce that she would expect her daughter there as soon as possible, and hung up.

'What was all that about?' Lewis demanded to know.

Ginny was dazed. 'I haven't the faintest idea. She arrived in Scotland yesterday, she's in a hotel in Kirkudbright and she's flying back to Spain tomorrow. And she needs to see me immediately, but I don't know why.'

'Then you'd better go.'

'But I've got these women coming to see the kitchen garden and they'll want to know all about the various herbs and vege-tables we grow. I was planning to give that talk I've done before because it usually goes down very well with women.'

'You have to get yourself changed and then go to Kirkcudbright to find out what she wants. If you don't go to her it means that she'll come here. I'll get Jimmy to show your group round the kitchen garden and I'll ask Jinty if she could be there as well, to talk to them about how various vegetables and herbs are used in cooking. Go on,' he urged, steering her towards the door. 'We'll manage – somehow!'

Twenty minutes later, Ginny, face and hands scrubbed, work clothes replaced by a clean sweater and clean jeans, drove the camper van out of the Linn Hall gates. On the road to Kirkcudbright she met a minibus on its way into Prior's Ford with a full load of cheerful women clearly looking forward to a good day out.

She sighed, wishing that she could turn the camper van about and join them.

'Ginny, you have no idea of the problems you're causing me at the moment,' was Meredith Whitelaw's greeting to her daughter when Ginny found her in the hotel lounge.

Ginny bit back a similar accusation, saying instead, 'I wasn't aware of being a nuisance, Mother. What have I done?'

'It's this wedding of yours – what else? I'm doing my best to organize my daughter's wedding while I'm working far away, and you've thrown it all back in my face. Do you realize how popular that wedding planner I've found for you is? She spends most of her time working on celebrity weddings and weddings among the nobility. It was absolutely humiliating having to tell the woman that my daughter didn't want her. Not that I did tell her that, of course. I had to say that you and Lewis had broken up. Fortunately, being a skilled actress, I was able to sound quite emotional about it. Have you heard from your father?'

'Not for many years, other than Christmas cards.'

Meredith sighed. 'I wrote to him, of course, to tell him how difficult you're being over this wedding business, and I urged him to support me for once, but I'm not entirely surprised to hear that he ignored my plea.'

'Mother, I've already explained that Lewis and I just want a quiet local wedding. He and his parents are greatly liked in the village; everyone's looking forward to seeing us get married in the local church and, with any luck, attending the wedding reception at the Hall. There's good news in that direction – work's going to start on renovating the entire ground floor in the autumn, which means that it should be completed early next year. That's when we plan to get married.'

'And you didn't think to explain all this to me as soon as it was arranged, and save me having to rush over to see you? Who's doing the renovation?'

'Angela Steele.'

'That woman? Are you sure that she's entirely suitable for the task?'

'She's very suitable. Lewis and his parents are delighted with her plans for the rooms. There's more good news as well; we've just heard that Lewis's daughter is coming to live with us in the summer. She'll be thrilled when I tell her that she's going to be my flower girl on the big day.'

Meredith sighed heavily. 'So you've got everything organized concerning this wedding – wherever and whenever it's going to happen.'

'That's all for the moment; Lewis and I are both very busy, but I'm confident that we'll manage to get everything arranged in time.'

'You must let me know as soon as the date's arranged. I'll need to have a lot of notice. Being the lead in this long-running sitcom, my absence causes a great deal of disruption for the entire crew and cast.'

'You'll have the date as soon as we do, Mother.'

'About your wedding dress—'

'It will be very simple,' Ginny said firmly, and her mother sighed, then reached over, took one of Ginny's hands and turned it over, shuddering.

'I use an extremely good hand cream – expensive, of course – I'll send you some. Start using it every night from now on, and never go to bed without gloves on.'

Ginny opened her mouth to point out that she was a gardener, then realized that it was of no use and said instead, 'Thank you.'

'What about your hair?'

'What about it?'

'It's very – mannish.'

Ginny ran her hands through her short black hair. 'This is the way I like it.'

'It's all wrong for a wedding.'

'I think it'll be all right for *my* wedding.'

'But not for my daughter's wedding. It will have to be a wig,' Meredith announced.

'A what?'

'I know a very good wig-maker in London. I'll try to come over early next year and take you there. We can organize your wedding dress at the same time.'

When Ginny got back to Linn Hall, Lewis, who had been watching out for her, arrived just as she was climbing out of the camper van. 'What did she want?'

'Wedding talk.'

He groaned. 'Such as?'

Ginny stretched her arms and then scrubbed her fingers hard through her hair. 'Don't ask,' she told him. 'Don't ever ask!'

Twelve

By the end of Elma Armitage's first week in the village, people began to realize that the slightest sign of sympathy towards her was dangerous, leading as it always did to self-pitying tears and an outburst against the missing husband and his new love.

Because Stella was at work every weekday and Elma seemed unable to be alone, she was constantly out and about. Following her first visit to the Village Store, when Sam Brennan had the bad luck to be behind the counter, he managed from then on to disappear into the back shop every time Elma came through the door.

'It's unfair,' Marcy objected. 'When I'm busy in the back shop I don't want to have to stop what I'm doing just to let you hide from that woman.'

'It's the things she says,' Sam protested. 'She just opens her mouth and doesn't seem to care what spills out. She stood there for ages yesterday maligning her husband and the woman he's gone off with while a queue was building up behind her with every ear flapping. I didn't know how to stop her.'

'It's all part of our job. We work with the public because we need their money.'

'Marcy, I've got news for you – I'd rather rob the public to get their money than have to listen to that woman,' her partner told her firmly.

Much the same conversation was going on in the butcher's shop next door, the Neurotic Cuckoo, and everywhere that Elma went. Even Naomi Hennessey, so used to listening patiently to all those who consulted her day in and day out and trusted her with their deepest secrets, found great difficulty in easing Elma out of the vestry following a tearful two-hour session.

After Elma attended a meeting of the local Women's Rural Institute Alma Parr, the very efficient chairwoman, told Marcy that she had had to struggle to prevent Elma from more or less taking over as that afternoon's speaker.

'Fortunately, in a way, it happened to be a Bring and Buy afternoon to raise funds, but I don't think it would have made any difference if we'd invited someone to give us a talk. That woman was extremely difficult to control. To be quite honest,' Alma continued as she packed her groceries into her shopping bag, 'most of us agreed afterwards that our sympathies were very much with her husband. She came over as a totally self-centred person. Also spoiled – most of us got the impression that she's used to having her own way no matter what.'

Nobody suffered more than Stella Hesslett. It was generally agreed by those using the mobile library regularly that Stella was beginning to look both tired and unhappy, although when they mentioned such concerns to her and suggested that she may be in need of a holiday she always summoned a smile from somewhere and assured them that she was absolutely fine.

On the one occasion when Malcolm Finlay managed to meet her for lunch in the pub, after discovering that Elma was going into Kirkcudbright to have her hair done and would be away for most of the day, Stella pinned a bright smile on her face and insisted that everything at home was 'absolutely fine'.

'I'll admit that it can be a little bit stressful, having a long-term visitor when one is used to living alone, but poor Elma badly needs company at the moment, and since our parents are no longer with us, it makes me the only person she can turn to in her hour of need.'

'Has she got no friends she can speak to? My sisters always had friends, and still do as far as I know. I've never really had many friends of my own,' Malcolm said thoughtfully, 'but I can't say that I've ever really felt the need for friends. In fact, you are probably the first person I can actually call a friend – if I may take the liberty.'

Stella blushed. 'Really? Oh my goodness – I've never thought of myself as the sort of person anyone would want to have as a friend!'

'I can't think why. As I understand it, a friend is someone that a person can feel comfortable with. A person one can trust. And that's the way I think about you – if I may be so bold.'

'Of course you may. In fact, I'm very flattered.' Stella put a hand to her burning face. 'I feel rather foolish – I'm not used to having such a frank conversation with someone.'

'Neither am I. It feels strange, two people in our age group suddenly realizing that they share a friendship – that is, if I may take it that you enjoy my company as much as I enjoy yours.'

'Oh, certainly.'

'Dessert?' Gracie Fisher enquired. 'Today we have jam roly-poly, custard and fruit or lemon meringue pie.'

Startled by her sudden arrival, the two of them floundered for a moment before agreeing that they would just have coffee.

'Won't be a moment,' she assured them and bustled off.

'Er – what were we saying?' Malcolm pondered when they were alone again.

'I'm not sure. Oh yes, you were asking about Elma's friends and then we seemed to go off on a tangent.'

'I was actually wondering if she wouldn't be better off staying with a friend. As far as I can gather, you and your sister haven't seen much of each other since you grew up. From what I remember of my sisters and their friends, they were as thick as thieves and knew every intimate detail about each other.'

Stella frowned thoughtfully for a moment before saying, 'To tell the truth, nobody in my family had friends. I wasn't good at getting to know people and since I was quite a few years older than Elma we never really had much in common. And our parents – my mother and Elma's father – were such a devoted couple that they never seemed to need friends, just each other. I recall being quite envious of them, having each other and being so close. Then when Elma married I got the impression that her entire life was built around her husband and the two children who came along.'

'The two children who are now with their father and the new woman in his life. Your sister must miss them very much.'

'She doesn't say much about it but I'm sure that she misses them badly. Once she's got over the shock of her husband's desertion she'll want them to live with her,' Stella was saying as Gracie arrived with the coffee.

'There's something about these two,' Gracie said to her husband as she arrived back at the bar.

'Which two?'

'Stella Hesslett and that nice Dr Finlay. When I went over to ask if they wanted any dessert they both looked quite flushed and confused.'

'Confused about what they wanted for dessert?'

'No, silly! Confused about whatever they were talking about. She was quite red in the face and he was blinking a lot. D'you think that they might be beginning to fall for each other?'

Joe looked over at the two people under discussion. 'Don't be daft! They just enjoy each other's company.'

'I'm not so sure. They seem to enjoy meeting for lunch, though they haven't done that since that whiny sister of hers arrived. I hope,' Gracie said, 'she goes back to where she belongs soon, because Stella and Dr Finlay could make quite a nice couple.'

'Give over, woman,' said Joe. 'It's high time you stopped reading those romantic Lilias Drew books you're so mad about.'

As soon as her children had gone off to school – Gregor, Gemma and Lachlan to Kirkcudbright Academy and Irene to the local primary – Helen Campbell snatched up her purse and her shopping bag before rushing out of the house, leaving the breakfast dishes in the sink and all the beds unmade for the first time in her married life.

She sped along the road and out into the main street, throwing breathless greetings to the people she met and then dashing on, leaving them wondering what the rush was about.

Reaching the Village Store she bounded up the two steps and through the door, almost falling over a small child wandering about as it waited for its mother, who herself was waiting for

Marcy to total her purchases. Otherwise, to Helen's relief, the shop was quiet. She hurried around the shelves, taking items down and putting them into her basket with the speed of a practised shopper.

As soon as the other customer had paid for her goods and left she made for the counter. 'Have they arrived?'

'Didn't you see the window? I taped a copy on to the glass so that everyone passing by or coming in can see it.'

'I didn't take time!' Helen turned towards the door and then came back to the counter when Marcy called, 'You can see it when you go out. Have a look at these before somebody else comes in.' She gestured to a large pile of magazines further along the counter. 'You walked past that lot too – have a look at the front cover.'

Helen dumped her basket and bag on the counter and picked up the top magazine with trembling fingers. Then she gasped at the sight of her own name in large letters: *Along came a Stranger – our enthralling new serial by Helen Campbell.*

'Oh! I didn't realize it was going to be right there for everyone to see!'

'They always announce the new serial on the cover. It's intended to catch the eye and make people want to buy the magazine. It looks good, doesn't it?'

'It looks absolutely wonderful,' Helen gulped. With shaking fingers she opened the magazine and leafed through it until she found the beginning of the first episode of her very first published story. 'Oh, Marcy, look at that – my name in print in a real magazine! And the illustration is lovely – I can't believe that it's finally happened!'

'Believe it, Helen, you're a published writer. We've sold at least two dozen copies already.'

'Really?'

Marcy grinned at her. 'Don't look so surprised – you're our local published writer now.'

'I'll take six – no, make it ten.'

'I hope Duncan's going to take you out for a meal tonight to celebrate,' Marcy said as she counted them out.

'If so, it's going to be a big surprise. Duncan's never been impressed by my writing.'

'Keep going as you are and he'll be impressed one day. Don't you have any plans to celebrate this milestone?'

'I'm going to Jenny's for coffee,' Helen said as she gathered up her shopping. 'It's her turn this week and I'll enjoy celebrating this –' she flourished one of the magazines at Marcy before tucking it into her shopping bag with the others – 'with my friends. I hope you're coming.'

'I wish I could, but Sam's off to the warehouse so I've got to stay here. Hang on for a minute,' Marcy disappeared into the back shop and returned almost immediately with a bottle of wine. 'Here you are, something from me to serve up with dinner tonight.'

'I can't take that!'

'You can, and you deserve it!'

After hurrying home to wash the dishes, make the beds and make sure that the house was reasonably tidy Helen emptied her shopping bag of everything but the wine and one copy of the magazine before heading over to Jenny's house. The front door was slightly ajar – a signal to go straight in. When she arrived in the living room she was greeted by cheers from Jenny and Ingrid, both waving copies of the magazine.

'Hail the conquering heroine!' said Ingrid, while Jenny shouted:

'Author! Author! Are you pleased with it?'

'Pleased? I've never been so thrilled and excited in my entire life!'

'So are we – now we can claim that we actually know a published author,' Ingrid said, and hugged her friend while Jenny disappeared to the kitchen. 'Have you read it yet? Do you like the illustrations?'

'I've only just bought it – and several others.'

'We've both read it and we think it's great. We can't wait to see what happens next,' Ingrid told her.

'Anyone for champagne?' Jenny arrived back with a tray holding a bottle and three champagne glasses.

'Oh my goodness! I nearly forgot—' Helen delved into her bag and produced the wine. 'Marcy can't come today because Sam's at the warehouse, but she gave me this to have with our dinner tonight. Between your champagne and tonight's wine I'll be an alcoholic by this time tomorrow.'

'When something fantastic happens you're entitled to celebrate.' Jenny began to open the champagne. 'Nobody leaves until this bottle is empty.'

'I've just remembered – Bob Green's coming to the house this afternoon to collect the Agony Aunt page for the *Dumfries News*,' Helen said anxiously. 'I can't afford to get tipsy.'

'You won't get all that tipsy on a third of a bottle of champagne,' Ingrid told her calmly as she held the glasses out to be filled. 'And even if you do, you've got every right to celebrate something like this. We know how hard you've worked to get to where you are today. Ladies, a toast. To Helen – may this be the first publication of many!'

'To Helen,' Jenny echoed. 'and to the first of many.'

'To me,' Helen agreed, 'and to my lovely friends and the faith they've always had in me.'

When she finally made her way home Helen was walking on air, partly because of excitement and partly because of champagne. It was fortunate that her three older children no longer came home for lunch and Irene had recently decided to start taking a packed lunch to the primary school so that she could stay with her friends during the break. It meant that Helen was able to make a pot of strong black coffee and find the time to sit down and read the first episode of her serial not once, but several times.

Looking at it in print she found it hard to believe that she had actually written it herself. She was already halfway through a novel and couldn't wait to get back to it.

She glanced at the clock and saw that she had just over an hour before Bob, the journalist who had persuaded her to take over the Agony Aunt page a few years before, was due.

She went upstairs, turned on the bath taps and tossed in a generous double handful of sweet-smelling bath salts.

While Helen Campbell was enjoying the pleasure of a lazy afternoon bath Malcolm Finlay was comfortably settled at a quiet corner table in the Neurotic Cuckoo, a pint of beer in front of him with an opened book beside it. He was totally immersed in the book when a voice said, 'Oh hello – aren't you the man I saw in Stella's house when I arrived last week?' He looked up to see Stella's half-sister looming over him.

'Er – ah—' It took a few moments before he remembered her name. 'Mrs Armitage—' As he began to struggle to his feet one knee was trapped beneath the table, which lifted slightly. The beer glass began to tip and he grabbed it just in time to prevent it from emptying itself on to the precious open book.

'Oh my goodness – don't get up!' Elma pulled out a chair and sat down opposite him. 'I just popped in for a quick drink and thought I recognized you. May I join you?'

There was no point in trying to refuse because she was already sitting, and clearly had no intention of moving. 'Of course.' Malcolm collapsed back into his chair, rubbing his knee. 'Can I buy you a coffee?'

'How kind,' Elma said as Joe Fisher approached, 'but something a little stronger, if I may. A vodka and tonic, please.' Then, as Joe returned to the bar, 'I'm so glad to meet you again; I've been hoping for the chance to apologize for my very clumsy arrival at Stella's house, Mr – oh, I believe it's Dr—?'

'Malcolm Finlay.'

'Malcolm, what a lovely name.' She used the spread fingers of both hands to push her shoulder-length red hair back from her face. 'I was so dreadfully upset at the time we first met. You see, my husband had just walked out on me after fifteen years of what I thought was a perfect marriage. I was totally distraught, as I'm sure you'll understand. Are you married?'

'I have never seen myself as the marrying type.'

'I can't believe that!'

'I mean it. I've been a scholar all my life; books are my main interest.'

'That explains why you were visiting my sister. Poor Stella's terribly bookish – I'm afraid it makes her rather dull, but she's probably quite a good librarian.'

'An exceptionally good librarian, and also a very kind and helpful librarian. I write articles for academic publications and your sister has gone to a great deal of trouble in the past to secure the research material that I need.'

'She's actually my half-sister, eleven years older than I am. That's why we're entirely different, both in looks and temperament. My father and Stella's mother both lost their partners, and when they met each other it was love at first sight, apparently. Thank you,' she said without looking up at Joe when her drink was set on the table. She picked it up, took a drink, and then went on, 'It was love at first sight with me and Douglas as well – at least, that's what I thought. But how very wrong I was!'

She took another drink and then leaned across the table towards him, her brown eyes moist. 'Suddenly one day, right out of the blue, he told me that he had met someone else and he was going to leave me and live with her! Can you imagine my heartbreak?'

'Well—' Malcolm floundered, 'I really couldn't begin to, being a bachelor.'

'His betrayal has damaged me deeply; he might as well have picked up a bread knife and plunged it into my heart.' She spread her hand, lavish with rings, over the area of her heart. 'We were so happy together! I even bore his children – twins, a boy and a girl. What greater sacrifice can a woman make for the man she loves than go through the agonies of childbirth for him?'

Malcolm, about to take a much-needed mouthful of beer, choked and spluttered, then hastily put the glass down in order to dab at his mouth with his handkerchief. When he was able to speak again he apologized, then asked where the children were.

'They're with their father, of course, and his new woman. I couldn't possibly cope with them on my own, not while I'm still trying to recover from the shock of his betrayal. Let her look after his children, I decided; let her know what it's like to have to cope with them day in and day out!' Elma drained her glass and then said, 'Stella tells me that you're a writer.'

'In a way. I write specialized articles for academic magazines.'

'Well that's writing, isn't it? I was just thinking,' Elma said, 'that my story would make a wonderful novel, filled as it is with love and passion and betrayal . . .'

Malcolm leapt to his feet, again banging one knee against the edge of the table without realizing it.

'N–not that kind of writer – excuse me – suddenly remembered that I'm expecting an important phone call . . .'

'Oh – we can talk about it another time. Thank you for your

company,' Elma said sweetly. 'And for your understanding. Could you order another vodka and tonic for me on your way out?'

He did, and paid for his unfinished pint and both her drinks before limping back to the peace and safety of his home.

Thirteen

When Helen opened the door to Bob Green the first thing she saw was a large bouquet of flowers. 'Congratulations, love! These are from all the staff at the *Dumfries News*.'

'You remembered about the serial?'

'Of course we did – we've all been waiting with bated breath for this day. You may not work in the office but you're still one of us. Everyone bought a copy this morning and all the girls have devoured your first episode already. I'm to tell you that they all think it's great and they can't wait for the next part. It's not my kind of thing but I got a copy to take home to the wife. I brought a camera,' he added as he followed her into the living room, 'because the editor wants your photograph.'

'What for?'

'We're going to do an article about you. Our Prior's Ford correspondent has just been published – as well as *writing* the news, kid, this week you *are* the news, or a part of it.' He produced the camera from the rucksack he always carried over his shoulder and glanced around the room. 'Probably best at your desk; where is it?'

'Upstairs, in our bedroom.' Helen led the way, glad that she had got around to making all the beds.

'This'll do fine. Sit down at your computer and look as though you're reading your serial.' Bob dipped into his rucksack, produced a copy of the magazine and laid it on the desk.

'Just a minute—' Helen found her comb and peered into the wardrobe mirror.

'Ach, you look fine, lassie. See women,' Bob grunted as she fussed with her hair, 'they never believe anything a man says. Right,' he went on when she finally sat down, 'open it at your serial, turn a wee bit to face me, and here we go.'

He took three photographs in all before deciding that he had enough. 'So how does it feel to see your name on the front of a women's magazine?' he asked as they went back downstairs.

'Fantastic! Would you like a cup of tea?'

'Love one, but I'd better collect the Agony Aunt page and be on my way. I'll email the article we're doing about your serial to you so that you can check it over before it goes to print. Hang on, I'd better get some details about you – the names of your kids and your husband and that sort of thing.'

Downstairs, he dug out a notebook to collect the necessary information, and then tucked the notebook and the envelope containing the Agony Aunt page into the rucksack.

On his way to the front door he paused. 'I just remembered – have you ever read any books by someone called Lily Drew?'

The sudden question took Helen by surprise. 'Lilias Drew?'

'Aye, that's the one. Have you heard of her? She writes books for women – quite racy according to my wife, who's mad about her stuff.'

'I've read a few of her books and I know that they're very popular with our local mobile library readers. Why are you asking about her?'

'The editor's heard a rumour that she's living in this area.'

Helen's heart skipped a beat. 'Living here in Dumfries and Galloway?'

'Apparently. If it's true, he'd love to get an interview with her, though it seems that she's quite a secretive person – there's no information or photograph on her books and her publishers say that she likes to keep a low profile.' Bob opened the front door. 'If you hear anything, let me know. Bye, and congratulations again from all of us.'

Helen's first thought when Bob left was to go straight round to Malcolm Finlay's house, but a glance at the clock showed that the children would soon be home from school, and she would have to wait until tomorrow.

Even her sons were awestruck when she showed them the magazine with her name on it. Fourteen-year-old Gemma sat down and read the first episode of the serial at once, then hugged her mother and said, 'It's absolutely brilliant and I can't wait to see what happens next. I'm going to tell everyone about it at school tomorrow, even the teachers. I want them all to know what a clever mum I've got!'

To Helen's astonishment, Duncan handed her a beautifully wrapped parcel when he arrived home from work.

'What's this?'

He went red and then said sheepishly, 'Jinty and Mrs Ralston-Kerr both had copies of some magazine for women and they were showing your serial to everyone. I didn't even know it was going to start this week. You never said.'

'I didn't think you'd be interested.'

'Of course I'm interested. That's why I bought this for you from Colour Carousel – it was made by that foreigner who's moved into a building at Tarbethill Farm. And I looked in at the pub on the way home and arranged for us all to go there on Saturday night for dinner to celebrate.'

Helen had opened the parcel to reveal a glass paperweight. 'Oh, Duncan, it's lovely!'

'Let me see, Mum.' Gemma took the paperweight and examined it closely. 'It's beautiful!'

Helen threw her arms around her husband's neck and planted a kiss on his lips.

'Give over, woman,' he said as the children giggled. 'Not in front of the kids!'

'Marcy gave me a bottle of wine so that we can celebrate tonight.'

'I'll drink to that,' Duncan said, and went upstairs to get washed before dinner. He was feeling very guilty, because if it hadn't been for Jinty he would never have remembered about the serial being published.

'Here you,' she had said when he was about to go back to work after the midday meal in the Hall kitchen, 'take this –' she pushed the little parcel into his hand – 'and give it to Helen. Mind to tell her that it's from you!'

'What is it?'

Jinty sighed and shook her head. 'Just as I thought – you've not only forgotten that her serial was going to begin in the magazine this week, you've probably not even thought about giving her a wee gift to celebrate it. So I bought this from Anya's shop. As far as Helen knows, you chose it specially for her. And here's the receipt – you can pay me at the end of the week when you get your wages.'

As soon as the four children went off to school on the following morning Helen raced from room to room, making beds, picking up the discarded clothes her family had left on the floors for her to gather up and wash, then filled the washing machine and switched it on before pulling on a jacket, grabbing her purse and shopping bag and leaving the house.

Instead of making for the Main Street shops, she went in the opposite direction, towards Thatcher's Cottage.

Fortunately Malcolm Finlay was still at home, washing his breakfast dishes and planning to do a little gentle gardening before he started work on his latest academic article. He opened the front door, dishcloth in hand, and beamed when he saw his visitor.

'What a pleasant surprise. Come in, come in – I haven't got any typing for you to do yet. Should I have? Is there something I've forgotten?'

'No, there's something I have to tell you.' She followed him into the living room. 'Something very important.'

'Oh dear, that sounds serious. Perhaps we should have some coffee? There's still plenty in the percolator.'

'That would be lovely.'

'And shortbread from the village shop. Make yourself at home, my dear lady, I won't be long.'

Left on her own, Helen sank into a comfortable chair. All the rooms in Thatcher's Cottage were small, but Malcolm Finlay, a large man, had managed to furnish the living room with three big armchairs and two bookcases without making it look crowded. Every time Helen visited the cottage she felt as though the entire room, like the chair she sat in, welcomed her as though she was an old friend. She could never understand how it managed to make her feel so comfortable.

Perhaps it had something to do with Doris Thatcher and her husband, a gentle, popular local couple who had spent many years in this cottage and left something of themselves in its very stones when they died. Perhaps it was because this place lacked the things that were a constant daily irritation in Helen's life – the discarded clothes, toys, books, newspapers and magazines, empty sweet wrappers and single shoes and socks she had to pick up and put away day after day.

'Here we are—' Malcolm bustled in, set a tray down on a small side table and began to pour out the coffee. Once he had attended to his visitor he sat down with his own cup and said cheerfully, 'What's worrying you?'

'The fact that I've just been told of a rumour going around. Apparently well-known novelist Lilias Drew has come to live in this area.'

Malcolm had begun to lift his cup to his lips; now his arm froze halfway and his eyes widened almost into circles behind his spectacles. 'What? Where did you hear that?'

'A journalist from the local paper came to my house yesterday to collect the—' Helen remembered just in time that nobody other than her closest friends, Ingrid, Jenny and Marcy, knew that she wrote the Agony Aunt page for the *Dumfries News*. 'The Prior's Ford news column that I write for them every week. He told me about the rumour and asked if I'd heard anything about it. I denied it, of course, but I thought I'd better warn you.'

'They won't put anything in the paper, will they?'

'I don't think so – as I said, it's only a rumour, and surely they wouldn't put it into the paper unless they had confirmation.'

'I wonder where they got it from.' His arm finished lifting the cup to his lips and he took a gulp of coffee.

'Could it be from your Lilias Drew publishers?'

He shook his head. 'No. It was a friend who showed the manuscript of the first book to a publishing company he knew, and persuaded me to let them publish it. I told them about my work for academic publications, and how it would destroy my reputation if anyone found out that I had also written what they called a women's novel. I was assured that they would keep my secret. But I'll check with them right away, just in case.'

'There's another side to it – if it ever came out that you were Lilias Drew you'd be mobbed by your fans from miles around,' Helen pointed out, and then, as he shuddered, she wished that she had held her tongue. 'But nothing will come of it,' she added swiftly. 'As I said, it's only a rumour.'

She herself had discovered Malcolm's secret by accident. On his arrival in the village the year before he had been searching for someone to type the academic articles that he wrote by hand. Helen used her computer to type work for other people, since the Ralston-Kerrs couldn't afford to pay Duncan a generous salary. It was only after she discovered the handwritten chapter of a Lilias Drew novel mixed up in the serious article she was working on and returned it to Malcolm that he admitted everything to her.

A shy man who tended to avoid women like the plague, he had grown up with parents and three sisters who had all led – and as far as the sisters were concerned, still led – promiscuous lives. After retiring from his work as a university lecturer, Malcolm had rid himself of his ongoing embarrassment over his family by putting everything down on paper. A friend he had confided in read the finished work and passed it to a publisher, who immediately offered Malcolm a contract. The book, described by reviewers as 'racy chick-lit for older women' was such a success that Malcolm was still writing Lilias Drew books.

'I hope you're right,' he said now, his voice uneasy.

'I'm sure I am, but I just felt that I should let you know about the rumour. If I hear any more I'll keep you informed.' She finished her coffee and shook her head as he offered another cup. 'It's delicious, but I have to get some shopping in before I return to the housework.'

'Of course. You're a very busy lady and I'm grateful to you for all you've done for me.' He eased himself up from the armchair, glancing out of the window as he did so.

'It's my pleasure.' Helen got to her feet and was heading for the door when her host suddenly grabbed her arm, rushed her out into the hall, and instead of turning towards the front door, almost threw her into a small cloakroom at the rear of the hall and then followed her in and shut the door.

'What are you—?'

'Shhhhh!'

The cloakroom wasn't meant for two people, especially when one of them was as large as Malcolm Finlay. They were jammed in stomach-to-stomach and Helen had to tip her head back as far as possible in order to look up at him.

'What's happening? Why are we in here?' she hissed, just as the front door bell rang.

Malcolm jumped, and as he was so close to her, she herself was forced to give a little hop. 'I knew it – I knew she was coming here!'

'Who is it?'

'That *woman*!' he whispered, so vehemently that she could feel his breath stirring the hair on top of her head. 'Miss Hesslett's dreadful sister. Saw her coming along the pavement – thought she may be coming here.' Then he uttered a soft moan as the doorbell rang again, swiftly followed by the sound of someone knocking to demand entry.

It was probably over in a matter of a few minutes, but to Helen, looking back on the situation later, it felt as though the two of them had been crammed together and unable to move for at least quarter of an hour, listening to the bell ringing and the door knocker being vigorously wielded. Helen began to feel claustrophobic, but since she had been pushed into the cloakroom first, there was no way that she could get past Malcolm to reach the door.

Even when the noise stopped he insisted on counting to a hundred in a hissing, hair-stirring whisper before he finally opened the cloakroom door. Once the two of them were back in the hallway he signalled to Helen to stay where she was while he himself crept into the living room, finally returning to report that the coast was clear.

'I am so sorry,' he said as Helen hurried towards the front door. 'That woman terrifies me. The other day when I was enjoying a quiet drink in the pub she came in and insisted on sitting at my table and telling me about her husband's desertion in the most embarrassing detail. And now, it seems, she's going to begin stalking me.'

'It's not just you,' Helen assured him. 'The whole village is getting tired of her, and we're all so sorry for Stella Hesslett. She must be having a dreadful time.'

'I think she must be; if only that woman would just leave! I'm going to have a brandy – would you like one?'

'No thank you, I must go and get some shopping now that the coast's clear.' Helen opened the door and glanced out before stepping on to the path. 'Not a sign of her,' she told Malcolm, who heaved a sigh of relief.

'At last!' Lewis flourished the official-looking letter. 'Just when I was beginning to think we would never get good news again, here it is.'

'Here what is?' his father wanted to know. The summer back-packers had all eaten a hearty breakfast in the kitchen before going off to their various tasks on the estate and the family were now having their own breakfast in the pantry, while Jinty, who had just arrived, was washing a great pile of dishes at the large kitchen sink.

'The bank's agreed to advance the loan I've been looking for. We've finally got the money we need to start putting the ground floor to rights!'

'That's wonderful, Lewis – another step forward,' Ginny enthused.

He nodded, his eyes running over the letter again. 'We're finally getting there – the house is weathertight with no more need to rush up to the top floor to put out every jug and chamber pot we possess to catch the drips—'

'Your father and I are so grateful about that, aren't we, Hector?' Fliss put in, and her husband nodded.

'—and the gardens have been brought under control,' Lewis went on. 'Only one large job to do now – the Hall itself – and now we're going to get the money to start on it. We'll be able to get married right here in Linn Hall, Ginny.'

'You can't start work until the autumn,' she reminded him. 'It would be absolute chaos having work done in the house while people are visiting the gardens.'

'You're right, but I'm going to phone Angela Steele and let her know that it's now definite instead of just maybe.' He folded the letter and tucked it back into its envelope then got to his feet. 'She's a very busy lady and she'll need plenty of warning if we want her to take over the job – which we definitely do. She'll probably want to come back for another look at the place first.' He glanced at his watch. 'Forty minutes to go before we open to the public.'

'Is it that time already?' Ginny shot to her feet. 'I said I'd spend the day at Fergus's garden.'

'Is he picking you up?' Lewis asked.

'No, he's got other things to do. It's just going to be me and the team. I'm taking the camper van. I'd better do a quick check to make sure that I've got everything I need for the day.'

Left on their own, Fliss and Hector looked at each other for a long moment before Fliss said, almost sadly, 'So it's really going to happen.'

'I'm afraid so.'

'I hate the idea of living in those big rooms, Hector. This has been our home for most of our married life.' Fliss gestured to the pantry they sat in and the kitchen beyond. 'I like living here; it's cosy, and it means we can be warm in the winter.'

Hector nodded. 'And we never get rained on down here – not that we'll get wet anywhere else, now that the roof and the windows have been fixed.'

'The official rooms frighten me and I hate the idea of all that walking involved in just closing the curtains at night or going into another room across that huge hall.'

'I never liked it when I visited here as a boy,' Hector admitted. 'You're quite right when you say that there's far too much space.'

'Perhaps we could live in one of the gatehouses once Lewis and Ginny are married. Hopefully they'll have lots and lots of children and they'll need the space. Younger people quite like space, don't they?'

'The gatehouses will probably always be needed for the summer workers now that the estate's open to the public every summer, my dear. Lewis and Ginny will always need the money coming in from the visitors.'

Fliss sighed. 'You're right. Pity – I rather like the idea of you and me tucked into one of those nice little gatehouses.' She sat in silence for a moment, and then her face brightened.

'We could buy a house in the village and live among all the people we know, and we could come here every day during the summer to help with the visitors and to see Lewis and Ginny and their children.'

'Yes, we could, but let's not worry about the future until it arrives. As Lewis said, work on the ground floor can't start until the autumn and it will probably be well into next year before the rooms are ready to be occupied. Perhaps he'll decide to open the public rooms to the people who come to see the gardens; if he does that we can just go on as we are, living here in the kitchen area.'

'That,' Fliss said, 'would be the best idea. Let's put it out of our minds for the moment and get on with what we have to face today, shall we?'

Fourteen

Ginny arrived back at the Hall that evening to find Lewis and his parents having dinner in the pantry.

'Sit down, dear, and I'll get your dinner. It's being kept warm in the oven.' Fliss began to get to her feet, then sat down again as Ginny, peeling off her coat, said, 'I'll get it. I need to wash my hands anyway.'

'Did you phone Angela Steele?' she asked Lewis when she arrived back with her food.

'Yes, we had a good chat. She's delighted to know that she's going to be able to work here – she says it's going to be a terrific challenge and she was hoping to get the job. As we thought, she's got a lot of work on hand at the moment and so the autumn suits her as well as us. She's coming here on Friday to have another look at the place and talk things over with us. So how was your day?'

'Really good. The gardeners have been doing extremely well and now we can all see the new layout clearly. It looks just as I had hoped.'

'Fancy a drink down at the Cuckoo this evening?' Lewis asked.

'That would be lovely,' Ginny agreed.

'Isn't it a perfect evening?' she said later as the two of them strolled down the driveway hand in hand. 'I love summer evenings in the country – that sudden pause that happens when all the wild animals and the birds and even the plants begin to settle down for the night. It makes me feel so relaxed because it seems as though there's all the time in the world. It's such a change from during the day, when I tend to feel that there's never enough time to get through everything that needs to be got through.'

'I know what you mean – but I think that part of the reason why I feel relaxed at the moment is down to knowing that we're definitely going to get the money to start work on the Hall itself, and knowing that your work's well ahead too. It helps me to feel that the better times are definitely on the horizon, when projects are completed and we've got more time for each other – time to think about you, me, and us.' Then, as they went through the gates and turned to go down the hill leading to the village, 'There's still one big snag, though—'

Ginny squeezed his hand tightly. 'I know – when are you going to find out what's happening about Rowena Chloe? We can only wait, my love, and keep our fingers tightly crossed.'

'You're right. I've just got to keep on being patient, though it's hard.' They were walking down the side of the public house, only yards away from Kilmartin Crescent and the village green, and he paused, turning to take her in his arms and kiss her while they were still unseen by others.

'To what do I owe that very pleasant pleasure?' Ginny wanted to know when he released her.

'Just to say that it was lovely having the time to wander down here, you and me together on such a lovely peaceful evening; but I bet that when we get into the pub all the peace and quiet will disappear.'

'But we'll still have a drink or even two to look forward to,' Ginny said as they turned the corner and were met by a babble of voices from the pub's open doorway.

As Lewis had predicted, the place was full. Most of the Hall's summer workers were there, together with a number of locals. As Lewis and Ginny searched for an empty corner table, Cam Gordon, Lewis's best friend from childhood, called from a crowded table, 'Hey, Lewis – Ginny – someone here wants to see you both. There's still room for another two.'

'Told you it wouldn't be quiet,' Lewis said as they worked their way across the busy room. Then his hand, now holding her elbow to guide her around chairs and tables, tightened so suddenly that she gasped.

'Ouch – Lewis—' she protested, looking up at him. Then,

seeing that his eyes were fixed on the table where Cam sat, she turned her head and saw what he had just seen.

Several local people were at the table – Cam's girlfriend, Anya Jacobsen, Steph and Grant McDonald and some of the summer workers from the Hall. But Lewis's eyes were fixed on the red-haired young woman sitting beside Cam. She smiled at them and raised her glass as though in a toast.

'Hello, Lewis,' said Molly Ewing. 'Hello, Ginny.'

For a moment Lewis stared at his former fiancée, lost for words.

'Aren't you going to say hello?' Cam asked, grinning. 'Don't tell me you've forgotten her already? From what I know of Molly, I'd say she's not that easy to forget.'

'Not at all easy to forget.' Lewis's voice was tight with anger. 'In fact, I've been waiting every morning for a letter from you or your solicitor,' he told Molly. 'But not a word – then suddenly here you are, socializing in the pub as if you don't have a care in the world.'

'I don't,' she said cheerfully, 'but now that we've met up again, why don't you and Ginny sit down so that we can have a chat?'

The others round the table, recognizing the sudden tension between the two of them, were already rearranging the seating so that they were clustered together, leaving two empty seats opposite Cam and Molly. Lewis pulled one back for Ginny and then sat down beside her.

'That's better.' Cam signalled to Joe Fisher. 'What are you going to drink?'

When Joe had taken their orders and the others at the table had fallen into conversation with each other Lewis glared at Molly. 'So – why haven't you been in touch? And why are you suddenly turning up without letting us know you were coming?'

The table was so crowded that Ginny was close enough to Lewis to feel the tension in his body. She covered his hand with hers in an attempt to warn him to keep calm and stay in control.

Molly, sitting opposite, gave him a sweet smile. 'I haven't been in touch because Bob and I both work in a bar that's very popular with tourists, and at this time of year we're kept very busy. I'm only in the country for a few days – I've booked in here for tonight and tomorrow night because remembering what the Hall's like, I knew I'd be more comfortable here. I was going to call you tomorrow morning. The day after tomorrow I'm going to Inverness to see Weena and my parents for an overnight stay, then it's back to Portugal.'

The drinks arrived and Lewis, who had uncharacteristically ordered whisky, emptied his glass almost immediately and slammed it down on the table.

'Another?' invited Cam. To Ginny's relief Lewis shook his head, then said evenly to Molly, 'It's going to be quite interesting for you, seeing our daughter. It doesn't happen very often, does it?'

'Working in a bar and living in two rooms above it isn't the best place for a little girl, and I didn't want to upset you by taking her away to Portugal. You should be grateful to me for that. In any case, Bob and I needed time to decide on what to do for the best. I may not be able to spend much time with her, but I do think about Weena's best interests.'

'Her best interests lie in being with at least one of her parents on a permanent basis instead of being switched between one place and another. She's about to start school, Molly, and more permanent decisions have to be made quickly. I know that your mother and father look after her well, and they love her, but if she was here with me she'd have my parents for company as well as me and Ginny. And she loves Linn Hall; you know she'd be safe with us.'

'Of course I know all of that, and now that you and Ginny are engaged – I'm so sorry, Ginny, I haven't congratulated you. I'm so pleased to know that Lewis has found someone much more suited to his lifestyle than I was. Has he given you a ring? May I see it?'

Ginny held her hand out and Molly took it in her own hand, which was much softer than Ginny's. 'It's very sweet, isn't it?'

'It's exactly what I wanted.'

'Are you talking about the ring, or about Lewis?'

'Both.'

'How nice.' Molly spread her own left hand out on the table, palm down to display the sparkling ring, much larger than Ginny's, on the third finger. 'Cam was telling me just before you came in that you're working on an interesting project at the moment, Ginny.'

'Ginny's been booked to redesign someone's garden,' Lewis told her. 'It's being televised for a series to be shown next year. She's done a magnificent job with our estate.'

'Yes, I've been hearing all about that as well. As I said before, you two seem to have been made for each other, just like me and Bob. I've never been happier in my life than I am with him.'

'When are we going to discuss what's to happen to Rowena Chloe? Is she coming to live with us or is she not?' Lewis's voice, and the way his fingers drummed on the table, showed that his temper was fraying.

'Why don't you and Ginny come down here to the pub for lunch tomorrow?' Molly suggested. 'I can book us into the little dining room; it will probably be quiet and we can get a proper talk. Cam's taking me to Kirkcudbright in the evening and I'm planning to leave for Inverness first thing next morning. Twelve o'clock suit you?'

'I'm working tomorrow,' Ginny said, 'but in any case, I think this is a matter best discussed between you two.'

'Then it's just you and me, Lewis, like in the old days. If you can fit me into your busy schedule?'

'Twelve o'clock. That'll give us plenty of time to thrash things out.'

She raised her eyebrows. 'I hope that's only a figure of speech.'

Cam laughed, and then said, 'Play nice, you two. Now that that's all been arranged, how about another drink?'

'Better not,' Lewis said without conferring with Ginny. 'We've both got a busy day ahead of us so we're going back to the Hall. Thanks for the drinks, Cam.'

'I wish you didn't have to work for Fergus tomorrow,' Lewis said as he and Ginny walked back to the Hall. 'Are you sure you can't phone him and put it off?'

'I can't, and in any case I think it's better that the two of you talk alone. It means that you'll both be able to concentrate on the subject in hand, which is Rowena Chloe. One way or the other you have to have the matter settled before Molly leaves – it's going to be your last chance. And if I'm not there she won't be able to keep trying to taunt me.'

'She did, didn't she? I was finding it difficult to keep my temper every time she had a go at you!'

'I'm well aware of it, and I know that that's the reaction she was hoping for. You'll have to bite your tongue, Lewis; don't give her any excuse to punish you by refusing to let Rowena Chloe live here. Concentrate on what you want, stay calm and stay in control – and whatever you do, ignore any jibes.'

'I don't know what I ever saw in her!'

'Don't you? I do. She's gorgeous, Lewis, and nobody could blame you for falling for her.'

'I put it down to stupidity,' he said grimly. 'I realized when she dumped me and went off with the fellow she's living with now that what she'd wanted from the start was Linn Hall. Even when she was trying to get me to agree that once I inherited the place I'd sell it and spend the money travelling all over the world with her, it didn't really occur to me that that had been her plan all along.'

'Well, I'm very glad that she finally gave up and walked out on you because that was when you began to look at me as a woman instead of a gardener. By that time I was beginning to think about moving away and trying to forget you.'

He made a sound that sounded like a half laugh, half groan. 'Thank God I came to my senses before it was too late, then.'

'But you did, and that's all that matters. Just concentrate on the fact that by this time tomorrow we may be looking forward to Rowena Chloe coming here to live.'

'If I can keep my temper under control – that's what you're trying to emphasize and I promise that I will,' Lewis said. Then, as they went up the dark drive, 'If my parents are still up I suppose I'll have to tell them that Molly's here.'

'I'll come in with you just in case you need any moral support – or would you rather tell them on your own?'

'Tonight or tomorrow morning, whenever I tell them I want you to be there. You're a member of the Ralston-Kerr family now – a very important member.'

Fliss and Hector were in the pantry, watching the news on television, when Lewis and Ginny arrived back. Fliss switched the programme off at once. 'Nothing cheerful, just the same not-very-interesting news. Shall I make some tea?'

'Not for me, dear,' Hector told her. 'I think I'll just go up to bed.'

'I've got something to tell you both before you go upstairs. When Ginny and I went into the pub this evening, Molly was there.'

'Molly?' Fliss's voice rose to an astonished squeak, and Hector, who was rising from his seat, fell back into it. 'Your Molly?'

'Not my Molly, Dad – though unfortunately, she used to be. Molly Ewing, my daughter's mother.'

'But how – what – when did she get here?' Hector asked feebly.

His wife said at the same time, 'Is she staying here tonight? Where is she going to sleep? There's only the room that Rowena Chloe uses, the one connected to your bedroom, Lewis, and that's not very suitable, is it?'

'Don't worry, Mum, she's staying the night at the pub. She's only here for a day, and I'm having lunch with her tomorrow.'

'Did she say what she's decided about Rowena Chloe? Will she be allowed to come and live here?'

'That's what we're going to talk about tomorrow. The place was crowded, and we couldn't discuss any of it. But I'll definitely find out tomorrow, once and for all. In the meantime,' Lewis said, 'let's all go to bed because there's nothing we can do tonight but worry.'

Ginny had a very busy day and when she arrived back at Linn Hall it was later than she had hoped. Eager to find out how the meeting between Molly and Lewis had worked out, she went straight to the kitchen instead of to the camper van to make herself presentable, as she usually did.

The kitchen was quiet, for once. The backpackers had eaten dinner and dispersed, Jinty had washed the dishes and gone home to see to her own large family, and now Fliss and Hector were sitting down to their own evening meal, but Lewis was nowhere to be seen.

'It's good news,' Fliss told her happily. 'Lewis was away for most of the afternoon but when he came back he said that Molly has agreed to let Rowena Chloe come and live with us here at Linn Hall. We're delighted about it, aren't we, Hector?'

'It's going to be good to have the wee lassie here with us,' her husband nodded.

'And it's lovely to have some good news after all the ups and downs of the past few years,' Fliss chattered on. 'We're not sure when she's coming because Lewis was anxious to catch up with some work, but we'll get all the details later. You'll be ready for something to eat, dear.'

Although the news was good, Ginny still felt slightly uneasy; she had fully expected Lewis to be waiting for her to come home. 'I think I'll go and look for Lewis first – I can't wait to hear all about it.'

'I'll keep both dinners in the oven, and reheat the soup when you come in, but don't take too long.'

'Did he say what part of the estate he was going to be working in?'

'I don't think he did,' Fliss said.

Lewis could have been anywhere on the estate, but after checking the places where she would have expected him to be without success, Ginny climbed the hill at the back of the estate and made for the stone grotto, where she shinned up the tangle of ivy that acted as a ladder.

Lewis was sitting on the flat roof, knees drawn up to his chin and his arms clasped tightly around his legs. He didn't have the look of a man who has just been granted his dearest wish.

'There you are – just as I thought.' She sat down beside him. 'Your mother told me the good news. When's Rowena Chloe going to move in?'

'Hopefully, early July.'

It's not all that long, and in the meantime you'll now be able to enrol her into the local school for the start of the autumn term.'

'Mmmm.' He had been staring down over the estate laid out below, to the village roofs. Now he turned towards her, putting an arm tightly around her. 'It's so good to see you!'

'And you. It was difficult trying to concentrate on work today. All I could think about was how things were going between you and Molly. Was she very difficult?'

'Surprisingly, she wasn't. To be honest, I think she's relieved about Rowena Chloe coming to live with us. I got the feeling that her parents were beginning to miss the old days when they could just pack their bags and go on holiday whenever they felt like it.'

'You can't entirely blame them, Lewis. They've raised both their girls, and like Molly, they enjoy being free to travel around when and where they wish.'

'But unlike Molly, they raised their children. I can't understand her, Ginny. At first she seemed to be a really good mother, although she was still insistent on continuing with her travels around the world, and she had to rely on her parents for help with that; but since this fellow Bob came into her life she seems to have lost interest in Rowena Chloe. How could she do that?'

For a moment Ginny hesitated. Even before she herself fell in love with Lewis she had known that Molly was never going to be the right partner for him, but although everything was now different she was still reluctant to criticize the woman who had given him his beloved daughter.

Finally she opted for honesty. 'It was never deliberate, Lewis. I'm quite sure that Molly loves Rowena Chloe, but in her own way.'

'What do you mean by "in her own way"?'

'In the way that a little girl loves her dolls. Dolls are inanimate objects that can be played with when you feel like it and put in a cupboard when you want to go and do something else. Some women never lose sight of that feeling – they love their children as babies to be looked after and cuddled, but when the children get older and start to become individuals in their own right, that makes them less interesting. Molly could be one of those women – she still loves Rowena Chloe, but now that she's got Bob and a new life in Portugal, Rowena Chloe doesn't fit in the way she used to.'

'Where on earth did you learn a thing like that?

She shrugged. 'That's the life I used to have. After my father went to Australia and my mother began to concentrate on her career I was lonely. I remember thinking that I must've done something bad to make them both lose interest in me; I remember looking at all the photographs she kept of us as a family for years, wishing that I could turn the clock back to the way it was; then one day when I was round about seven it suddenly occurred to me that it wasn't my fault after all. My mother had enjoyed having a baby to cuddle, but she wasn't so good with older children. I felt a lot better after that because I started to concentrate on becoming my own person.'

Lewis hugged her tightly. 'Poor you, feeling so lonely!'

'It wasn't that bad,' Ginny protested. 'I survived, and now everything has worked out just as I wanted it to. I've got you and your lovely parents, and I can't tell you how much I'm looking forward to being a stepmum to Rowena Chloe. She's not going to grow up as a lonely only, the way I did. Not if I can help it!'

'Nor me.' Lewis looked out over the view that they both loved, then said, 'There's something I haven't told my parents, but I can't keep it back from you.'

'I thought there might be, because you're remarkably glum for a man who's just been told that he's finally got the news he's wanted so much to hear. I take it that Molly gave you a bad time?'

'She gave me a shock that I wasn't expecting. She's not so much giving Rowena Chloe to me as selling her.'

'*What?*'

'She wants ten thousand pounds, Ginny, before she'll agree to let Rowena Chloe live here.'

Fifteen

'Ten thousand pounds? But that's ridiculous!' Ginny exclaimed. 'Molly can't seriously be thinking of selling her own child!'

'Oh yes, she can.' Lewis's voice was thick with disgust. 'Apparently the owner of the bar where she and Bob work is retiring. They're desperate to buy the place, but they don't have enough money.'

'Neither do you. You've had to work hard for those grants and loans, but you never let the constant struggle get you down.'

'She's found out about the loan I'm getting from the bank

to start work on the Hall. I'd mentioned it to Cam and I can only assume that he passed it on without realizing that telling Molly was a bad move. And of course she knows that the gardens are finally bringing in some money. Thanks to that, we've got almost enough in the bank to pay her, and knowing that we're definitely getting the money to start work on the house helps. But I'm not sure when we'll get that. Until it arrives, things are going to be sticky, and I realize that Molly and Bob will need that ten thousand now or they'll lose the bar. I'm going to have to do some juggling. For a start, the work Angela Steele's planning for the house will have to be undertaken bit by bit, until I can get the bank account built up again, but it's going to be very tricky between now and when the loan arrives. I've to see Molly again first thing tomorrow morning before she leaves, to let her know whether or not I'm going to be able to pay her off. I have to, one way or the other, or I may lose Rowena Chloe for good.'

'You won't,' Ginny said. 'I haven't told you yet that I was paid five thousand pounds for that documentary Fergus made about the Hall, and it's still sitting in my bank account. And apparently I'm going to be well paid for the work I'm doing for him at the moment. When – if – the series he's planning on putting together about his garden's restoration appears on television I'll get some more money, apparently. Even if it doesn't become a series I'll be paid for the work done. Meanwhile, the money in my account at the moment, plus another five thousand from you, will pay Molly off, and you'd still have some money left in your bank account to keep things going.'

'But I can't and won't take money that you've earned!'

'The decision's not just up to you – I'm going to be Rowena Chloe's stepmother, and for that I would sell the coat off my back.' Ginny put her fingers to his mouth as he began to protest. 'You and I are getting married, which means that for the rest of our lives, beginning here and now, we share everything. It's the only way we get Rowena Chloe *and* save this place, so no more arguing – please!'

For a moment he looked as though he was going to ignore the request, and then, to her relief, he nodded. 'Thank you a million times. I'm the luckiest man in the world!'

'Sadly,' Ginny told him, 'you're not. As I said, from now on we share everything – the good things and bad things – and that doesn't just apply to your daughter, it also applies to my mother. And now that everything is decided and put right, can we please go down to the Hall and have some dinner? I'm absolutely starving!'

Normally everything else disappeared from Ginny's mind when she was working on Fergus's garden, but on the following day she had to concentrate hard in order to stop from thinking about Lewis's meeting with Molly.

Fergus had driven her there, and on the way home he again tried to persuade her to let him take her for a meal before driving her back to Linn Hall.

'All I want after a day's work is to get washed and changed,' she told him.

'A drink, then – that wouldn't take more than fifteen minutes.'

'Lewis had an important meeting to attend today and I want to find out how it went,' she said, and he sighed.

'Very well, but why don't you bring a change of clothes with you when you're working on my garden? The shower in the house is working adequately, so you could shower and change there, and enjoy a leisurely meal with me before I take you home.'

'That's not part of the job description, Fergus,' she said firmly, and he laughed and then said, 'I must remember to write it into the contract the next time you work for me.'

As they headed towards the entrance to Linn Hall Ginny saw Lewis leaning against one of the gateposts.

'You can drop me here, Fergus, and I'll walk up with Lewis.'

'He must have really been missing you today.' There was a sarcastic note in Fergus's voice as he slowed the car down.

'Perhaps almost as much as I miss him when we're apart,' Ginny couldn't resist saying as she got out and closed the door. 'Thanks for the lift, Fergus – I'll take the camper van tomorrow because I've got some cuttings that I want to bring with me.'

'Hi, Lewis,' Fergus called out of the driver's window, 'Here she is, safe and sound.' And then, as Ginny got out of the car, 'See you tomorrow, Ginny, and don't forget what I said about that change of clothes.'

As the sports car reversed into the driveway in order to change direction before roaring back down the hill, Lewis asked suspiciously, 'Did he just say something about a change of clothes?'

'Just Fergus being silly. He keeps suggesting that he should take me for a meal on the way home after work, and I keep pointing out that after a day's gardening I'm not really dressed for dining out. On the way here he was pointing out that the shower in his house works, and I could freshen up there.'

Lewis frowned. 'And are you going to take a change of clothes from now on?'

'Absolutely not and absolutely never.' She kissed him, and then said as they began to walk up the drive, 'I couldn't wait to get back to find out how things went with Molly today.'

'That's why I was waiting for you at the gate, so that we could talk without being overheard. It went well, and now she's on her way to her parents' place and then Portugal with a cheque for five thousand pounds, to ensure that she and Bob will get their pub. I've promised that they'll get the other half as soon as everything's signed and watertight.'

'So everything's definitely going to be legal?'

'It is, thank God. I've already arranged to go and see our lawyer tomorrow, and I have the address of Molly's lawyer in Portugal. Having only half the money she wants at the moment should ensure that nothing goes wrong on their side of the bargain. We've roughed out a contract between us – she'll promise that from now on I'm Rowena Chloe's legal guardian, and I've promised that she and her parents will have reasonable access when they want it.'

'That's wonderful! I've been worrying all day in case something went wrong again.'

'I think it's going to work out for everybody – at last!' Lewis said.

When Helen assured Malcolm Finlay that the *Dumfries News* wouldn't print the rumour that Lilias Drew had moved to their area she firmly believed it – until the following Friday, when Marcy, totalling Helen's purchases, which included the local paper's new edition, said, 'When I saw the article in the paper this morning about the successful author I thought for a moment or two that it was you.'

Helen blinked. 'What are you talking about?'

The shop was quiet, with only two other shoppers still browsing round the shelves, so Marcy had time to flip the paper open and point to a short article on an inside page. 'This headline.'

'Let me see.' Helen almost snatched the paper from her friend's hands and turned it around so that she could read it. It was a small article, but the headline, *Does Successful Author Live Among Us?*, seemed to jump off the page and slap her in the face.

'It's about Lilias Drew, that woman who writes the sexy romances everyone's reading just now,' Marcy chattered on, 'What are they called? Oh yes – chick-lit for the older woman. I've never got time to read but I really must try one of her books. Apparently someone's got the idea that she's moved to this area. Certainly not to this village; the only female who's come here recently is Stella Hesslett's sister Elma, and I doubt if *she's* a highly successful novelist. We'd all be a lot happier if she stopped going on day after day about her broken marriage and just wrote about it instead.'

One of the other shoppers arrived and dumped her basket on the counter, giving Helen the chance to pay Marcy and escape from the shop. It was her intention to go at once to Thatcher's Cottage, but as she turned off Main Street she saw Malcolm hurrying towards her.

'Have you seen the local paper?' he asked as soon as they met.

'Yes, and I was coming to find out if you had. It's clearly still a rumour,' she tried to reassure him.

'If so, why would they write about it at all? It's supposed to be a newspaper, not a rumour-paper!'

'Newspapers often seem to publish unproven stories nowadays. It's my guess that it's in this week's edition because they needed to fill a space and had nothing else to hand. Or it may be that they hope one of their readers will give them a clue, such as mentioning some woman who's moved into their area and is still a bit of a mystery to them. Whatever the reason, they're clearly under the impression that Lilias Drew's a woman, which shows that your secret is still safe.'

'I certainly hope so, because I recently signed a new three-book contract.'

'That's good news for all your readers, including me.'

'Perhaps you should ask your friend the journalist why they put the article in when they don't appear to have any proof?'

'That's the last thing I should do. If I show too much interest in this rumour he'll probably wonder if I know something.'

'I didn't think of that. Perhaps you're right, and we should just ignore it,' Malcolm said, to her relief.

Ginny and Lewis both felt safer now that Molly had been paid off and was back in Portugal. It had been agreed that her parents would deliver Rowena Chloe to Linn Hall in July, when her nursery school closed for the summer, and so the little girl had already been enrolled for the local primary school's autumn term.

Fliss was now happily involved, with Jinty's help, in getting the small bedroom attached to Lewis's room ready for her arrival.

As Lewis walked round to the front of the house with Ginny to wait for Fergus, who had arranged to take her to work, he said, 'I feel so guilty about Angela Steele. When she comes to have another look at the ground floor rooms this afternoon I'm going to have to tell her that although the loan's been confirmed, we may not be able to pay her in full as we had expected. I just hope she doesn't ask why.'

'But even if she has to get the money in a series of payments instead of a lump sum, she's still going to be paid in full. I think she'll accept that – she strikes me as a sensible businesswoman. In financial circles it's called cash flow.'

'She's also a professional who has the right to be treated fairly. It's not her fault that we've had to pay Molly off. But at the same time, Rowena Chloe has to come first. I'd rob the nearest bank rather than lose her.'

'I know that, and if you hadn't had any other option I'd have gone along with the bank robbery and offered to be your getaway driver,' Ginny said, and he took her hands in his and kissed them.

'Thank goodness you're here; I'd go mad if I didn't have

somebody to talk to about this Molly business! I wish you could be with me for moral support when Angela arrives.'

'And I wish that you could come with me. I'd enjoy this new job so much more if the two of us were working on it together,' she told him. 'We make a great team.'

'I think so too.' Then, as Fergus's sports car came roaring up the drive, Lewis added, 'If it's any help, you know that I'll be thinking about you all the time.'

The car almost burst from the driveway to circle the open area before the house, gravel spraying from its wheels. 'I wish he wouldn't *do* that!' Lewis said irritably, 'especially not on open days – it always means that the gravel has to be raked all over again!'

Fergus brought the car to an abrupt halt in front of them. 'Good morning, good morning – and isn't it a perfect day?' he greeted them as he leapt out. 'How are things going, Lewis? Lots of visitors?'

'So far so good – we're getting about double the visitors we did last year,' Lewis said, and then winced as Fergus gave him a hearty and unexpected slap on the shoulder.

'That's all down to this magnificent fiancée of yours. Didn't I tell you, Ginny, that your fantastic performance in the documentary would be a success?'

'Personally, I think the increase in visitors is down to the work Lewis and his team have put in on the estate; it looks better every year.'

'This young lady is modest as well as beautiful, eh, Lewis?' Fergus looked at his watch. 'We'd better get going. She may be late back; we're going to have a very busy day.'

'That reminds me, Ginny, now that I've been co-opted on to the village Progress Committee I'm attending my first meeting this evening, so I might be out when you get home. Good luck!' Lewis was preparing to kiss her when Fergus slipped an arm about her shoulders and began to steer her to the car, calling over his shoulder, 'Not to worry, Lewis, I'll take good care of her.'

He helped Ginny into the car tenderly, as though she were unable to do it for herself, and shut her door. As he went round to the driver's door Ginny turned and blew a kiss to Lewis. He blew one back and saw her catch it and then put her fingers to her lips as the engine revved up.

'Bloody idiot!' he muttered as the car began to roar down the drive.

As it happened, Angela was quite relaxed about the financial arrangements and merely nodded when Lewis asked her if it was possible to pay the fee in smaller amounts as each area was completed, rather than beforehand.

'I'm not going to start until after the estate's closed, because having visitors around all the time would be chaotic for you and for me. And since I've got other commitments and may even have to take time off from this project on a couple of occasions, I'm quite happy to be paid bit by bit if that helps you.'

'It's very decent of you.'

'Sensible rather than decent, Lewis. Look at this place—'

They were standing in the entrance hall, and now Angela spread her arms wide. 'Clearly, your lovely home has been neglected for years, and it's also clear that you and your parents love the place and would never have allowed it to fall into such disrepair if you'd had the money to look after it. To be honest, I'm really looking forward to this task. And I'm confident that at the end of the day you'll all be delighted, and I'll be paid in full.'

'Thank you for being so understanding.'

'And thank you for being so honest.' Angela shook his hand firmly. 'Now that the financial situation has been discussed and dealt with I'd like to go round the entire area on my own to refresh my memory, and start making detailed notes.' She indicated the door at the rear of the hall, overshadowed and dwarfed by the staircase. 'As I recall, that leads to the kitchen. When I'm finished I'll go through it, and if you're not there I'm sure someone will tell me where to find you.'

'I'll have to leave you to it any case; we've got quite a few visitors around this afternoon and I'm supposed to be staffing the stable shop. I'll arrange for someone to bring you tea or coffee, and biscuits.'

'No biscuits, but a pot of strong black coffee would be lovely,' Angela said briskly, 'without milk, cream or sugar.'

Sixteen

'Isn't it time we decided who's going to open the festival?' Muriel Jacobsen suggested at that evening's meeting of the Progress Committee.

'Hannah's right,' Naomi Hennessey agreed, 'we're at the end of May now, and we don't have all that much time left.'

'We should list several possible names,' suggested Alastair Marshall, who together with Lewis had recently been co-opted on to the committee. 'If we only choose one person they may not necessarily agree to do it, then we'd have to start all over again. If we come up with a few names today we can arrange them in the order we'd prefer and in that way, if it comes to it, nobody needs to know that they weren't the first choice.'

'Should we ask the villagers to put names forward?' The idea came from Pete McDermott, but immediately met with disapproval from the others.

'That way lies madness,' Muriel said firmly.

'I don't see why.'

'She's quite right, Pete,' Robert Kavanagh told him. 'For one thing, we could end up with people who just wouldn't be capable of doing the job properly, and for another, the suggested names would then be known to everyone and they'd all start lobbying for support. We could end up with a village war.'

'Surely people wouldn't be so small-minded,' Pete said, and Muriel gave a grim laugh.

'You'd be surprised. Not everyone in this village is as fair-minded as you are. I'm probably not the only member of this group who can think of at least one person that I'd never ask to open any of our festivals.'

'Let's start thinking of names,' Robert said impatiently. 'Time's moving on and there are other items to discuss.'

'That television and stage actress, Meredith Whitelaw – Ginny Whitelaw's mother – made a good job of opening the Hall's garden party once, didn't she?' Lachie Wilkins volunteered. 'And she's got quite a high-profile name. That sitcom she's in is very popular at the moment.'

'Apparently so,' Muriel said, 'Though personally, I can't stand it.'

'Nor me,' Robert agreed, 'but the wife thinks it's brilliant.' And then, remembering that Lewis was present, 'Sorry Lewis, I forgot that the lady's future son-in-law was among us.'

'Me too,' Muriel said hastily. 'My apologies.'

'Don't worry about it,' Lewis assured them. 'She and I don't really care for each other. But in any case, I don't think there's much sense in putting Meredith's name on your list because she's spending most of her time in Spain and she's always so busy that she'll probably not manage to fit in a visit to us this summer.'

Lynn Stacey, a good friend of Ginny's, caught his eye and winked at him, then said, 'I opened the Scarecrow Festival last year, and I was honoured to be asked, but I don't think anyone, even someone as famous as Meredith Whitelaw, should do it more than once.'

Robert nodded. 'I've done it once, being Chair of this committee, and I agree with Lynn.'

'Poor Mrs Ralston-Kerr would be delighted to hear you say that once is enough,' added Helen Campbell, busily recording the meeting, but taking time off to say her piece. 'She's had to open the Linn Hall garden party several times, and I know that she always hated doing it because she's such a shy person.'

'You're right, Helen − my mother was delighted to hear that our annual garden party's going to be part of the festival this year instead of a separate entity. She's hoping that since it's such a big event she won't be asked to open it. She and I would both appreciate it if you didn't approach her.'

Muriel put up a hand. 'I've just thought of someone − there's a writer called Lilias Drew whose books are very popular here and everywhere else as far as I can tell; the *Dumfries News* had an article in last week, saying that she's moved into this area. It might be worth getting in touch with her, if we can. Having our festival opened by someone as popular as she is at the moment would bring in more people.'

There was a general murmur of interest, and Robert Kavanagh asked, 'Does anyone know how we could get in touch with her?'

'I don't think that's possible.'

'You sound very definite, Helen,' Naomi said. 'Do you know something about her that we don't?'

Helen flushed. 'I do, in a way; you all know that I write about what's going on in Prior's Ford every week in the *Dumfries News.* The last time Bob Green collected the notes from me he mentioned the rumour about Lilias Drew. He said that they had tried to get information from her publishers, but they refused to give any comment whatsoever. It seems that Lilias Drew is a very private person and doesn't like publicity.'

'So why put an article in the paper saying that she lives in this area when they don't know if it's true?'

Helen shrugged. 'I don't know much about how newspapers are run, but I suspect that they used it to fill an empty space on one of their pages. What I do know for sure is that the newspaper wasn't able to find out anything about her, or where she lives. I doubt if we'd have better luck.'

'I suppose we could try her publisher ourselves,' Lachie suggested. 'Just to make sure.'

'No harm in it.' Robert looked around the group, eyebrows raised, and everyone nodded. 'Helen, would you do it, please?'

'If you want me to, but if they refused to speak to the press I doubt if they'll speak to me.'

'Helen is probably right,' Muriel put in, 'and I don't think we should waste time on something that's probably untrue.'

Alastair suddenly snapped his fingers. 'What about Steph McDonald? She's a local girl and she recently won that scholarship to the drama college in Glasgow. That's a terrific achievement – we should all be very proud of her, and she surely deserves to be honoured by the village she was born in.'

'That's a great idea,' Lynn Stacey said at once. 'Steph isn't only a very nice girl, she's a brilliant actress too, and our drama group is going to miss her very much when she goes. Modest, as well. Having directed her onstage, I can confidently say that I wouldn't be surprised if she became quite well known. And I believe that she'd be thrilled to be asked to open our festival before she leaves us.'

'I second that,' Naomi agreed warmly. 'The McDonalds are a terrific family, especially Jinty. A marvellous mother, and a very hard worker.'

'She has to be a hard worker,' Muriel said drily, 'Her husband certainly doesn't contribute much to the family finances, judging by the time – and money – he spends in the local pub.'

'Who votes that we ask Steph McDonald to open this year's festival?' Robert Kavanagh looked around Naomi's small study, where the committee usually met, then when every hand immediately went up, 'As we seem to be unanimous, I think that Steph McDonald should be contacted without any more delay. In the meantime, we can try to think of other names just in case she's too shy to take it on.'

'I doubt if she'll be too shy,' Lynn said drily. 'After all, the girl hopes to become a professional actress, and actresses can't afford to be shy.'

Robert grinned at her. 'Foolish me! Lynn, would you be willing to approach Steph on our behalf?'

'I'd love to.'

'Thank you. And now,' Robert referred to his notes, 'we can move on to the next point, which involves Linn Hall. Lewis, can we start discussing activities that can be held on your estate?'

As always, Ginny's day sped by. Now that the weather was improving the entire team had got into the habit of bringing packed lunches to work, picnicking on the lawn, now well mowed, on good days and in the house if the weather was poor. By the time they finished for the day she was delighted with the progress they had made.

'If we can keep going at this rate,' she said to Fergus as the others began to leave, 'we're going to get the entire place hauled into shape before autumn.'

'I've got no doubt about it. I've never met such a hard worker as you are, Ginny.'

'It's the gardeners you should be praising, not me. You chose them well and they're doing a magnificent job. I just wish that Lewis could have had gardeners like them when he started tackling the Linn Hall estate.'

'Sometimes, Ginny Whitelaw, I despair of you.'

'Why? What was I doing wrong?'

'Absolutely nothing at all. It's just that I don't think you're fully aware of your own talent. You're so incredibly knowledgeable

about gardening, and so natural and relaxed in front of the cameras.'
The others had gone and they were the last to leave. As always,
Fergus opened the car door for her and helped her in. Being
treated like valuable china irritated her, but she couldn't find a
way to say so without offending him.

'Yet again, I have to say that you could definitely have a good
future as a television presenter,' he told her when he had driven
the car out on to the lane. 'You're a natural, but I don't think
you realize that. I'm sure that I could put a lot of work your
way.'

'I've already got a lot of work ahead of me. Once this job's
over and the Linn estate closes to the public in the autumn, Lewis
and I have to get started on renovating the interior of the Hall and
keeping the estate going, not to mention planning our wedding.
I forgot to tell you the best news – his little daughter's coming
to live at the Hall permanently and we're both so excited about
it. So I'm going to have lots to do,' she ended happily, 'with no
time for any extra television work.'

'You really should try to consider the larger picture. Lots of
people could do what you're planning to do with the rest of your
life, but not many of them have your particular talents. You could
make a heck of a lot of money – enough to hire a good nanny
for the child and get the entire Hall renovated – if you would
just let me make a better use of your gardening skills. Think of
the pleasure of being able to help Lewis and his parents to stop
worrying about money all the time. There's a nice little restaurant
not far along this road,' Fergus suddenly changed the subject.
'Fancy stopping for a bite to eat?'

'Dressed like this?' she laughed, indicating her jeans and T-shirt.

'I've noticed that you haven't taken up my idea about bringing
a change of clothes to work.'

'I've no intention of doing that.'

'Fortunately, this isn't a fancy place.'

'I'm expected for dinner at home. Lewis will be wondering
where I've got to as it is.'

'He's going to be at some kind of a meeting, isn't he?'

She'd forgotten about the Progress Committee. 'Yes, he is, but
his parents will be waiting dinner for me.'

'We don't need to take long – we're almost there.' He began

to slow the car down as the restaurant came in sight. 'If you're so fussy about being home for dinner you could at least make time for a pre-dinner drink.'

Ginny began to feel irritated by his insistence.

'I'm hungry, and I'd love a drink, but I'm also longing for a bath and the comfort of a fresh outfit – so the sooner I get home the better.'

'That's a great pity. Another time, perhaps – no, not perhaps, let's make a definite arrangement.' He gave her a sideways glance, as though expecting her to agree. But Ginny stared straight ahead and said nothing.

Seventeen

On the evening following the Progress Committee's meeting Lynn Stacey went to see Steph McDonald. Normally, the council house where Jinty and Tom McDonald had raised their eight children was filled with noise and activity, but on this pleasant late-May evening most of them were out and about. Jinty's husband Tom was in the Neurotic Cuckoo, where he spent most of his evenings, and Steph's twin brother Grant, a professional footballer, was at a training session.

The other three boys were enjoying a noisy game of football in the back garden, while Jinty and her daughters were watching television. As soon as Jinty opened the door to her, Lynn, hearing the television set blaring and the girls giggling, said, 'Am I interrupting something interesting? It's actually Steph I've come to see.'

'Of course you're not interrupting; we're just watching a repeat of *The Last of the Summer Wine* – the kids can never get enough of it and I quite like it myself,' Jinty said as she drew Lynn into the hall. 'It's better than some of the sitcoms shown these days. But they'll probably make a fuss if I switch it off and then we won't get any peace at all. Would you mind terribly if you and Steph talked in the kitchen?'

'Of course not.'

'That's good of you. I'll put the kettle on,' Jinty said as she led the way, 'and send Steph through so that you can have a good chat in peace.'

'Come with her, I think you'll be interested to hear what I've got to say.'

'That sounds intriguing. We'll be with you in just a moment,' Jinty promised.

Looking round the kitchen, which was immaculate, Lynn marvelled over the way Jinty managed to fit housework in with looking after her large brood and working at Linn Hall, plus keeping the Village Hall and the primary school clean.

Hearing voices and shouts of laughter from the back garden, she went over to the window to watch the boys enjoying their football game. Nineteen-year-old Jimmy was throwing his tall, bony body around recklessly, arms flailing, freckled face crimson with exertion and laughter, his red hair brilliant in the last of the evening sun. Norrie and Frankie, his younger brothers, seemed to be more interested in throwing themselves at Jimmy and trying to trip him up than in concentrating on the game.

'It's hard to believe,' Lynn said as she heard the door from the hall open, 'that when the next school term starts in August there won't be a member of the McDonald family there. It's the end of a tradition.'

'I feel much the same myself,' Jinty said sadly. 'They all seem to have grown up so quickly. I miss having little ones running around. Steph, love, get the biscuits out.'

'Don't tell me you're beginning to feel broody, Jinty.' Lynn turned back into the room. 'I think you've done more than your fair share when it comes to populating the primary school.'

'I wouldn't mind having more children,' Jinty admitted, 'but I don't think Tom's very keen, so I'm just going to have to wait for the grandchildren to come along.'

'Don't count on me for that, Mum,' Steph advised her. 'I'm going to be busy for the next few years; you should look to Heather for your grandchildren. All she's ever wanted is to get married and have babies. Merle wants to be a teacher and Faith's still determined to be a lady wrestler. Tea or coffee, Miss Stacey?'

'Coffee would be lovely, and you always call me Lynn at drama rehearsals, Steph.'

The girl laughed, flushing slightly. 'I think it must be a habit – when you're told that your former teacher wants to talk to you, you tend to switch to schoolroom mode.'

'I know what you mean. A few weeks ago I was at my class reunion and one of our teachers was there. My best friend insisted on calling her Miss Marshall, although the rest of us were all calling her by her first name. When the teacher said, "Elizabeth, my name is Jean," Elizabeth went crimson and said, "Oh, Miss Marshall, I couldn't *possibly!*"'

'I can understand what she felt like.' Jinty took her seat at the table. 'I remember gaping at my primary teacher when I was about six years old and met her in the Kirkcudbright Woolworth's. I had this vague idea that teachers had been put on earth to teach, and that they were put away in cupboards at the end of every school day.'

'I believe I thought something like that when I first started school.' Lynn stirred her coffee. 'Anyway, enough of going down memory lane. Steph, the Progress Committee asked me to have a word with you.'

'With me? What about?'

'We wondered if you'd be willing to open this year's festival for us.'

Steph, who had picked up her coffee cup, stared at Lynn, her mouth dropping open, while her mother gasped and then said quickly, 'Steph, you're spilling your coffee!' and jumped up to get a cloth, while Steph hurriedly clattered the cup back down into its saucer, spilling hot coffee over her fingers as she did so. 'Ow!' she said, sucking her burned fingers.

'Now it's going everywhere!' Jinty mopped the table with one hand while picking up the cup and saucer with the other.

'Sorry,' Lynn apologized, 'I should have asked you before the coffee arrived.'

'Did you say that you wanted *me* to open the festival?' The last word was almost a squeak.

'Yes, that's right.'

Jinty dumped the dishcloth, cup and saucer on the draining board and turned, her face glowing. 'Oh Steph, what an honour!'

'But why me? What have I done that's so special?'

'You're special to this village, Steph, because you were born

here, you grew up here and you're one of the best actresses
the drama group has. For all these reasons you're going to be
sorely missed when you go off to Glasgow,' Lynn told her
sincerely. 'We all know how desperate you've been to get to
drama school, but because your parents couldn't afford to pay
for it you started to train as a nursery nurse without a single
complaint. Now, at last, the dream's come true, and we're all
so proud of you. Asking you to open the festival is our way
of thanking you for the past and wishing you every success in
the future.'

Tears sprang into the girl's eyes. 'I can't believe this—' Her
voice quivered and she gulped hard. 'I don't know what to say.
Mum, tell me what to say!'

'Well *that's* a first.' Jinty, too, was on the verge of tears. 'But I
know you have to say yes. This is the best thing that's ever
happened to us – apart from the day Grant became a professional
footballer.'

'And who knows – one day Steph may be invited back to
open a future festival because she's become a famous actress, Jinty.'
Lynn, too, was beginning to feel emotional. 'Your children are a
real credit to you – though I must say that they always were. Will
you do it, Steph? The committee are all waiting for your answer.'

Steph nodded, pulling a handkerchief from the sleeve of her
sweater and dabbing at her eyes. 'I'd love to, and thank you all
so much for asking me.'

Jinty hugged her daughter. 'I can't wait to tell the others!'

'And I can't wait to tell Robert Kavanagh. He'll be delighted
to know that that's been decided.' Lynn finished her coffee and
got to her feet.

'What do I have to do? I've never had to open anything before,
apart from doors and envelopes.'

'You'll be expected to make a short speech, but don't worry
about that – it's not until August, and you and I can work something out before then,' Lynn assured her.

Cam Gordon made his way along the row of former almshouses
then stopped and knocked at one of the doors. When there was
no answer he strolled back along the row and round the side
of the last house to the garden at the rear, where, as he expected,

he found all the residents having one of their communal afternoon teas.

Everyone was there – Robert and Cissie Kavanagh from number six, Dolly and Howard Cowan, number five, Hannah Gibbs and Muriel Jacobsen from numbers four and two respectively and Charlie Crandall, who lived at number three. The youngest residents, Derek and Tricia Borland, were missing, but with this being a Saturday, Cam knew that Derek would be working in his father's butcher shop in the Main Street and Tricia, being Tricia, would no doubt be shopping in Kirkcudbright, the nearest town. Today they were represented by Layla, their four-month-old daughter, who was sitting on Harold Cowan's knee, happily playing with the buttons on his shirt.

Cam was made welcome by everyone, including Layla, who turned her curly little head to inspect the newcomer. 'Gah!' She beamed at him, showing two front teeth.

'She's quite the little chatterbox now, aren't you, my darling?' Dolly Cowan said fondly. And then as Layla blew some bubbles and turned back to counting Harold's shirt buttons. 'Harold seems to be her favourite person at the moment.'

'Sit down, Cam,' Cissie Kavanagh invited. 'There's a spare chair and plenty to eat. Tea or coffee?'

'No thanks, but I wouldn't mind some of that ginger cake.'

'Help yourself, I made it this morning,' Cissie told him.

He picked up a thick slice of the cake and bit into it. 'It tastes even better than it looks,' he said, and Cissie beamed. 'So where's Tricia today? Shopping or getting her hair done?'

'Her nails, actually.'

'She's landed on her feet, has our Tricia. Moving into the house that old Ivy McGowan used to live in has provided her with plenty of babysitters,' Cam observed as he finished off the cake and helped himself to another slice.

'We don't mind looking after the baby now and again,' Cissie protested, 'She's such a placid little thing, a pleasure to be with.'

'Cam's right, though,' her husband said. 'Tricia should be spending more time with her own daughter.'

'I don't mind looking after the little moppet now and again,' Dolly Cowan said warmly. 'We never had children, just Minnie and Maxy – and we love the two of you to bits, my little darlings,' she added hurriedly as the poodles lying at her feet lifted their heads on hearing their names, 'but it's lovely to have a human baby around sometimes. Layla adores all of us, Harold especially, and we all adore her.'

'Perhaps we should encourage Tricia to spend more time with Layla now that she's old enough to differentiate between people,' Hannah Gibbs said thoughtfully, then, to Cam, 'Robert tells us that Steph McDonald is to open the Festival in August – have you heard?'

'Yes, and I'm pleased for her because all she's ever wanted to do is act. And I know that she's thrilled to be asked to do it.'

'We all are – a wonderful choice,' Hannah said warmly. 'Help yourself to more food, there's plenty left.'

'I'm fine, thanks. Actually, I wanted a word with you, Harold – just between ourselves if you don't mind.'

'Certainly.' Harold began to get up and then remembered Layla. 'Dolly—'

'Come to Aunty Dolly, darling.' Dolly got to her feet to lift the baby from her husband's lap. As soon as she realized that she was being taken away from Harold Layla began to protest, squirming in Dolly's arms and trying to reach out to him.

'Let's dance,' Dolly said quickly, and started to whirl her way across the grass, singing a song. Layla began to chuckle, while Minnie and Maxy, clearly used to this form of entertainment, jumped up to join Dolly, alternately prancing about on their hind legs and then dropping down to weave around her feet without ever tripping her up.

'It's about this festival,' Cam said as the two men strolled across the grass towards the flower beds. 'I was just thinking that it would be a good idea to have a clown present.'

'I don't think so,' Harold said at once.

'It would be terrific – the kids would love it – a mysterious and unexpected clown appearing from nowhere, then disappearing just as suddenly, like the Scarlet Pimpernel. "Now you see him, now you don't." And we'll have the adults all wondering who this mysterious stranger is, and where he came from.'

'And then finding out,' Harold said, 'and expecting the poor clown to entertain at their children's parties forever more, and on all sorts of other occasions.'

'They won't find out, I'll make sure of that,' Cam promised. 'The few people who already know that you used to be a circus clown haven't breathed a word, and I'll make sure that they know what's going on and that they mustn't give you away. You looked fantastic that time we got together to scare off those kids who were trying to sabotage our first Scarecrow Festival, and they never tried it again.'

'It wasn't just down to me that night; the others played their part as well.'

'It's true that the others making a lot of noise startled the little vandals, but it was you who sent them fleeing back home – a clown in full costume suddenly appearing from the dark and walking slowly towards them when the car headlights were switched on.' Cam chuckled at the memory. 'It was one of the great occasions of my life!'

'When Dolly and I retired we settled in Prior's Ford because we wanted a quiet, peaceful retirement far away from circus life.'

'Just one more appearance, and I promise I'll never ask you to dress up as a clown again,' Cam coaxed. 'Talk to Dolly about it and see what she thinks.'

When he and his mother moved to Tarbethill Farm Jamie Greenlees had thought that his cup of happiness was full to the brim, but life had just become even better with the arrival of Stefan Krechevsky, Berta, and her horse. Every day became a new adventure with so much to do.

True to her promise, blonde, brown-eyed Berta had begun to teach him to ride Titan. She was an excellent tutor, and Jamie had very quickly begun to feel comfortable in the saddle. He loved watching Stefan at work, and could happily spend hours in the glass-blower's workshop, making sure that he didn't get too close to the furnaces. He was even beginning to wonder if it would be possible to combine glass-blowing with farming when he grew up.

He was also learning, with Ewan's help, to start training Paddy, the puppy he had chosen as his own from Bess's litter. Paddy was an appealing little dog with a white face, stomach and paws, and a black back and tail. Although it would be quite a while before he was old enough to become a fully trained working dog he was interested in everything and quick to learn.

'It looks to me as if Jamie chose the best of the litter,' Ewan told Alison. 'The pup's already showing signs of becoming as good a working dog as Old Saul was. My dad couldn't have chosen better. And Jamie's working well with Paddy – I'm thinking that next year the two of them might be worth entering for the young sheepdog owners' trials.'

All in all, Jamie's days were full of activity and happiness, the only drawback being that his mother and stepfather steadfastly refused his frequent suggestions that with so much to do at Tarbethill, and given that he was determined to be a farmer, school was getting in his way and they would be wise to allow him to give it up in order to concentrate on more important things closer to home.

Eighteen

After spending a week in London in order to visit both his publishers – one to discuss Lilias Drew's next book and the other to make plans for a series of academic articles he had been asked to write, Malcolm Finlay was delighted to return to the relative calm of Prior's Ford. As soon as he stepped into Thatcher's Cottage he felt the place welcome him back, and knew for certain that this was where he wanted to stay.

He was vexed at having missed one of the mobile library's visits to the village. Since her half-sister's arrival, his only chance of seeing Stella Hesslett was when she brought the van to Prior's Ford, and even then they only spoke together for the few minutes it took to have books stamped in or out, or to collect books that he had specially asked for.

Even more, he missed their lunches at the Neurotic Cuckoo, when they always seemed to find such a lot to talk about. Although Stella was considered by most of the villagers to be a quiet, shy woman, Malcolm had discovered a completely new side to her character. As far as he was concerned she was a woman with a brain like an encyclopedia and a wide know-ledge of literature, both fiction and non-fiction. As time went on and their friendship deepened he had even discovered that she had considerable knowledge of some of the subjects he himself had specialized in.

As their friendship developed he had also discovered her sense of humour, something she had, for some reason, preferred to keep to herself. Malcolm had never known a woman like her; listening to his three older sisters talk together in front of him he had grown up convinced that all women were predators, constantly hungry for physical contact with the opposite sex.

As a result of this belief he had avoided close contact with any of the females he met during his university years as a student and then a lecturer.

He was comfortable with Helen Campbell for the simple reason that as she appeared to be happy in her marriage she was therefore no threat to him, and with Stella because she, like Helen, made him feel safe. But now that Elma Armitage was in Prior's Ford Malcolm was uneasy again, concerned not only for himself, but for Stella.

The day after he returned from London he worked hard in his study until mid-afternoon, when he decided to have a break and a leisurely drink at the pub.

The place was quiet and Gracie Fisher, behind the bar, welcomed him with her usual friendly smile.

'It's nice to see you back among us again, Dr Finlay. A pint of beer – or is it a coffee this time?'

'I'll have a pint today, thanks.'

She nodded. 'Perfect day for a nice long cold drink.' Then, as she returned to the bar, 'You and Miss Hesslett haven't been in for lunch for a while.'

'She's kept busy now that her sister's visiting her. I take it,' Malcolm said carefully, 'that Mrs Armitage is still in the village?'

'Oh yes, she's got her feet well under Miss Hesslett's table,' Gracie said. 'We're all beginning to wonder if it *is* just a visit, or more like a case of moving in and making herself comfortable. It's not my way to criticize anyone, Dr Finlay, but nobody in this village likes that woman.'

'Really?'

'For one thing, we're all sick and tired of hearing her going on about how her husband's deserted her. If I've heard her ranting on about it once I've heard it twenty times. And for another, I don't think she's very nice to Miss Hesslett.'

Malcolm's ears pricked up. 'In what way?'

'Stella Hesslett's a very nice woman – everyone says so. Quiet but friendly. Never has a bad word for anyone and she's always so helpful when it comes to choosing library books. And I've known her to help people in other ways too. But that sister of hers keeps putting her down and talking about her being dull, which she's not. The last time she was in here I thought she was looking definitely under the weather, and I'm not surprised, since she's the one who has to listen to that woman moaning on about herself day and night.' Then, as she brought his drink over to the table, 'It's the husband *we're* all sorry for – everyone hopes that he and his children are very happy with this new love of his.'

She set the brimming glass carefully on the table before him.

'Thank you. Did you say something about Miss Hesslett's sister moving in? D'you mean she might live here permanently?'

'It's beginning to look that way, and I'm not the only one who's saying so,' Gracie informed him, and then, changing the subject, 'I heard that you were in London all week. Did you have a good time?'

'It was all to do with work, I'm afraid.'

'You were missed. You've become part of this village.'

'Have I?' Malcolm asked, both surprised and pleased.

'Oh yes. It's so nice to see the right kind of person living in Thatcher's Cottage now. Doris Thatcher's and her husband were both born here, I've been told, and they lived in that cottage all their long married life. That's why the cottage eventually got its name. Me and Joe only came here a few years ago, long after Doris's husband died, but I got to know her well when I joined the local Women's Rural. Such a sweet little old lady. She died in the Village Hall when the Rural was holding a fashion show – just slipped away quietly while she was drinking a cup of tea.'

'Good gracious.' Malcolm, about to put the glass to his lips, set it down again.

Gracie took the movement as a sign of interest. 'Everyone hated seeing the cottage empty after that but it wasn't empty for long. The first to rent it were a husband and wife with twin daughters – his, from a previous marriage. They'd lots of money, but it turned out that she was earning most of it, and not in a way that we'd have expected, if you know what I mean. So they didn't last long, and then there was a very nice couple – she was Laura Tyler, a well-known cookery expert, and he was a retired police officer who'd been very high up in the Force. He was writing his memoirs. Unfortunately it turned out that you can never tell a book by its cover because they weren't here for all that long before she went and murdered Kevin Pearce.'

'What? Did you say that someone who used to live in my house committed murder?'

'Not actually in your house,' Gracie hurried to assure him. 'She strangled him in the Village Hall with a feather boa belonging to the drama group. Kevin ran the drama group at the time. Quite a nice man – not much of a drinker, though, so we didn't see him in here often. His widow Elinor still lives in the village, just a few doors along from here.'

Just then a young couple came in and Gracie hurried to welcome them, much to Malcolm's relief.

'When did you last hear from Amy?' Alastair asked as he helped Clarissa to clear the breakfast table.

'Come to think of it, not for a while. She should be letting me know any day now about whether or not she'll be able to come over for the festival. I hope that nothing's got in the way of that.'

'Why don't you call her?'

Clarissa, neatly stacking the dishes ready for washing, looked at him in surprise. 'I never thought of that! Amy always seems to phone me, but it never occurs to me to call her unless I've got something really important to say. Isn't that silly?'

'Very. Perhaps it's a case of thinking that for some reason it's easier to call here from America than to call to America from here.' He picked up the dish towel. 'Your turn to wash, my turn to dry.'

She took the towel from him. 'My turn to do both – aren't you supposed to be on your way right now to the school to run an art class?'

He looked up at the kitchen clock on the wall. 'Good grief – you're right! I'd forgotten all about it!'

'I thought you might have,' Clarissa said as he made a rush for the door. As she turned on the tap she heard him charge up the stairs to collect his rucksack and as she added washing-up liquid to the hot water he came charging back down two steps at a time.

'Back in an hour – consider yourself kissed – and remember to phone Amy!' he shouted, and then the front door slammed and he was gone.

'Hello, you're talkin' to Amy Rose. What can I do for you?'

'You can tell me that you're coming over to Prior's Ford soon to see all your friends again.'

'Clarissa! Now there's a coincidence,' Amy Rose said, 'I was plannin' to phone you today. Sorry about the silence but I've been helpin' a friend who got herself into a whole lot of trouble.'

'I'm sorry to hear that. What sort of trouble?'

'Every which way sort of trouble. Now that it's over I don't even want to talk about it, and believe me, you wouldn't want to know. But as I said, I was goin' to phone you to tell you that my travellin' arrangements have just been completed.'

'So you're coming to Scotland this summer?'

'You'd better believe I am – I've got so that I can't do without some of that Scottish air for long. Hang on, I can't remember where I put the arrangements, darn it! As I recall it's the middle of July, that's in six weeks' time. Does that suit you?'

'It sounds perfect. I hope you're going to be here for the festival in the second week of August.'

'I certainly am. I'm stayin' till the end of August, but not sure when I'm comin' home because I want to get to know a bit more of your country before I head back here.'

'Is your cousin Patsy coming over with you?'

'Is she heck as like! She was plannin' to, right up until a couple of weeks ago, then she met Ambrose – he's loaded and he's single, so Patsy's gone a-courtin' again.'

'Good heavens!'

'I know. That hip replacement she had seems to have given her a new lease of life. Anyway, enough about my man-mad cousin; how are you an' Alastair?'

'Very happy indeed. At the moment he's teaching art to the

children in the local primary school. He's got a lot of work on just now because he's helping to organize the festival, and there's going to be an art exhibition as well as a lot of other things.'

'You sound different,' Amy said.

'Do I?'

'Definitely different. More confident – so what's been goin' on?'

Clarissa launched into an explanation about the visit she and Alastair made to Glasgow when he agreed to help Nuala with her art exhibition, and her own sudden metamorphosis from self-conscious, unsure older woman with a young lover to a confident older woman with a young lover.

'Good for you, girl,' Amy crowed when she'd heard the entire tale. 'I always knew you had it in you – and thank goodness you've finally let it out. Alastair must be delighted too.'

'He is – we both are. I feel totally liberated now, Clarissa. And it's an added bonus to have won Alexandra over as well. She's now officially engaged and going to have a Christmas wedding – I'm looking forward to that very much!'

'I'll bet you are! And how's Stella?'

'Not so good at the moment. It turns out that she has a half-sister she hasn't seen for years. Elma – that's the half-sister's name – suddenly arrived here a few weeks ago. She and her husband have separated because he's found someone else, and Elma's furious about it. As far as I can gather, she dumped their two children on the husband and his new love and then arrived on Stella's doorstep out of the blue. She's driving the entire village mad by insisting on telling everybody the story of her husband's desertion and expecting lots of sympathy in return.'

'She doesn't sound as though she deserves sympathy.'

'You're right. All our sympathy is for poor Stella. She's looking stressed and Elma's showing no sign of moving on.'

'We can't have that, can we? Listen, Clarissa, you tell Stella from me that I'll be over there in six weeks' time an' this sister of hers will be out of there in six hours!'

'You've got an idea already?'

'No, but I'll have one by the time I get there,' Amy promised grimly. 'So what else is goin' on in your part of the world?'

'Mainly preparations for the festival. As well as the scarecrows, quite a lot of the local people are going to open their gardens to the public, and Linn Hall's involved this year, with various concerts and events held on the estate, which is already open to the public and looking wonderful. You have to see their gardens.'

'Can't wait! A big kiss for Alastair and one for yourself,' Amy said.

Nineteen

Following his London meetings with both lots of publishers, Malcolm Finlay was now facing the task of writing an outline of the next Lilias Drew novel and researching information to do with a new series of articles.

But for the first time in his life he found himself unable to concentrate on work. Instead, he kept remembering Gracie Fisher's comments about Stella Hesslett and her sister.

More than once he thought of visiting or phoning Stella, but each time he either turned back at the garden gate or put the phone down before he had finished dialling her number, just in case Elma was at home with Stella, or, worse still, Elma answered the door or phone. Finally he decided that he would wait until the mobile library van's visit to the village.

By the time it did arrive he had written out a formidable list of books required for the new article series. He now knew from experience when the van was most likely to be quiet – round about noon, when the many readers who frequented it, sometimes buzzing around like bees going in and out of the hive, were likely to be at home either making lunch or being served lunch made by someone else. At that time, he knew, Stella would close the van for an hour and either eat a packed lunch within it, go home or go to the pub.

On the next library day he left Thatcher's Cottage just before noon carrying a briefcase containing the list of books that he needed, plus half a dozen sandwiches, a packet of biscuits and a Thermos filled with coffee. When he got to the village green the van was in its usual place near the Neurotic Cuckoo. Just as he arrived a man and a woman came down its steps, both carrying books – and then someone else came hurrying along and entered the van.

Malcolm strolled casually along to the church, where he stood and admired the building for a few minutes before turning back to look at the van. Nobody was leaving it, but nobody was approaching it. He took a few tentative steps across Main Street and then retreated to the pavement again as someone else appeared and went into the van.

The butcher's window turned out to be quite useful, as it meant that Malcolm, under the guise of studying the meat on display, could also see the van reflected in the glass. In the five minutes that he spent there another four people either trickled in or trickled out of it. Then Stella herself appeared, carrying a shopping bag. She locked the door and was hurrying down the few steps when she came face-to-face with a slow-walking, small elderly woman. They spoke for a moment before Stella turned back, unlocked the van door and then went back down the steps to help the newcomer into the library.

After some time she reappeared and assisted the old woman to get back down the steps and on her way just as a man coming out of the pub hurried to the van and Stella waved him in. Frustrated, Malcolm walked along to the church again, where he could watch for the man leaving.

He was standing at the church gate, checking the van, when a voice said, 'Hello – Dr Finlay, isn't it?'

He spun round guiltily to see the Reverend Naomi Hennessey approaching him from one corner of the church.

'Ah – good morning – I mean, good afternoon—'

'Are you by any chance looking for me?' she asked, and then, as he tried to think of a reply, 'I just wondered because I was tidying up over there,' she held up one brown hand which, he saw, clutched a few bits of paper, while the other hand indicated the corner of the church, where a few bushes grew here and there among the old gravestones, 'picking up some of the rubbish that tends to blow in, and I noticed you hovering about. Some people do that when trying to decide whether or not to come in and talk to me, so I thought I'd better ask if that's what *you* were trying to decide. If so, please don't hesitate. I'm always available, and I make a good cup of tea into the bargain.'

Malcolm felt his face grow hot. 'I wasn't – I mean, I was just taking some time to admire the church building itself. It's a case of always being too busy to notice places—'

She smiled at him. 'I know what you mean, but any time you do feel that you want to talk to someone, or to be shown around the church, please don't hesitate.'

'Thank you – so kind, but I must go,' Malcolm said, and fled. This time, realizing that he was making a complete fool of himself and that the minister may not have been the only person to notice it, he went straight across to the library van.

It turned out to be the right move at the right time. The van door was still open and the only person inside was Stella Hesslett. She was working at the desk but looked up as he entered.

'Miss Hesslett – Stella, I've been hoping to find you on your own.'

'I was about to close down for lunch, but you're very welcome.' She glanced at the sheet of paper in his hand. 'Are you looking for some more books? If you give me the list I'll start working on it as soon as I return to the library.'

'Thank you. As a matter of fact I brought some sandwiches and a Thermos with me. I thought we might be able to have lunch here, since I haven't seen you for a while. I've been in London to talk to my publisher about a new series of articles, hence this rather long book-list.'

She took the list from him. 'It's very kind of you to think about sandwiches and coffee, but my sister's expecting me home for lunch today. I'm so sorry.'

'No, don't be. It was just an idea. Don't let me hold you back, I expect you're in a hurry since it's well past noon.'

'If you're looking for some books from the shelves—'

'I'm not,' Malcolm said, 'but if you're closing up now I'll wait, and we can walk part of the way together.'

Once the van had been locked and they were crossing the green he got the chance to look at her on the pretext of telling her about his time in London. He was concerned to see that Gracie Fisher was quite right – Stella's face looked quite drawn and there were shadows beneath her brown eyes.

When they reached the parting of the ways he ventured to ask, 'How is your sister? Is she feeling a little better than she was when she first arrived?'

Stella hesitated, and then said, 'She still seems to feel very depressed about her situation. I've tried to help her, but I'm not very good at assisting with that sort of problem, never having experienced it myself.'

'Perhaps she needs to accept what's happened and learn to face up to it and rebuild her life. By that I mean going back home and – well – getting used to being on her own,' he ended lamely.

Stella shook her head. 'I'm afraid she just can't seem to find a way of doing that. She says that she couldn't cope without company.'

'Your company?'

'There doesn't appear to be anyone else.' Stella said almost apologetically. 'I'm all she's got.'

'And yet, as far as I can understand, you haven't actually seen her for quite some time?'

'She didn't need me then because she had her husband and children.'

Malcolm seized on the final word. 'Her children – they must be missing her, and she must be missing them. Children make very good company, I've been told by colleagues who have them.'

'As far as I can tell, they appear to be quite happy with the father and his new partner. As for Elma, I get the impression that she needs looking after, rather than having to look after the children.' They had reached the turn-off to her house. 'I must go – lunch will be on the table by now and she can get quite upset if she's kept waiting. I'll let you know as soon as I have those books you're looking for,' Stella said, and hurried off.

As Malcolm watched her walk away it seemed to him that her shoulders were slightly bowed, as though they bore a heavy burden.

Back in Thatcher's Cottage he sat down to his sandwich lunch, eating his share and gulping down coffee until the Thermos was empty. Then he went out into the back garden to feed the sandwiches that should have been Stella's to the birds. As he often did when stuck with whatever writing project he was doing at the time, he went to sit at the small garden table near to the river, where the sound of running water usually had a soothing effect.

Today though, it sounded rather like Elma Armitage's voice babbling on and on – and on.

Something, Malcolm thought as he returned to the house, had to be done to get rid of Elma and save Stella. But he didn't know what that something was.

It had been a profitable day for Linn Hall and the Ralston-Kerrs. The weather was excellent and the gardens were looking extremely good. There had been a steady stream of visitors throughout the day and closing time was near when a man wandered into the stable shop, where Lewis was on duty.

There were several people in the shop at the time and the newcomer strolled casually around the shelves, selecting several items and finally reaching the counter as the shop emptied. He laid down his purchases and when Lewis had totalled them up he fished a note from his wallet and handed it over.

'This is a very nice place you've got here.' He sounded English but with a faint hint of something added, as though he had spent a lot of time elsewhere. He was tall, tanned and strikingly good-looking, with a thick mop of silver hair. 'It must take a lot of looking after.'

'It does, but it's all worthwhile now that we've managed to pull the place together. It had been badly neglected for years, both the house and the gardens.'

'I realized that when I was having a good look at the before and after photographs.' He nodded at the wall given over to Linn Hall's story. It had been Ginny's idea, when she and Hector were going through piles of old family papers and photographs, to set up three large panels, one with grainy black and white photographs of Linn Hall in the days when it was cared for by servants and gardeners, and Lewis's great-grandparents held house parties for their friends; the next bearing pictures taken by Cam Gordon of the neglected house and gardens before the restoration work began, and the final panel displaying pictures, also taken by Cam, of the work done on the gardens and the exterior of the Hall after it had been made wind and watertight.

'We're hoping that by the time we open next summer we'll have a fourth panel showing the house interior,' Lewis explained. 'We've just managed to get a bank loan for that, and work on the ground floor rooms will start in the autumn once the place is closed to the public. We might even open the public rooms to visitors next year.'

'It's good to see such a lovely old house being looked after.' The man's voice was rich, every word clear and easy on the ear.

'Did you enjoy the gardens?' Lewis asked as he handed over the visitor's change and his purchases.

'I just arrived, so I haven't had time to go round them yet.'

'That's too bad.' Lewis glanced at his watch. 'We're just about to close, so I'm afraid you're not going to manage to see them today.'

'That's not a problem. I'm going to be here for a few days – I've booked a room at the pub down the road. I plan to come back here tomorrow.'

'In that case I'll probably see you again,' Lewis had started to say when they heard the handbell signalling the estate's closure being loudly and vigorously rung by Duncan, who insisted on doing it himself because sending everyone packing was his favourite time of the day.

'That's the signal for the visitors to start leaving,' Lewis said, but instead of picking up his purchases and going the man lingered, studying him with interest. His eyes were quite striking – grey, but when animated, as they were now, almost silver, framed by surprisingly long lashes for a man.

'Are you employed by the owners?'

'I grew up here – my father inherited the place from his father.'

'So you're Lewis Ralston-Kerr?'

'That's right.'

'Then you'll be able to tell me if a young lady by the name of Genevieve Whitelaw happens to be on the premises today.'

'You know Ginny?'

'I wish I could say that I do, but sadly I can't, though I'm very much looking forward to getting to know her. I should introduce myself.' The stranger stuck a hand across the counter. 'My name is Adam Whitelaw, and I believe that you are my future son-in-law.'

Ginny always loved talking to the people visiting the estate, especially those who showed signs of liking it as much as she did. But today, now that the crowds were leaving, she was suddenly tired, thirsty and hungry. Instead of heading for the kitchen and the meal awaiting her there she felt more inclined to spend some time on her own, so she climbed the hill behind the house and then climbed further, to the roof of the grotto. Unwinding there was the perfect end to a busy day and she looked on it as a way of catching up with herself.

She was sitting cross-legged in the midst of the ivy, looking down over the estate and the village, when she heard Lewis call her name. 'I'm up here,' she shouted back.

'Come down – there's someone with me who wants to speak to you.'

'Oh – drat!' Ginny muttered as she unfolded her legs, then with an ease born of habit she scrambled to the edge of the roof, took a strong grip on the ivy covering the little summer house, tipped herself over the edge and reached the ground, using the ivy for handholds. After running her fingers through her hair to dislodge any twigs or bits of ivy that might have become entangled she looked up to see Lewis and a tall silver-haired stranger watching her.

'Oh, hello. You want to see me?'

'I do, and I have for a long time.'

'Excuse me?'

'Ginny, love,' Lewis said, 'this is your dad.'

Twenty

'I can't believe,' Ginny said, 'that I didn't recognize you. I've got some photographs in my camper van; when I was growing up I kept looking at them so that I wouldn't forget what you looked like if we ever met. I forgot that you would have changed over the years.'

'I had photographs of you, too, but a lot of water has gone under the bridge since then and I knew that I couldn't expect you to still look like a three or four-year-old,' Adam told her. 'I'm ashamed to have to ask – what age are you?'

'Thirty-one next month – or as my mother would put it, eighteen next month.'

Adam laughed. 'Thirty-one's fine with me.'

'I'm glad that at least one of my parents doesn't mind having an elderly daughter.'

It was mid-evening and the two of them were alone in the Neurotic Cuckoo's dining room. Adam had met Fliss and Hector, and as Lewis had a Progress Committee meeting that evening, Adam had suggested that he should take Ginny to the pub for dinner to give them both a chance to catch up. Lewis was going to join them when the meeting was over.

'I owe you a lot of birthday presents,' Adam said now.

'No need. I got all my birthday presents rolled into one today when I met you.'

'I wish I'd had my camera with me; I would have loved to have taken photographs of you suddenly appearing up on the top of that stone summer house and then shinning down to the ground.'

'I do that a lot, so you can take a photograph any time. I love that little grotto – I go there when I need to think or to be alone.'

'Lewis told me when we were coming to find you that it was your favourite place. He said that he and his friends used to play there as kids but he'd forgotten about it until you discovered it. I like him, Ginny – I like him very much. And it's clear to see that he's mad about you. He talked about you all the way as we went through the gardens and up that hill. He said that the place wouldn't look as good as it does if it hadn't been for you. What brought you here?'

'My mother. She was one of the main characters in a television sitcom until they suddenly decided to write her out. She promptly went into a decline and insisted on going somewhere quiet to help her to get over it.'

'Meredith was always a prima donna. Did she insist on your company?'

'She did, and I agreed because I was actually quite worried about her. I was working in a garden centre at the time and beginning to feel as if I needed to do something different with my life. I was even thinking about giving up the job once I'd saved enough to go to Australia and find you.'

'I wish you had.'

She shook her head. 'I'm glad that I never managed it because the best thing that ever happened to me was coming to this village and finding Lewis and his parents and Linn Hall. I talked Lewis into taking me on as a gardener. And now you've found me, so everything worked out after all. Does my mother know you're here?'

'Good Lord no! The only good thing that resulted from Meredith and I meeting and marrying is you, and now I've finally got the chance to tell you how sorry I am that I deserted you when you were so young, and didn't even keep in touch. I've been a lousy father.'

'What happened all those years ago?'

'The truth?'

'And nothing but.'

He thought for a moment, and then said, 'We were both too young and Meredith was gorgeous – looking back over old publicity photographs, to be honest, I know that I was gorgeous too. We fell madly in love, married, and you were born. It all happened so quickly. The problem was that we were both very ambitious. That's what got in the way.'

'I was always given to understand that it was me that got in the way.'

'From your mother?' he asked, and then when she nodded, 'if anything, Meredith was more ambitious than I was and being young and at the beginning of our careers it was very difficult trying to cope with work and a home life and a baby. Meredith's career forged further ahead than mine, which in itself caused problems between us, and then I got the chance to do a film in Australia. It was my big break and we both thought that it would be good for us to be apart for a while. By that time Meredith was earning enough to pay for a nanny for you, which left me free to go. I loved Australia from the moment I arrived, and although I didn't have the lead in the film I enjoyed the work. When it went into the cinemas I suddenly became popular and more work offers started flowing in. I haven't stopped working since; in fact I'm heading back in a week's time to do a play that looks like having a long run.'

'You're only here for a week?' she said, dismayed, 'Why come to the UK after all those years for such a short while?'

'Meredith sent me a long hysterical email, the first contact between us since I came over briefly for the divorce. She said that you were making a dreadful mistake, rushing into marriage and possibly pregnant—'

'Which I am not.'

'I realized that when you came tumbling over the top of the – grotto, do you call it? She told me that she was spending most of her time in Spain and insisted that I take up my fatherly duties and fly over at once to talk sense into you. I did as she asked because it gave me the chance to finally meet you.'

At that point Lewis arrived and accepted a glass of wine. 'I could do with this, because the Progress Committee had quite a heavy session. The village is holding a summer festival in August,' he explained to Adam, 'and this time the estate's going to be very involved.'

'What exactly do you mean by "very involved"?' Ginny immediately wanted to know.

'Marquees on the lawns, concerts, a dance display by the school-children, and there's talk of some sort of treasure hunt down by the lake. So you and I have got quite a few things to plan out.'

'When are you two planning to marry?' Adam asked.

'Not for a while,' Ginny told him. 'I've got quite a big job on at the moment, designing someone's garden from scratch – you must come and see it while you're here – and we've got the festival coming soon, and once the estate ends its open season in September work will start on renovating the ground floor rooms. And then there's Rowena Chloe – I can't believe I forgot to tell you about her!'

'You've both had quite a lot to talk about,' Lewis said, 'so it's not surprising that her name hasn't come up yet. Rowena Chloe is my five-year-old daughter,' he explained to Adam, 'and up until now she's been living with her mother's family, but I'm delighted to say that I've managed to win custody and she'll be moving into Linn Hall by the end of this month.'

'You've been married before?'

'Engaged, but Molly decided eventually that travelling the world was much more tempting than spending the rest of her life helping me to keep Linn Hall going. She's living in Portugal now with her new partner, which is why we're getting Rowena Chloe.'

'She's a wonderful little girl, and I can't wait to be her stepmother!'

Adam looked from one to the other. 'You two seem to be living more interesting and hectic lives in this small village than anyone else I know. No wonder you both look so full of life. One of the reasons why I'm over here is to ask if you'd be willing to consider a month-long honeymoon with us in Australia, as our gift and to make up for my appalling neglect of you, Ginny.'

Lewis and Ginny glanced at each other, and then both shook their heads.

'It sounds wonderful,' Ginny said, 'but we can't possibly find the time. Right now we're not even sure if we're going to be able to take enough time off for a wedding ceremony, let alone a honeymoon.'

'I can see that, but never mind – the offer stays open for the two of you – and your daughter. Laura's looking forward to meeting you. I'll bring my camera tomorrow and get lots of photographs to show her and the boys when I get back home.'

'I haven't even asked about your wife and your family,' Ginny said just as Lewis finished his wine, set the empty glass down and then gave a massive yawn.

'Tomorrow – and tomorrow and tomorrow, as Shakespeare puts it,' her father said. 'We've still got the best part of a week, so let's all get a good night's sleep. Can I come back to Linn Hall in the morning? I want to meet your parents, Lewis, and hear a lot more about all your lives. And I've got a lot of photographs to show you of Laura and our boys.'

'I can't believe it,' Ginny marvelled as she and Lewis left the pub and started to walk up the hill towards Linn Hall. 'When I first came to Prior's Ford there was no one else in my life except my mother – not that we had ever spent much time together before that. And now look at me! I've got you and your parents and so many friends here; we'll soon have Rowena Chloe living with us, and now I've got a father, a stepmother and two stepbrothers. I feel as if I've suddenly won millions of pounds in the Lottery. No, it's even better than that – because I've won people, not just millions!'

★   ★   ★

The few days that Adam spent in Prior's Ford more than made up for the many years Ginny had been without a father. At last she was able to show him round the entire estate, explaining how she had managed to turn the neglected and overgrown kitchen garden into the vibrant place it was now, stocked with vegetables, fruit and herbs and telling of the day she had discovered the grotto and, later, the valuable collection of rare plants.

She described the fun she and Jimmy had shared as they waded knee-deep in the neglected lake's sloppy mud, both determined to create the picture they had formed in their minds of a stretch of clean water bearing rafts of water lilies and surrounded by banks of water-loving flowers.

'All you really need to do,' she explained earnestly, 'is to fix a picture in your mind of what you want to achieve and hold on to it – and if you work hard enough at it, it will happen. That's the only way I can explain it, and luckily Jimmy understands that, though not everybody does. Do you?' she added uncertainly as Adam stared at her as though astonished by her stupidity.

'You haven't stopped amazing me since the first moment I met you,' he said. 'You're not only an excellent gardener, Ginny, you're extremely creative. You're my daughter – mine and Meredith's – in every single way. We've both used the gift of creativity by becoming actors while you've used yours to create this beautiful garden.'

'Not on my own,' she said hurriedly, embarrassed by such praise.

'Of course not. Meredith and I make speeches that were written by other people – our creative contribution lies in our ability to speak them well and convincingly. Lewis tells me – and you've just confirmed it – that his original plans for the estate changed dramatically when you came along. I can see now that that's because you introduced the creative touch to everything. You had the ability to look beyond his ideas and discover the extra touches.'

'Golly!' Ginny was stunned. 'Nobody's ever told me anything like that before.'

'There's something else I've gathered from Lewis,' Adam went on, 'he tells me that Meredith is constantly putting you down and refusing to believe that you're capable of anything. Don't ever let it bother you again because it only proves something that I came to realize through living with Laura – your mother is a very talented actress and an incredibly beautiful woman, but she's also rather single-minded. She wanted you to follow in her footsteps and become an actress, though at the same time, never to be as talented as she is. When Meredith looks in the mirror she sees the most important person in her life, the only person she really loves. When we married I was crazy about her – but the more I got to know her the less I loved her until it reached the stage where I had to escape. That's why I grabbed the chance to do that film in Australia. I just wanted a bit of space and I was fully expecting to come back to her and to you, but then I met Laura and found out what love was really like.'

'Tell me all about Laura. What's she like?'

His eyes softened. 'She was one of the make-up artists on the film, but now she's a successful and respected theatre director. She's very down to earth, she's practical, sensible, and outspoken. To me she was like a breath of fresh air – still is. She's also got a fantastic sense of humour. You and Lewis and his little girl are going to have to come over as soon as you can to meet her and our boys.'

That evening Adam had dinner in the kitchen with Ginny and the Ralston-Kerr family, and afterwards showed them the photographs he had brought of his family. His wife Laura had short blonde hair and a wide smile that crinkled up her eyes. For the first time Ginny saw her half-brothers, twenty-three-year-old Tom, who worked for a sheep farmer and was aiming to have his own farm one day, and Alec, younger by three years, just starting on an acting career. Both, fair-haired and smiling, resembled their mother rather than their father.

'But at least I can now say that my daughter's got her dad's looks,' Adam said, reaching over to ruffle Ginny's black hair. 'Alec shows a lot of promise but he's just out of drama school and he's still got a lot to learn. He's had a couple of television ads and he played the lead in one play that ran for just over a month and I think he's got a good future ahead. In the meantime he's financing himself by taking on odd jobs while waiting for the next call from his agent. From the time they left school Laura has insisted on them standing on their own feet – and doing well enough to be able to help their parents once the two of us are too old to work,' he added, grinning.

On the following day Ginny was due to work on Fergus's garden. She drove there in the camper van with Adam in the passenger seat. As always, it was a long and busy day, and although Ginny was feeling slightly nervous at the thought of her father watching her work in her other environment, she very quickly forgot about him once she got started, just as she always forgot about the cameras.

He and Fergus got on extremely well – so well that to Ginny's embarrassment Fergus promised to make sure that when Adam returned to Australia he would take with him a copy of the Linn Hall estate documentary that had already been shown on television.

'I can't wait to see it,' Adam said as he and Ginny drove back to Linn Hall at the end of the day, 'and I can't wait to show it to Laura and the boys. It's much better than photographs.'

'Just promise me that you won't ask to watch it at Linn Hall,' she begged.

'But Fergus said that you were so natural in it, and I've heard the same from Lewis and his parents. Haven't you watched it yourself?'

'Under protest, the night it was on television. Lewis and I watched it in the camper van, and I couldn't face another hour of squirming!'

'I told you the other day that you had definitely inherited creative talent from me and Meredith – but now I've discovered something you didn't inherit from us, and that's vanity. Laura's always accusing me of it, and I have to admit that I enjoy watching myself working in a film or on video. I don't always approve of what I've done, but I still want to see it. I tell Laura that it's important for me to find out where I went wrong and learn to improve it, but truth to tell, it's vanity. And I'm quite sure that the same goes for Meredith, although I doubt if she ever sees any flaws in her performances.' Then, changing the subject, 'I love what you're doing with that garden, and it's clear that Fergus is delighted with your work. He's very professional.'

'And very successful.'

'I can believe that.' He shot a sidelong glance at her. 'He was telling me during the lunch break, when you were making plans with the gardeners, that he reckons you're a natural presenter, which I could see for myself. And he's also keen for you to consider it as your next step.'

'He's told me that several times but it's not what I want for myself. My future lies with Lewis and Rowena Chloe, and Linn Hall.'

'So my daughter is going to be the next mistress of a mansion house?'

'I'm going to be Lewis's wife and Rowena Chloe's stepmother; because Lewis can't leave Linn Hall and wouldn't even if he could, I'll be there too because I want to be where he is. In any case, I love Linn Hall as much as he does.'

'You know that Fergus has taken a real shine to you? Not just because you're a good gardener and designer as well as a natural presenter.'

'I couldn't help but notice,' she said drily. 'But he's wasting his time.'

'Good for you – that's my girl,' her father said.

Twenty-One

Helen Campbell's fingers were flying over the computer keys and her mind working overtime as she tried to complete another chapter of her novel. Most of her typing was done for other people; for years she had earned much-needed extra money by typing out work for clients such as Ingrid MacKenzie's husband Peter, a college lecturer, or local students who wanted to deliver more legible copies of their handwritten essays to their tutors.

Thanks to Malcolm Finlay she was now earning more money than ever by typing up the articles he wrote, not to mention his Lilias Drew novels. After winning the magazine serial competition and finally becoming a published writer, she had been able to afford a brand-new computer – a great relief, because the elderly machine she had used for years was clearly coming to the end of a very long and hard-working life. Being able to work at a much better speed meant that as well as coping with work for others and dealing with the fortnightly Agony Aunt page and the weekly Prior's Ford news column, both for the local paper, she was now finding a little more free time in which to do her own work.

She was in the middle of a particularly nostalgic scene which was almost moving her to tears when the doorbell rang.

'Oh, drat and darn it!' Suddenly she was wrenched cruelly away from her heroine's sobs to land, with a crash that almost physically hurt, in her own bedroom. She waited for a moment in the hope that whoever was at the front door might give up and go away, but when the doorbell rang again and then again she had no option but to go downstairs, hoping that she would be able to remember the rest of what looked like a really important scene in the book.

Her heart sank when she opened the door and saw Stella Hesslett's sister on the doorstep, an envelope in her hand.

'We've seen each other in the village but you probably don't remember me.' The woman started talking as soon as the door opened. 'I'm Elma Armitage.'

'Yes I do remember seeing you in the village store, Mrs Armitage.' Then as Elma opened her mouth to go on, Helen looked pointedly at the envelope. 'You've probably heard that I do some typing for people – is that what you've called about? I've got quite a lot of work on at the moment but if it's something important I'll do my best to help.'

She held a hand out for the envelope but Elma held on to it.

'No it's not – well, yes it is in a way. Can I come in?' She was already advancing.

'It's not really convenient at the moment—'

'It won't take long, and I believe that it would be well worth your while to hear me out.'

The woman kept coming forward, leaving Helen with no alternative but to move backwards. Before she knew what was happening Elma had surged past her and was in the hall. 'In here?' she asked briskly, and when Helen nodded she walked into the living room, used a thumb and forefinger to remove a discarded cardigan from an armchair, put it over the back of the sofa and sat down.

'My sister tells me that you're a novelist.'

'Not exactly – I have a serial running in a women's magazine at the moment but I've never actually published a book—'

'You may have heard why I'm in Prior's Ford.'

'Yes I have and I'm sorry to hear about your misfortune.'

'It has nothing to do with misfortune,' Elma said impatiently. 'I've been treated shamefully – betrayed and abandoned by a man who stood before a church altar and promised to love and cherish me for the rest of our lives. It's a story that needs to be told, and as a writer you can do that for me.'

Helen was appalled. Almost everyone she knew, especially those who were unable to flee at sight of this woman, such as Gracie Fisher, Marcy, Sam, and the others who worked in local shops, dreaded seeing her approach. And now, it seemed, she was going to be expected to turn Elma's grievances into a novel.

'It would, of course, be published under both our names as a collaboration,' Elma rattled on. 'I've written it all down – the suggestion came from some woman recommended by my doctor when I consulted him regarding the black depression that had closed over me at the time. This woman who, sadly, turned out to be useless, told me that writing it all down would get it out of my system and help me to start a new life but of course she was wrong. However, her advice turned out to be useful in that when I sat down this morning to look through the notes I had written I realized what a wonderful novel it would make. And fortunately, I haven't had to look far for a co-writer.'

'Mrs Armitage,' Helen began just as the phone rang. 'Excuse me.' She fled gratefully into the hall to pick up the phone. 'Hello?'

'Mrs Campbell – Helen,' Malcolm Finlay said, 'I've just completed another two Lilias Drew chapters and I wanted to make sure that you were home so that I could bring them round to be typed.'

'No!'

'Oh, my dear lady,' he said at once, 'I'm so sorry. I didn't mean – I'm taking you for granted and that's very wrong of me. I know that you have other people to think of and of course, your own work to do. The chapters can wait until you have time to work on them.'

Helen cupped her hand around the receiver and hissed into it. 'It's not that at all – Mrs Armitage is here!'

'Oh you poor woman! I'll leave it until tomorrow—'

'No, I have to see you – I'll phone as soon as she leaves,' Helen said, and hung up. When she returned to the living room Elma had opened the envelope and was scanning through several hand-written pages. When she looked up, Helen saw that her eyes were filled with tears.

'Reading it brings all the unhappiness back,' she said in a choked voice, laying the pages on her lap so that she could find her handkerchief and mop her eyes. 'How does anyone ever get over a broken heart? I'm told that some people do, but when you're as sensitive and vulnerable as I've been all my life, terrible wounds can never be healed!'

'Would you like a drink?' The words were out before Helen could stop them from spilling across her lips.

'Do you have any brandy? Or a little vodka would do.'

'Actually, I meant tea or coffee; we can't afford to keep anything stronger in the house.'

'In that case, no thank you.' Elma started to fold the sheets of paper and put them back into the envelope, which she held out to Helen. 'I'm going now – when I get emotional I find it best to lie down in a darkened room. I'll leave you to read my full story, which I'm sure will grip your imagination. Every detail's been recorded and as I expect to be staying with my sister for some time you can be sure that when you start work on the book I'll be within easy reach to elaborate on any points you may need more information on.'

Once she was out on the garden path she turned and said with a brave and tremulous smile, 'I feel that our collaboration will be most successful. Goodbye.'

Back indoors, Helen immediately telephoned Malcolm. 'Mrs Armitage has just left,' she said as soon as he answered. 'You can bring that work over now – and I'd really like to ask your advice.'

'Where is she going now?' He sounded nervous.

'She said that she was going back to Stella's house, and I watched as she began to walk up the road, moving away from your direction, so I'm sure that she really is going home. You're quite safe.'

'I certainly hope so – I'll leave now.'

Helen watched from the window and as soon as she saw him hurrying towards her house she went to open the front door. When he saw her standing there he broke into a rapid trot and almost launched himself up the path towards her.

Once in her living room he collapsed breathlessly into the chair that Elma Armitage had recently vacated.

'I'm so glad that I telephoned you before setting out to your house,' he wheezed. 'I simply cannot stand that woman – she terrifies me!'

'She has certainly terrified *me*,' Helen said, and sat down to tell him why Elma had called on her. 'What am I going to do?' she wailed. 'I'm far too busy to write her story for her, and in any case I'm already trying to write a novel of my own!'

'Of course you can't do as she asks – it's out of the question and she had absolutely no right to ask you!'

'She's even written it all down for me – every single detail – do you want to read it?' She held the papers out to him and he shuddered, waving them away.

'I have already heard her story in detail, and so have most of the people in this village, possibly more than once. The woman is quite deranged and the sooner she goes back to where she belongs the better for all of us, especially poor Miss Hesslett.'

'From what she told me today she has no intention of going back to where she belongs,' Helen told him, and he shot upright in the chair.

'Are you sure?'

'She said that although she had written everything down for me, she was going to stay on in Prior's Ford so that she would be available should I have any questions while I'm writing the book – which I have no desire to do. I've only just started to feel that I finally have a chance to become a proper writer –' Helen heard her own voice wobbling and felt frustrated tears prickling at the back of her eyes – 'and she's going to ruin it all for me, I know she is!' She was embarrassed to hear her voice start to rise on the final few words.

'No!' Malcolm thundered, thumping a fist down heavily on the arm of his chair. 'I will not have it! I'll not allow that – that *poisonous* woman – to upset you or Miss Hesslett! Something has to be done!'

'But what?'

He suddenly seemed to sag back into the chair. 'I don't know.'

'That's the problem – neither do I. Some people seem to be so strong that nobody can fight them,' Helen said sadly. 'Not me, and not you, because we're just too nice.'

For a few minutes they were both silent, then Malcolm said, 'But not everybody is too nice, and some people are trained to deal with difficulties.'

'What do you mean?'

'In the university where I worked one of my colleagues was a professor of psychology. A very approachable man – we still exchange Christmas cards. I'm going to contact him and ask his advice regarding Mrs Armitage. If anyone can help us it's him.' Malcolm, rejuvenated, almost bounced out of his chair. 'And I shall go and telephone him now. Don't worry. my dear young lady – we shall win the battle!'

Although Adam Whitelaw was only able to spend a few days in Prior's Ford he managed to make friends with most of the villagers – entertaining everyone in the pub's public bar with fascinating stories of life in Australia as well as life as an actor. Lynn Stacey managed to get him to come and give a short talk to some of her older pupils, almost all of whom immediately decided to become actors when they grew up.

'I've never known some of these children to be so quiet and well-behaved when listening to a visitor,' she told Ginny. 'And once it came to question time even the shyest child had a hand up. He was so patient with them, especially when it came to signing autographs, and I particularly like the emphasis he put on the importance of concentration and hard work in order to learn to become whatever they wanted to become. He even managed to make the effort sound exciting. They hung on every single word and afterwards everyone wrote a really good composition about his visit. I'm going to have them copied so that you can send them to him. As for the staff,' she added, eyes twinkling, 'we've all fallen madly in love with your father because he's so gorgeous!'

As well as spending as much time as he could with Ginny and the Ralston-Kerrs, Adam found time to visit the local shops, buying several items from Anya at Colour Carousel and from the Village Store. He also went to Tarbethill Farm to watch Stefan Krechevsky at work and got several pieces of his beautiful glassware.

He always had his camera with him as he was determined to show his wife and sons as much as he could of the life Ginny led and the people she knew; he also commissioned Cam to make copies of all the before, during and after photographs of Linn Hall and the estate he had seen on the walls of the stable shop.

'I'm so proud of you,' he told Ginny just before he left. It was early morning and he had come up to the Hall to have breakfast with the Ralston-Kerrs and all the workers before leaving the village. He and Ginny had walked round to the front of the Hall to share a few final moments together. Jimmy McDonald was down at the end of the drive to watch for Adam's taxi, which was almost due to collect him and then pause at the Neurotic Cuckoo for his luggage.

'I've always been proud of my boys and what they've achieved, but at least they had me and Laura rooting for them,' Adam went on, 'and they knew that we were there when they needed support or advice. But you've had to do it all on your own, and that makes me especially proud. Promise me that you and Lewis and his daughter will come to Australia as soon as you can. I can't wait to see all my family gathered together!'

'We'd love to see where you live, and meet everyone, but as you know, it might take a while.'

'I know, and I'm willing to wait. In the meantime, this is for you and Lewis.'

She opened the envelope he gave her and gasped at the size of the cheque inside.

'Dad – no! This is far too much!'

'Where you're concerned it can never be too much. It's made up of what Laura and I would have paid to get you over for a visit, plus a wedding gift from us both.'

'But the money you would have spent giving us our honeymoon in Australia would have been the wedding present,' she protested.

Adam sighed. 'You're a very determined and independent young woman, aren't you?'

'I've had to be, and in any case, I like it that way.'

A slight shadow crossed his face. 'I know, but even so I wish that I could have done more to help you. But now that we've finally met up and I've discovered that I have a daughter to be very proud of, I want to make up for all those years of neglect. And the best way to do that is to help you achieve your ambitions by giving you the money that you and Lewis need. Fortunately for us both, I can afford it. If nothing else, think of it as the money I would have spent on you had we been a normal family.'

She threw her arms around his neck and hugged him tightly. 'Thank you, Dad!'

He kissed the top of her head. 'It's worth all the money I have just to hear you call me that.'

'What am I going to tell Mother?' Ginny asked as they drew apart. 'About your visit, I mean. She's going to be jealous and perhaps even annoyed at us meeting without her knowledge.'

He laughed. 'Of course she will – I wouldn't expect anything other than that from Meredith, but on the other hand it's really none of her business. Tell her as much or as little as you want to – but don't forget to send her my love and congratulations for all her successes. And I mean that, though she'll probably tell you that I don't,' he added as Jimmy came racing up the drive screaming:

'Taxi's coming – taxi's coming!'

By the time the taxi came into view, Jinty, Lewis and his parents and most of the backpackers had appeared round the corner of the house to say goodbye to Adam.

The cheque burned a hole in Ginny's pocket and she could scarcely wait for an opportunity to show it to Lewis. Her chance came the next day when the two of them were in the kitchen garden discussing some possible changes before Ginny left for Fergus's garden.

He, too, gasped when he saw the amount. 'We can't accept this – it's far too much!'

'That's what I told him, but he insisted. He said that part of it is the money that he and his wife would have spent to give us a honeymoon in Australia with them, plus a wedding gift.'

'But that's not right – the honeymoon would surely have been the wedding gift?'

'I said that, but his reply was that it was also the money he never spent on me when I was growing up. He was very determined. Lewis, this cheque is going to make all the difference to us – for one thing, it means that we can pay Angela Steele in full without having to worry.'

'If you're sure you want to use it for Linn Hall.'

'What else would I use it for? Linn Hall is my future – *our* future,' she said firmly. Then, as he tried to hand it back, 'You put it away safely for me.'

'Are you're sure? I feel a bit nervous about being responsible for this amount of money.'

'So do I, and that's why I want you to look after it until we can put it into the bank.'

'I'm going into Kirkcudbright today anyway, so I'll bank it.'

'Good – then we'll both feel happier about it.' They had reached the stable courtyard and Ginny opened the driver's door of the camper van then paused. 'I should phone my mother soon, to tell her about my father's visit.'

'Wouldn't it be wiser to let sleeping actresses lie?'

'Normally it would, and I'm pretty sure that it's going to annoy her, but it would be wrong not to tell her. She's bound to find out one way or the other and I'd rather it came from me. She told me that she had contacted him to demand that he talk me out of marrying you, so she's bound to ask sooner or later if I've heard from him. At least,' she added, brightening slightly, 'I'll be able to report that he likes you and he's all for us getting married.'

'You're a brave woman, Ginny Whitelaw, and I salute you.' He kissed her on the forehead.

'I know I am, but a woman's got to do what a woman's got to do. I'll phone her today.' She opened the camper van's door. 'See you later.'

'I look forward to it,' Lewis said, and kissed her properly.

During the break for lunch Ginny retired to the camper van to telephone her mother.

As soon as she recognized her daughter's voice Meredith began to panic. 'What's wrong? You haven't got married without telling me, have you? You're not—?'

'Mother, I'm not married, and I'm not pregnant. Everything is fine.'

'Then why are you calling me? You know that when I'm working I need to keep calm – stress and worry play havoc with my vocal chords,' Meredith fretted.

'I'm sorry about your vocal chords, I wouldn't damage them for the world, but I felt that I had to tell you something.'

'What? Tell me what?'

'It's nothing to worry about,' Ginny soothed. 'It's just that I recently had a visit from my father.' Then, after a long silence, 'Are you still there?'

'Adam? Do you mean – Adam?'

'How many fathers do I have?'

'Don't be facetious,' her mother snapped. 'And don't be impertinent – of course you've only got one father! And how *dare* he visit my daughter after all those years with not a word!'

'He said that you contacted him to demand that he come over here and forbid me to get married.'

'Yes I did, but I didn't expect him to actually do it,' Meredith said impatiently. 'He could have written to you; I gave him the address. He's never bothered to visit you before.'

'He feels very bad about not being in touch with me.'

'I should think he does! All those years I spent raising you—'

'Actually, I was raised mainly by nannies and housekeepers.'

'Yes you were – because I had to work to clothe you and feed you and pay for those nannies and housekeepers.'

'I know, and I'm very grateful to you, Mother.'

'If he's still there, put him on the phone at once,' Meredith ordered. 'I have a great deal to say to him.'

'He was only here for a few days – and he's met Lewis. They both got on very well and he's pleased about us getting married.'

'I must go and lie down,' Meredith said, 'I'm about to go before the cameras and I can feel a headache coming on.'

'Mother, I'm sorry—' Ginny began, but her mother had already hung up.

Twenty-Two

Although Malcolm meant it when he told Helen Campbell that he would find a way to remove Elma Armitage from Prior's Ford, by the time he returned to Thatcher's Cottage his firm promise had begun to take on a distinctly hollow feeling. A lifetime of being dominated by his family had taught him, when he moved into university life, to avoid close relationships by running away from them as often as possible. He was well aware that this attitude made him what he thought of as 'a bit of a coward', but it also kept him safe.

So far he had managed to avoid bad situations throughout his adult life, but clearly the time had come to set aside his fears and face adversity. He liked and admired Stella Hesslett and he couldn't bear to see her being bullied. He knew that she badly needed help and he genuinely wanted to provide it, but realized that he couldn't do it on his own. But at least he had remembered someone who might be able to offer advice.

As he had told Helen, his only contact now with his friend Max Turner was at Christmas, and it took him some time to find the seldom-used address book with Max's phone number in it. Once he had dialled, it only rang twice before the phone was picked up by Max himself.

'Malcolm – this is a very pleasant surprise. How are you and how do you like living in the depths of the Scottish countryside?'

'I've discovered that village life suits me very well.'

'Good. And I hope that retirement suits you as well as it suits me.'

'Semi-retirement in my case – I'm still publishing articles. Max, I have a problem and I hoped that you might be able to help me with it.'

'If it's academic, old man, I doubt that I can offer any assistance because you have a better brain than I ever had.'

'It's more in your line than mine. This is a very friendly little village, at least, it was until recently—' Malcolm launched into the story of the pleasant, helpful librarian and the extremely unpleasant half-sister.

The story took some time to tell, but Max, trained as he was to listen patiently to other people's problems, said nothing until Malcolm finally ended with, 'She's driving her sister into a nervous breakdown, and doing the same to just about everybody else in the village, including me. Something has to be done, and done quickly, but none of us know what. So I was hoping that you might be able to advise me.'

'It sounds like an idea for a novel,' Max remarked. 'Pity you're not a fiction writer rather than an academic, old man, because then you would be able to turn it into a good book. It reminds me of that children's story we all knew decades ago – the Pied Piper of Hamelin. Remember that one? It used to scare me when I was a kid because I was terrified of rats – mice, even.'

'I doubt if even a piper could scare this woman away, unless he was rich and wanted to marry her and take her off to a life of spoiled luxury.' Malcolm knew that he sounded irritable but couldn't help it. 'I was hoping for more positive help from you.'

'Oh dear, she's really frightening you, isn't she?'

'More than rats,' Malcolm said between clenched teeth.

'Enough of the levity, then.'

'I would appreciate that very much.'

'This librarian whose house has been invaded and taken over—' Max said thoughtfully, 'I gather that she's a good friend of yours?'

'She's an excellent librarian and I find her extremely helpful, which makes her important to me.'

'You seem to have a problem with the word "friend", Malcolm.'

'I don't understand what you're saying.'

'Like you, I'm single by choice. I enjoy being single and at the moment I intend to continue to be single. But I also have friends. There's nothing wrong with having friends, old boy; it's an inoffensive little word and there's no need to be afraid of it. It doesn't have a hidden agenda – it means what it says on the tin. Can I therefore suggest without offending you that you see this lady not just as a librarian but also as a friend?'

'I don't know why you're going on about it, Max, but if you're determined to discuss the situation, then yes, I do see her as a friend,' Malcolm said stiffly, and could have sworn that he heard a faint sigh of relief drift into his ear.

'It always was difficult to pin you down regarding relationships, old man. But the fact that you like this woman – as a friend,' Max added quickly, 'makes it just a little bit easier for me to try to help you.'

'Good. Can you hang on for a minute?' Malcolm asked. 'I'm just going to get pen and paper so that I can make notes.'

Although he would have liked to come to Stella's rescue immediately and get his meeting with Elma Armitage over with, Malcolm had to wait until the village's next library day to ensure that Stella wasn't at home when he called. The wait gave him time to study the notes he had scribbled down while on the phone to Max, but unfortunately it also gave him time to become more nervous of what lay before him.

When the day came and he left his house and began to walk to Stella's his heart was thumping and a large fist seemed to have got a tight grip on his stomach. Max's advice had sounded very positive on the phone, but as Malcolm read over his notes again and again he began to realize that the basic theme centred around the fact that in order to help Stella he had to stop thinking about what he was doing and concentrate his mind on the person he was doing it for.

'At the moment, old man,' Max had said more than once, 'you're frightened of this Armitage woman, but *you're* not the one who needs help, it's her sister. If you want to help her you must set your own thoughts aside and concentrate on what this woman is doing to her peace of mind. Don't be frightened, don't be angry, and don't try to reason with this Armitage woman because she'll see that as a weakness. Tell her, adult to adult, that you're extremely concerned about your friend's well-being and you feel that she's the cause. Tell her that whatever influence she is trying to impose on her sister has to stop. If she starts to argue, which she probably will, you must keep on thinking about what she's doing to your friend. Raise your voice if you must, don't hesitate to interrupt her, and whatever you do, don't let her think that she's winning, and don't back down.'

Despite concentrating hard on Stella's problem as he strode along the pavement Malcolm seemed quite unable to forget about his own nerves. By the time he reached Stella's house he had begun to hope that Elma Armitage was out, possibly – hopefully – for the entire day. But when he rang the bell Elma opened the door so quickly that he jumped.

'Dr Finlay – Malcolm! What a pleasant surprise. Do come in.' She opened the door wide. As it was too late to turn and run, Malcolm did as he was told and was ushered into the living room.

'I've just had my coffee but I'd be happy to make more if you—'

'No thank you.'

'Something stronger?' Then when he shook his head, she indicated the magazines scattered over the table. 'Forgive the mess, but I've been studying those interior design magazines in the hope of finding some ideas suitable for this house.'

'Is Stella – Miss Hesslett – redecorating?'

She shook her head. 'No, I am. Don't you find this colour scheme very bland? I really couldn't bear to live with those walls and this furniture, not to mention the carpets and curtains.'

Malcolm looked slowly around the room. 'Don't be angry,' Max had advised, but it was difficult not to be angry. 'I like this room,' he said, 'I'm quite surprised to hear that your sister wants to change it.'

'Stella's too wrapped up in books to know anything about how to create beautiful rooms. You really should see my home – I'm the artistic member of the family and my creative style has been greatly admired by everyone who has visited my house.'

'And when are you going to return to this beautiful house of yours? Several villagers have asked me that,' Malcolm lied.

'Oh, there's no hurry. I'm still grieving and I need something to do. I'm planning on redecorating this entire house as a form of therapy, and if it works for me then I may be ready to return home – if I can ever call it home again—' Her voice shook and she produced a handkerchief from her pocket, dabbing at her eyes. Then, with a suspiciously sudden change of mood, 'In fact, just before you arrived I was thinking that it might be a really good idea for me to consider a new career. I could advise people on how to decorate their homes.'

'The village already has a home decorating business called Colour Carousel.'

'I've been there, and it's rather a nice little shop, although the girl who runs it is very young. I'm thinking of approaching her with a view to the two of us considering a partnership; I believe that that would benefit the business, especially since I'm a British citizen. Some people are wary of doing business with foreigners. The girl who runs the shop is a foreigner, you know.'

'I have met Anya, she's a very pleasant young woman and I have always found her most helpful and easy to deal with.'

'I could bring different skills to the business,' Elma rattled on, ignoring him and totally unaware of his rising temper. 'For instance, once I've finished with this place it could be used to showcase my talents.'

'Mrs Armitage—'

'Elma, please.'

'Mrs Armitage, this is your sister's home, the place where she lives. It is not yours, and I very much doubt that she would appreciate having her home turned into a showroom for strangers to trek through!'

'You don't know Stella as well as I do – nobody here does. She's extremely shy and knows very little about the modern world – she hasn't even been engaged, let alone married.' Elma trilled a little laugh. 'To be absolutely honest with you, I don't even remember her ever having a boyfriend. She needs to be stimulated and to—'

Suddenly Malcolm had had enough – a lot more than enough. 'For God's sake, woman,' he stormed at her, 'shut up!'

Elma's torrent of words stopped as though they had been turned off like a tap. Her eyes and mouth were wide with shock and it was several seconds before she found her voice again. 'How *dare* you speak to me like that!'

Malcolm was coping with a sensation that he had never known before. He felt dizzy, and for a moment he wondered if he was going to fall at her feet; then he realized that the dizziness was caused by elation rather than fear. For the first time in his life he had spoken back to someone, and it felt wonderful because the victim was somebody who deserved it.

'And how dare *you* treat your sister as an entity? How dare you move into her house uninvited and unwanted, and then make the decision to stay here and change the whole place without asking her permission?'

Elma's mouth, still opened, closed and when she opened it again to speak all that came out was an inarticulate squeak. She swallowed so hard that Malcolm could see the muscles working in her neck, and then tried again. 'I am trying to help my sister. I am looking after her interests!'

'I doubt, madam, that you have ever in your entire life considered anyone's interests other than your own. And in saying that, I include your unfortunate husband. You and I have met only occasionally, but looking back on each meeting I've realized that it has been dominated by the sound of your voice, talking only about you. I can honestly say that your husband has my sympathy and I hope that he has found happiness with his new partner.'

She uttered a brief scream, which he ignored.

'As for Stella, she is greatly liked by all in this village. I've only known her for a short time but I consider myself honoured to have met her. She's twice the woman you are, and I don't intend to stand by and let you destroy the life she's created for herself. It's long past time you returned to wherever you came from; my advice is that you do so at once, and then concentrate on trying to emulate your sister and rebuild your own life – this time relying on improving yourself rather than searching for another unfortunate man willing to dance to your monotonous tune.'

Her eyes narrowed. 'You seem to be very interested in Stella, Dr Finlay. Could it be that you have plans of your own concerning my sister?'

'Warped minds have warped thoughts,' Malcolm told her coldly. 'As I said already, I admire Miss Hesslett very much and I would be honoured to think that she may consider me as a close friend and even as a good companion. And if our feelings for each other were ever to become deeper – as they may – that would be none of your business. I'll say goodbye now, Mrs Armitage, since I have a strong feeling that you and I will never be obliged to meet each other again. Please follow my advice and leave as soon as you can – because if you don't I think you may discover that I am not the only person to make it clear that your presence in Prior's Ford isn't welcome.'

She began to say something, but Malcolm strode past her towards the door.

'I've listened to you for the last time – goodbye!' He walked out of the room, went straight past a wide-eyed Stella hovering in the hall, and left the house.

As soon as Malcolm returned to Thatcher's Cottage he poured a generous glass of whisky and carried it into the back garden, where he sat and listened to the river running past his garden.

At first he shied away from thinking about his meeting with Elma Armitage because the way he had behaved and the things he had said to her filled him with shame. Today he had seen a side of himself that should never have been set free, and looking back on it frightened him. But as the level of whisky in the glass lowered and the river worked its magic his mind insisted on playing out the whole scene, and after some wincing and groaning he began to remember why it had happened at all.

'Don't be frightened, don't be angry and don't reason with her,' Max had said, 'because she'll see that as a weakness.'

Max was right. Elma Armitage wasn't the only one who had seen another side to Malcolm – he had as well, and although he hated what he had become for that short time he knew that it had been the only way. If it worked it would not only free Stella; it would please the entire village. And if that happened he would have done what he had set out to do. As for the way he had behaved towards Elma Armitage and the things he had said to her – Max was a trained psychologist, and he had managed somehow, in one phone conversation, to tap into a never-before-revealed part of Malcolm's mind in order to help Stella. A part of Malcolm's mind that had come to the fore in a time of need and could now be put back into its box, hopefully never to be set free again.

As he finished the whisky Malcolm slowly began to feel more like his old self. Suddenly he felt ravenously hungry and realized that it was long past his lunchtime. He went into the house and as he prepared a meal he allowed himself to go back over the confrontation with Elma Armitage, this time calmly.

Instead of wincing he was able to run it as though watching a film. He had done what he needed to do – he had tackled the woman, refused to let her bully him, told her what she needed to know and, hopefully, he had made it clear to her that her time in Prior's Ford had come to an end.

He had then left the living room with dignity, walked past Stella, and left the house, closing the door quietly behind him. He distinctly remembered closing it quietly and was pleased about that because it showed that he was completely in control of himself. Had he not been in control he would have banged the door shut.

He was about to carry his lunch to the kitchen table when he realized that there was something wrong with the mental picture of him leaving the house. He tried a quick rerun – out of living room, into hall, past Stella . . .

Stella had been in the hall. Stella had come into the house, her arrival unheard because of the raised voices. Stella had been there, listening . . .

Malcolm dropped his lunch on the floor.

Twenty-Three

'Good morning, everyone,' Jinty McDonald said cheerfully as she arrived for work at Linn Hall. Because she had her own family to feed in the morning and had to tidy up after them once they had all dispersed to work and school, the morning routine at the Hall involved setting out breakfast for the backpackers the night before. There was always a wide collection of cereals, an industrial toaster and plenty of bread, and those who insisted on a cooked breakfast prepared it themselves from the ingredients left out for them.

Lewis and Ginny had breakfast with them, while Fliss and Hector enjoyed the luxury of a long lie-in and usually came down to the kitchen around half-past nine. That was when Jinty arrived to share a cup of tea with them before getting down to the task, with Fliss, of washing all the dishes.

On that late-June morning Ginny had finished eating and gone out to check the kitchen garden before leaving for her other job. Fliss had arrived downstairs and while waiting as he did every morning for the postman, Lewis was filling in his time by washing the used dishes while his mother dried them. When Jinty waved a bundle of letters in the air and announced, 'I met the postman on the way up so he gave me the letters – and there's a legal-looking envelope among them, Lewis,' he immediately vacated the large old-fashioned sink and snatched up a towel to dry his hands.

'Let me see!'

Jinty brushed some crumbs aside and spread the letters out on the table. 'There's not much else, mainly the usual junk mail. We get a lot of it as well – I hate to think of the number of trees that are cut down to create that rubbish. Leave the washing-up, Mrs F, and come and sit down while I make a nice cup of tea.'

Lewis had ripped the envelope open and hauled out its contents. 'Yes!' He waved the papers in the air. 'It's from the lawyer – he's received the signed papers from Portugal! Rowena Chloe is coming to live here!' He thumped the papers on to the table, grabbed Jinty, who had just refilled the kettle and was on her way to the big stove, and began to dance her around the room. 'At last! At long last!'

'Let go of me, ye daft laddie!' she screeched, 'the kettle's spilling water all over the floor!'

'Who cares?' he said cheerfully, releasing her.

Jinty set the kettle down on the table, took his face in both hands and gave him a smacking kiss. 'I'm so pleased for you,' she said when she had released him. 'So pleased for all of you!' And fetching a cloth, she began to dry the floor as Hector wandered in sleepily, wanting to know what all the noise was about.

'Wonderful news, Hector,' Fliss said, beaming. 'Lewis, you go and find Ginny because she'll be leaving for that other garden any time now. I'll tell your father.'

Ginny was just coming out of the kitchen garden when Lewis emerged from the kitchen, calling her name.

'I'm right here – I'm just about to leave for Fergus's place.'

'He can wait—'

She gave a startled squeal as he picked her up and began to dance her around the courtyard, with Muffin, who had followed him out, skipping around the two of them and barking his excitement.

'What's all this for?'

'What do you think? I've had a letter – a lawyer's letter!'

'Molly's agreed? Please say that Molly's agreed!'

'Molly has agreed,' Lewis said triumphantly, and she hugged him.

'That's the most wonderful news, Lewis! When's Rowena Chloe coming to live with us?'

'As soon as possible. I'll phone Molly's parents when the estate closes today and try to pin them down to a date.'

'And use that money we got from my father to write a cheque for Molly. The sooner she gets it the better.'

'Not yet – I want to make absolutely certain that everything has been agreed before she gets the second half of her blood money.'

'You don't trust her, do you?'

'I trusted her once but I was an idiot. Never again,' Lewis said as he set her back on her feet. Ginny glanced at her watch, and gasped.

'Good heavens, look at the time! I should be halfway to Fergus's place!'

'And I should be checking to make sure that everything's ready for today's opening.' He kissed her quickly. 'Wine with dinner tonight, I think?'

'Sounds lovely. Bye,' Ginny said, and jumped into the camper van.

'You're late,' Fergus said when she finally arrived to find everyone waiting for her.

She beamed at him. 'I know – sorry about that, but just as I was about to leave the Hall, Lewis got a letter to say that all the legal papers have been signed and Rowena Chloe is going to come and live with us. Isn't it wonderful?'

'My congratulations to you both,' he said, but his voice and eyes were cool and it seemed to Ginny that he had a problem forcing the words through his lips.

It turned out to be a bad day. Fergus, normally so easy to get on with, seemed to find fault with everything and everybody. He and the cameraman fell out before the day was halfway through and when work stopped for their usual picnic lunch he ate on his own, his back turned to the rest of the group.

In the afternoon it was Ginny's turn to bear the brunt of his bad mood, but when he suddenly decided that her plan for the part of the garden they were working on needed changing she was ready for him.

'I don't agree,' she told him flatly. 'We're following the plan exactly as I designed it and as you'll remember, you were very happy with it from the start.'

'That was then and this is now. I don't think it's going to look right. It has to be changed.'

'Fine, that's not a problem.' Ginny stripped off her gardening gloves. 'There's so much going on at Linn Hall that I'll be happy to get back to my duties there. I'm sure you'll be able to replace me without any problem.'

It was a warm day, but suddenly the air in the part of the garden where the team was working seemed to turn chilly.

'Bye, everyone,' Ginny smiled at the group. 'I enjoyed working with you.'

Fergus caught up with her as she reached the patio. 'Ginny, you can't just walk out like that – we have a contract.'

'No worries – you don't need to pay me for the work I haven't done yet.'

'I'm sorry, OK? I've got things on my mind.'

'So have I, most of the time I'm here, but I'm learning to concentrate on the present and make anything else that's on my mind wait until I have time to deal with it.'

'Do me a favour – let's get on with today's work and then we'll talk things out.'

'If you're going to insist on changes at this stage, Fergus, then you'd be wise to wait until you have somebody else working on the project because I'm not changing anything at this late stage. Change one thing now and we'll end up with a domino reaction that ends with everything having to be changed.'

'I'm not going to change anything today. Let's get back to work.'

'Good.' Ginny started to put her gloves on again as they both returned to the others.

When the day's work had finished Fergus suggested that he and Ginny should meet each other at the small restaurant about half a mile away. 'Just for coffee,' he added hurriedly as she began to shake her head. 'We need to sort out what happened earlier so that we can all work together tomorrow.'

She agreed reluctantly, and phoned Lewis as soon as she got into the camper van to tell him that she would be later than usual.

'Today of all days? Jinty and my mother have been working on a special celebration dinner and the wine's cooling – not to mention calling.'

'There's been a bit of a hiccup today and Fergus and I have got to thrash it out before work starts tomorrow. It should only take half an hour – forty minutes at the most, I promise. I've been looking forward all day to getting back to you so that we can celebrate the good news.'

Fergus's car was already parked outside the restaurant when she arrived, and he himself was waiting at a table, a bottle of wine and two glasses in front of him.

Ginny walked over to the bar and ordered a cappuccino before she joined him. 'I've already ordered coffee,' she said as he began to pour the wine. 'We're having a special dinner at Linn Hall tonight to celebrate the good news about Rowena Chloe, so I can't stay long.'

'I can't drink all this on my own,' he protested.

'Then take the rest of it home with you, or stay here and take your time emptying the bottle. I have to leave in half an hour and I don't like drinking and driving. Nor do I like it when I'm told in front of the others that something you agreed to months ago has to change.'

He had the grace to look shamefaced. 'Sorry about that, I was just being difficult. I don't want you to make any changes – your designs are all good.'

'So why did you have to embarrass us all today?'

Her coffee arrived just then, and Fergus took the opportunity to drink deeply. He set down the half-empty glass and then said abruptly, 'Ginny, you're a terrific gardener and you've got a terrific eye for design. Why are you throwing your talents away on marriage and instant motherhood?'

'You know why. Because that's what I want more than anything, to be Lewis's wife and to be the best mother that his little girl could ever hope for.'

Fergus groaned and then said, 'As I've told you before, any woman can get married and have children, but only a few could hope for the good career that you could have if you'd only listen to me!'

Ginny stared at him in disbelief. 'Is that why you've been in a bad mood today? Because I told you about Rowena Chloe?'

He drained his glass and began to refill it. 'Ninety-eight per cent of women would be happy to marry and look after children, but the other two per cent – the gifted ones like you – they can do better than that.'

'You don't rate women very highly, do you, Fergus?' she said drily.

He drank from the refilled glass 'I rate *you* very highly, Ginny. You and I could make a wonderful team – and if you'd only listen to me, you could make more money than Lewis ever will. You could have a wonderful life!'

'You don't really know much about me. Let me tell you about my life so far,' Ginny began. 'You already know something about it – only child, parents both successful and well-known actors, father fled to Australia – but you have no idea what it was really like for me. I had no contact at all with my father until recently, and very little with my mother. I was brought up by nannies and housekeepers and occasionally my mother took time to use me as a prop for her beloved photoshoots, which meant being dressed up in frilly frocks and having my hair done and being told to look at my mother adoringly and not spoil the photograph. It was such a relief when I was about five and she decided that I wasn't pretty enough for any more photoshoots. At least it meant that she left me more or less to my own devices, and to the nannies and housekeepers. It also gave me the chance to become my own person, and when one of the nannies started taking me to the local park I discovered that I loved flowers and plants and trees. That's why I was working in a garden centre before my mother lost her television job and went into a decline and insisted on hiding away in Prior's Ford with me as her companion.'

Fergus opened his mouth to say something, but she kept on talking. 'Lewis very kindly let me try my hand as a gardener, and in doing so he changed my world for ever. He was the first person I had ever met who looked on me as *me*. That's possibly why I fell in love with him, but he wasn't in love with me – he was in love with Molly. It was a good while after she dumped him that he began to notice me. Unfortunately, once he did finally notice me and we got engaged, that's when my mother reappeared. I was going to marry someone with a big house and a big estate – both dilapidated, but nevertheless potentially worthwhile. So now that I had found a career and found a man who genuinely loved me for myself – guess what? My mother suddenly began to take an interest – not in me, but in my wedding, which has to be lavish because I'm Meredith Whitelaw's daughter. She wants to decide what wedding dress I'm going to wear, and where the wedding should be held; and no doubt she expects to interfere with the rest of my life – if she's allowed, which she won't be. And now, Fergus, I come to you.'

'Cheers,' said Fergus, now on his third glass of wine.

'I'm very grateful to you for appreciating the work I've done on the Linn Hall estate and for offering me the job I'm doing for you now. I've loved every minute of it – until today, but I'm quite sure that that unpleasant situation won't happen again. I've hated being filmed and seeing myself on television – and even hated knowing that hundreds of other people have seen me on television – but thank you for the money, it's been very helpful. I might even be interested in any small future jobs you may put my way—'

'Good.'

'—but that doesn't mean that I'll necessarily take them on. What I'm actually telling you, Fergus,' Ginny said, 'is that thanks to Lewis and his family I have finally been allowed to become my own person. Nobody – not my mother, and not you – will ever control me again. I'll see you tomorrow, same time and same place.'

'You haven't touched your coffee,' Fergus pointed out as she got to her feet.

'Get the waiter to heat it up when you've finished the wine, and then order another pot of coffee – hot and strong. Alternatively, take a taxi home. Good night,' Ginny said sweetly, and left.

'Half an hour you said, and half an hour it was,' Lewis said by way of welcome as Ginny walked into the pantry at Linn Hall to find the table set with an old but magnificent tablecloth, the

Ralston-Kerrs' best cutlery and china, two bottles of wine and a huge vase of flowers from the gardens.

The three Ralston-Kerrs were beaming. 'We've got another reason for celebrating tonight,' Lewis told Ginny. 'I spoke to Molly's parents today and they've been given the all-clear to bring Rowena Chloe anytime. And guess what?'

'There's even more wonderful news?'

'The best ever.' To her astonishment, he picked her up and whirled her around. 'They're bringing her on Monday!'

'This coming Monday?'

'This coming Monday,' Fliss confirmed. 'Isn't that lovely?'

Lewis set Ginny back on her feet. 'I think they were getting tired of not being able to just go on holiday whenever it suited them. Apparently as soon as they got the good news from Molly they booked a holiday in Spain there and then. Mum and Jinty are going to get her bedroom ready tomorrow. So we've got a lot to celebrate tonight! But what about you? Did you and Fergus get your problem sorted out?'

'All done, dusted and dealt with,' Ginny told him. 'And it's lovely to be back home!'

Twenty-Four

On the following day, Fergus arrived an hour late to find Ginny and the gardeners hard at work. They were being filmed, and Ginny was providing a commentary for the future viewers. Fergus slumped on to the garden bench already on site and watched until they stopped for a coffee break.

'You seem to be managing perfectly well without me,' he commented when Ginny joined him.

'We've got into the routine, but you timed your arrival well because I'm not sure what you had planned to do next.' She took a mouthful of coffee. 'You look hung-over.'

'Thanks for reminding me.'

'I thought I saw your car in the car park when I drove past the restaurant this morning.'

'The waiters wouldn't allow me to drive home so I had to get a taxi – and another taxi back to the restaurant this morning. It cost me a small fortune.'

'Luckily, you can afford it.'

'I seem to remember getting quite a lecture from you last night – something about nannies and housekeepers – and being taken to a park?'

'I was explaining to you why I'm not interested in fame and fortune, but I *am* interested in living my life the way I want to live it. I can explain it all over again if you want.'

He began to shake his head, and then groaned and clamped a hand on either side of his face. 'I think I remember the gist of it.'

'Good. I did say that I might consider work offers that don't take up too much time,' Ginny said before draining her coffee mug and getting up from the bench. 'And now that that's settled, let's get back to work.'

After a restless night, Malcolm got up early and went to his study, hoping that some good hard work would help to rid him of memories of the previous day.

But after sitting for the best part of an hour staring at an empty sheet of paper he gave up and went out to buy a newspaper.

It was a perfect June day and the people he met on his way to the Village Store all called out, 'Lovely morning, isn't it?' to him as they passed by. Malcolm, who hadn't noticed the weather and was so wrapped up in a strong sense of guilt that he would probably not have noticed if it had been snowing, was caught by surprise each time and only just managed to mumble back an unconvincing, 'Lovely.'

'Good morning, Dr Finlay,' Marcy Copleton greeted him as he stumped into the Village Store, 'Lovely morning, isn't it?'

'Lovely.'

'Particularly pleasant,' Marcy went on as she produced his regular newspaper from beneath the counter. 'Have you heard the news?'

'I didn't have the radio on this morning,' replied Malcolm, who rarely listened to the radio and didn't own a television set.

Marcy laughed heartily. 'I doubt if it's the sort of news the radio people would be interested in, although everyone here is delighted. I'm talking about that sister of Stella Hesslett's,' she went on as Malcolm stared at her, puzzled. 'She's gone back home, thank goodness. Left last night apparently, in a bit of a hurry.'

'Are you sure?'

'I haven't seen Stella herself, but one of her neighbours was in earlier and she told me that she and her husband were both working in their front garden last night when a taxi drew up and Stella helped her sister to load luggage into it, then Mrs Armitage got in and it drove off. Apparently Stella looked a bit upset and she hurried back indoors without stopping to speak to the neighbours.'

'Luggage as well, you say?'

'A few people who were in this morning mentioned it and they all said luggage. They all looked happy, too − it's as if a cloud has been lifted from over this village. Nobody liked her, you know. Personally, I'm delighted because now I'll be able to get Sam back behind this counter. The woman terrified him so much that after their first meeting he kept pretending that he had something important to do in the back shop, to ensure that he'd never have to come face-to-face with her again. Good morning, Ada,' Marcy called out to a newcomer.

'Lovely morning, Marcy − Dr Finlay. Have you heard the news?'

'I have indeed! You forgot your change, Dr Finlay,' Marcy called after Malcolm as he headed for the door.

'Just put it in one of the collection boxes,' he called back.

Outside the shop, he hesitated, wondering if he should visit Stella, then decided to go over to the pub in the hope that a drink might help him to make up his mind.

'Good morning, Dr Finlay,' Gracie Fisher chirped as he went into the public bar. 'And what a beautiful day it is! You'll have heard the good news?'

When he left the pub Malcolm fully intended to visit Stella, but at the entrance to the cul-de-sac where she lived, his courage deserted him and he decided to phone Max instead.

'At least you've achieved your objective,' Max said cheerfully once he had heard the entire tale. 'The dreaded sister has cleared off and from what you say the entire village is celebrating the fact. Do you realize that you are now the Pied Piper of Prior's Ford?'

'It's not a joking matter – the villagers might be pleased but I'm not so sure about Stella. She's a very kind and gentle person and although she may be relieved she's very possibly worrying about what's going to happen to her sister now. She may even be blaming me for being so cruel.'

'You won't know whether you're right or wrong until you speak to her, will you?'

'Perhaps I should wait for a few days to let her cool down.'

'Perhaps she'll come to you,' Max suggested.

'I wouldn't want that!' Malcolm said swiftly. 'I mean, if she came here to see me and she was angry I wouldn't be able to walk away because she would be in my house. She might even weep, and I couldn't face that!'

'You really care about this woman, don't you, old man?'

'Of course not – what on earth makes you think that? I like her and I respect her, that's all! I'm just seeking your advice as to whether I should go to speak to her now or leave it for a while.'

'In that case my advice is to go and see her as soon as possible. Apologize for any problems you may have caused her by getting rid of her overbearing sister.'

'I don't know if I can.'

'Malcolm, stop prevaricating. You didn't know if you could find the courage to face up to the dragon, but you did it and you won. There is absolutely no reason why you shouldn't be able to finish the task off properly. Go forth now and prosper,' Max said firmly, and hung up.

Malcolm would have liked to take a good stiff drink before facing Stella, but realizing that if she was as angry with him as he feared, it would not help to turn up smelling of alcohol before lunchtime, and he set off with dragging footsteps.

After ringing her doorbell he stepped back down on to the path, just in case. He half-hoped, as he did when about to face Elma, that she might be out, but after a moment the door opened.

'Oh – good morning, Dr Finlay,' Stella's face flushed poppy red.

'Miss Hesslett, I wondered if I – if I might—'

'Yes?'

Malcolm, falling back on his false reason for calling, produced a sheet of paper from his pocket. 'If I might ask you to order a few more books for me?'

'Oh – yes of course.' As he reached out to give her the paper she asked, 'Would you like to come in?'

'If I'm not interrupting anything—'

'Nothing at all. I wanted to talk to you in any case.'

'Ah.' Malcolm entered the house, thinking as he did so that this could be the way a man might feel when heading in the direction of the execution chamber. It came as a welcome shock when, once in the living room, Stella said, 'I had been thinking of calling on you, to thank you for what you did yesterday.'

'And I'm calling on you to apologize for what I did yesterday. I've been – I mean, most of the people in the village have been concerned in case you were finding your sister's visit –' Malcolm tried to find the right word and came up with – 'difficult. Yesterday I thought I may be able to suggest to her that the time had come for her to accept her unfortunate situation and try to rebuild her life, but I'm afraid I lost my temper.'

'Elma is my *half*-sister,' she reminded him, 'and you were quite magnificent.'

'Really?'

She smiled at him. 'Really. I have to admit that I was beginning to wonder if she was looking on her visit as a permanent situation, and I would have hated that. I'm used to living on my own and I like it.'

Malcolm nodded. 'I can understand.'

'My problem is that I've always been used to giving in to Elma, and I didn't know how to tell her that it was time to go. But you – you were so firm with her, especially when you told her that she wasn't popular in the village.'

'How much did you hear yesterday?'

'Quite a lot. I had forgotten something that I should have taken to the library van with me and when I came to the house to fetch it the two of you were arguing so loudly that you didn't hear me.'

Malcolm swallowed hard, trying to remember exactly what he

had said about his friendship with Stella. He had a terrible feeling that whatever it was, he had said too much.

'I was trying to explain to Mrs Armitage that you're well-liked and respected in the village. From what I recall she accused me of meddling –' his mind was working furiously – 'and I believe that I told her how helpful you had been to me in your position as the local librarian, and how much I appreciated that help. I tried to make it clear that I was speaking as a concerned friend of yours. A good friend, I hope, but no more than that. Just a friend. Afterwards, I wondered if she had misunderstood . . .' His voice trailed into silence.

'That's what I heard – you saying that we are friends. No more than that.'

Malcolm nodded eagerly. 'Friends – good friends. Nothing less and nothing more.'

'Exactly,' Stella said emphatically, and then they looked at each other for a moment, both wondering if they were protesting too much.

'I must go,' Malcolm blurted out. 'I'm busy – I mean, you must be busy too.'

'Do you have time for a cup of coffee?'

'That would be very agreeable,' Malcolm said, and sank into a chair as Stella went to the kitchen.

'Would you – could we perhaps meet for lunch tomorrow in the Neurotic Cuckoo?' he ventured half an hour later as he left the house.

'That would be very nice, thank you. Would one o'clock suit?'

'Admirably!'

There was a new spring in Malcolm's step as he strode along the pavement. A load had been lifted from his shoulders and everything was back to normal.

The nearer he got to Thatcher's Cottage the springier his step became, because, as Max had suggested, his meeting with Elma Armitage on the previous day had suddenly started to rewrite itself in his head as part of a plot line for the next Lilias Drew book and he was in a hurry to record it before it started to fade.

Despite the fact that the estate was open to the public, Lewis managed to organize things so that he had an assistant with him in the stable shop on Monday afternoon, and had also arranged to get a phone call from Jimmy, who was on duty at the front gate, as soon as the Ewing's estate car arrived.

He got the call mid-afternoon and immediately hurried over to the kitchen to alert his parents. The three of them, plus Muffin, were waiting in the courtyard when the car arrived with Tony Ewing at the wheel, his wife Val in the passenger seat and Rowena Chloe trying valiantly to get out of the child seat behind them.

'Do make an effort to stand still and let Val hug you, Hector,' Fliss appealed to her husband.

He shuddered. 'You know that I hate being fussed over like that. I always have!'

'It's just the kind of person she is.'

'Then I wish she wasn't that kind of person. It's her perfume that makes it worse.'

As soon as the car stopped Lewis jumped forward to open the rear door.

'Daddy! I've come to see you, Daddy, let me out! Let me out – now!'

'I'm trying to, sweetheart. Stop wriggling,' Lewis appealed as Val stepped out of the car and advanced on Fliss and Hector, arms wide.

'How lovely to see you all again! Fliss –' she enfolded Fliss in her usual heavily perfumed embrace and then released her in order to grab Hector, who shied back nervously but could not escape – 'and dear Hector!'

Lewis managed to get his daughter out of the car and she immediately started trying to greet everyone at once, her exuberance fortunately taking attention away from Hector, who had developed a sneezing attack.

'Granfliss – Jinty – Grandpa—' Rowena Chloe knee-hugged everyone before hurling herself on Muffin, who was frantic to lick her face.

'Are you sure that that dog's got a clean tongue?' Val asked anxiously. 'You don't know where he may have been in a big place like this. Weena, darling, please don't let the dog do that!'

'It's just doggy kisses, Gran,' Rowena Chloe told her happily, her arms wrapped around Muffin's neck.

'Come to Grandma,' Val begged, producing a handkerchief,

and when she was obeyed she rubbed vigorously at the little girl's
face. As soon as she was released, Rowena Chloe hurried back
to the car and began trying to open the rear door. 'I need to get
my luggage out,' she insisted, and Lewis went to help her.

'Is this your luggage?' He held up a small plastic suitcase, pink
with a pattern of blue flowers.

'Yes. Where's Ginny?' she asked as she put the case down on
the ground and squatted to open it.

'She's working in someone else's garden today, but she's coming
back soon because she can't wait to see you. D'you want me to
open that for you?'

I can do it myself – I'm nearly old enough to go to proper
school.' After a short struggle she opened the case and brought
out the elaborately dressed doll that her mother had given her
the year before.

'We've arrived, Carmen,' she informed the doll, briskly fluffing
up its velvet skirts with one hand. Then to the adults, 'I'm
hungry!' And she led everyone into the kitchen.

Twenty-Five

'This is probably a much better place for Weena to live than
where we are,' Val Ewing said later, as the adults sat at the kitchen
table. Rowena Chloe had wolfed down several sandwiches, three
chocolate biscuits and a glass of orange juice, and had then gone
off happily with Muffin and Ginny, who had arrived home, to
find out what changes had been made to the gardens since her
last visit. 'You have such a lovely big place for a little girl to play
in, and there are always people around to keep an eye on her.'
And then, hurriedly, 'But we'll certainly miss her dreadfully, won't
we, Tony?'

'She's a little ray of sunshine,' her husband agreed.

'She certainly is,' Fliss said fondly, 'and you know that you're
always welcome to come and see her, and have her for visits. It
can't have been very easy for you at times, with you working
part-time, Val.'

'It wasn't, especially once our girl left school and went away to university, and wasn't there to babysit for us.'

'Not that she was fond of babysitting,' Tony added. 'When she was younger and sitting at home with her nose stuck in school books we used to think that she wasn't a bit like our Molly, but that all changed when she started university. She chose a university so far away from Inverness that we hardly ever see her now. You spend the best part of your life raising kids and then as soon as they can get away from you they're off like greased lightning without so much as a goodbye and thank you. One of them in Portugal and the other in Durham!'

'Is she still at university?' Lewis asked.

'Oh yes, she seems to be doing very well, and now she's decided to do an extra year more than she needs to. She says that it will help her to end up with a really good job.'

'With her mother and me forking out the necessary cash,' Tony added, 'and wondering if we're going to get a sniff of the great wage she's eventually hoping to make.'

'Oh, give over, Tony,' his wife chided him. 'It'll all work out in the end. He's badly needing this holiday,' she told the Ralston-Kerrs. 'We're not used to spending so much time at home, but now that you're looking after Weena we'll be able to go away more often. We're the kind of people who need a lot more sunlight than we ever get in this country. Molly was always more like us, that way.'

'Does she like living in Portugal permanently?' Lewis asked, and Val beamed at him.

'She loves it, and so does Bob. And they're so thrilled about buying the bar where they work.'

'They're going to own the place where they work?'

'Yes, Fliss, and they're both so excited about it! The man who owns the bar decided to sell, which could have meant that they both lost their jobs, but fortunately for them they've both been working so hard that they had managed to save enough money to buy it from him. When Molly phoned to give us the news she said that they'd planned to save enough to be able to send for Weena, but as it turned out they had to use the money to save their jobs instead. And as she knew how much you wanted to have Weena here with you, Lewis, it all worked out well for everyone in the end, didn't it?'

'Yes, it did, and I'm very pleased.'

'So am I.' Val reached over and patted Lewis's hand. 'I had been so looking forward to my Molly being the lady of the manor here when the two of you got married, but although it wasn't to be, it's lovely to know that one day this place will be our Weena's.' Then she looked at the clock and gasped as she jumped to her feet. 'Tony, look at the time! We should be on our way. We're spending the night in a hotel at Glasgow Airport and flying out to Spain tomorrow morning.'

'I'm not sure where Rowena Chloe is,' Fliss said as they all began to move out to the Ewing's car. 'Lewis, could you go and find her so that she can say goodbye?'

'I don't think we've got the time to wait, have we, Tony?'

'Not if you want to be sunning yourself in Spain tomorrow at this time.'

'Oh dear, give her a big kiss from us, will you?' While Tony opened the car door for his wife she hugged Lewis and then Fliss. 'Where's Hector?'

'Val – get in,' Tony said impatiently.

'Hug Hector for me, Fliss. Bye!' Val got into the car as the engine was switched on.

Once the car disappeared round the corner of the house Hector joined his wife and son. 'Thank goodness that woman's gone,' he said.

Twenty-Six

By the time July arrived Prior's Ford had become a hive of activity. The festival was now only five weeks away and there was a sudden rush to get everything ready in time. The weather was kind, allowing preparations to be made for the Best Garden competition, and even those with quite small gardens were keen to open them to the public during the festival week. They were also busy making scarecrows, since the original Scarecrow Festival had been merged into the general festival.

The Village Hall was in constant use; the Women's Rural

Institute needed it as a store for all the items being collected or made for their stalls, Elinor Pearce, wardrobe mistress for the local drama club, required one of the rooms for herself and the women helping her to make costumes for all those who wanted to be dressed up for the festival, a hastily put-together dance group required it for rehearsals, and Alastair Marshall was busy turning its corridors into an Art Gallery displaying pictures created by the village school pupils.

Lewis and his staff were particularly hard-pressed, erecting two large marquees on the lawns, one being used as a tea tent, the other to house an orchestral concert. Linn Hall's large drawing room and equally large dining room were being pressed into use, one as a green room for the musicians and the other needed to store a vast collection of cutlery, china and, when the time came, food for the tea tent. As well as making certain that the estate was in pristine condition, the backpackers were also working hard on making small scarecrows to be dotted around the estate.

To Fergus's annoyance, Ginny insisted on taking a week off so that she could help on the estate while the festival was on. 'We have a contract for an entire year,' he protested.

'But normally I would be entitled to two weeks' holiday even though I never take holidays, and in any case, we've reached the stage where everyone here knows what they're doing. They can manage without me for a week. I've still got to organize a treasure hunt on the estate for the children.'

'You're my presenter – you have to talk the viewers through the work process.'

'I can do voice-overs when the series is being put together. Fergus, I'm taking a week off for the festival and if you don't like it you can sack me.'

There was a coolness in Ginny's direct gaze that made Fergus uncomfortable, and her voice was unusually firm. It reminded him of their recent meeting in the restaurant. He could recall little of what was said at the time because he had been working through the bottle of wine on his own, but he knew that she had been very angry. He also knew that if she walked away from his project it could never be completed.

'Yes, I suppose that you *could* do voice-overs. Take that week off.'

'Thank you, Fergus,' Ginny said sweetly. 'Now let's get back to work.'

Clarissa was setting the kitchen table for lunch and Alastair, who had spent the morning at the primary school helping the young artists to complete their paintings for the festival art exhibition, was upstairs washing the paint off his hands when the doorbell rang.

'I'll get it,' Clarissa called, and went to the door.

'I'm just tryin' to remember,' Amy Rose said as soon as the door opened, 'did I let you know that I was comin' a bit earlier than I first said?' Then, as Clarissa gaped at her, stunned into silence, 'Darn it, I've done it again! I never remember to check with you before I leave home. It's the excitement – I was so lookin' forward to seein' you two an' this quaint village that I got excited as a kid and when that happens everythin' goes out of my mind.'

'Don't worry about it, Amy – we knew that you were coming round about now and we've already prepared the spare room. This is a lovely surprise!'

'Good – I love surprisin' people.' Amy dropped the bags she carried in both hands and threw her arms around Clarissa. 'So how are you? You look great – I swear you get younger every time I see you. An' where's my favourite man? Don't tell me he's not home!'

'He's upstairs. We were just about to have our lunch and there's enough for three.'

'Good to hear that, 'cause I'm starvin'! Hey, here he comes!' Amy released Clarissa and hurried into the hall as Alastair came bounding down the stairs. 'Hello, handsome, guess what – I'm back in town!'

'Amy!' As he picked her up and whirled her around Clarissa had to move quickly to rescue a vase of fresh flowers from the garden before it was knocked off the telephone table. 'We didn't realize you were coming today!'

'I forgot to tell you. I do that every time, don't I? Put me down and let me have a look at you,' Amy ordered, and when he did as he was told, 'God, you're handsome! I wish I was thirty years younger.'

'You look great to me, blue hair and all. What colour was it last time we saw you?'

'I can't remember. You like it? I love this shade of blue; I thought about adding a bit of red and white in honour of my British friends but my hairdresser said it would be gildin' the lily and I looked fine as I was.'

'You do. Hang on, Clarissa, I'll see to that.' Alastair went to help Clarissa, who was gathering up the bags that Amy had dropped.

'The rest of the stuff's in the hired car. The door's open and the keys are in the ignition.'

'Interesting vehicle,' Alastair commented, glancing out at the small car parked at the curb. 'It looks quite old for a hired car.'

'I like little old cars, they're my kind of vehicle,' Amy said fondly, 'especially now that I'm a little old woman. We kind of go well together. Now what's happenin' with Stella? Is that sister of hers still botherin' her?'

'I'm glad to say that she's left Prior's Ford and Stella's beginning to look more like her old self.'

'Darn! I mean, I'm pleased for Stella but I was lookin' forward to dealin' with the sister. I like sortin' things out for people – it keeps life interestin'. Don't bother carryin' everythin' upstairs just now, Alastair,' she went on as Alastair arrived with the luggage. 'Just dump it all right here till later. Let's eat!'

As soon as Cam Gordon knocked at the door of Number Five Jasmine Cottages, the official name for the row of almshouses, there was a burst of yapping from Minnie and Maxy, the Cowans' two poodles, followed by the scrabbling of claws on linoleum as they raced each other to the door.

'Maxy – Minnie, for goodness' sake behave yourselves,' he heard Dolly scold as she followed the dogs. Once the door was opened and they recognized Cam the two poodles quietened, tails wagging.

'Cam, it's you. Come on in,' Dolly invited. 'We were just having a glass of wine – come and join us!'

'I've chosen the perfect time,' Cam said happily.

'Harold,' Dolly called as she led the way into the small living room, 'it's Cam. Fetch another glass, will you?'

'I recognized his voice and I've already done it,' her husband told her, emerging from the kitchen just as the two of them arrived. 'Sit down, Cam.'

'So what can we do for you?' Dolly wanted to know when the wine was poured and served.

'I think I know,' Harold gave Cam a suspicious look.

'Harold, have you been keeping something from me?'

Cam shook his head sadly. 'I should have spoken to you in the first place, Dolly.'

'About what? Tell me!' Dolly demanded just as her husband said, 'I'm not going to do it.'

'Do *what*?' Dolly was becoming exasperated.

'I asked Harold a few weeks ago if he'd be willing to wear his clown outfit at the Festival.'

'What a wonderful idea – Harold, you have to do it!'

'Over my dead body,' her husband said grumpily. 'Those days are gone, Dolly, and you know it.'

'But it would be such fun!' She clapped her hands and the poodles, who had just settled down at her feet, immediately got up again, looking at her expectantly. 'Oh, I'm sorry, darlings, Mummy forgot what that means to you. It's what I do before I give them their treats at bedtime,' she explained to Cam. Then, as the dogs stared up at her, 'Now I'm going to have to give them the treats – that means second helpings because they won't go to bed later on without them.'

She went into the kitchen and returned with two small unwrapped chocolate bars. The dogs took the bars carefully from her fingers and gulped them down.

'There now, back to business.' Dolly sat down again. 'Where were we – oh yes. Harold, it would be lovely to see you all dressed up again.'

'But what if someone recognized me, Dolly? I'd end up being expected to put the outfit on for every children's party within miles. I was a professional then, not just a party entertainer,' Harold insisted.

'You were the best in the business,' his wife agreed. She turned to Cam, her eyes shining. 'Oh, Cam, you should have seen him in the ring! That's when I first fell in love with him. I was Dolly and her Dancing Dogs and I was new to that circus, and the first time I saw Harold do his act I said to Minnie and Maxy – not you, sweethearts,' she added to the dogs, who had raised their heads at the sound of their names, 'the first Minnie and Maxy. I said, "I'm going to marry that clown!" The funny thing was that when I saw him working around the place during the day I didn't even know that he was the clown who'd stolen my heart. It was a week before I realized that it was the same man.' She smiled across at Harold, who shook his head and said affectionately, 'You read too many of those romantic stories you get from the library.'

'Dress up once more for me, Harold.'

'I've had an idea,' Cam told them both. 'How would it be if I wore a clown costume too? You could make up my face, Harold, and we could work together, appearing and then disappearing. If things got tricky I'd cover for you so that you could disappear back home and I'd stay. It doesn't matter if anyone realizes who I am. And that time you put on the costume to scare off those young vandals there were other people in on your secret and none of them has said a word about it since – Charlie Crandall and Hannah Gibb, Ewan McNair and Grant and Jimmy McDonald. They can all be trusted and I reckon we could ask them to help us out again. If they were all watching out for you and ready to help you to disappear I think you'd be safe enough. You don't have to appear as the clown all week,' he promised. 'Let's say just one day for you, and I'll do my clown act throughout the week.'

'You could do it for just one day, Harold. We'll all protect you and help you to get away if you need to. Think what fun it would be to dress up one more time!'

Harold looked from one eager face to the other.

'I'll think about it,' he said.

'He'll do it,' Dolly told Cam as she showed him out later. 'I'll see to that. I can't *wait* to see him in that costume again!'

The day after she arrived in Prior's Ford Amy Rose set about renewing her relationship with the village and its residents. One of the first people she contacted was Stella Hesslett, who happened to be in the mobile library that day. A few people were browsing contentedly along the shelves when she arrived, making heads turn with her yell of 'Hi, Stella, guess who's back?'

'Amy, how wonderful to see you! Clarissa didn't tell me you were arriving so soon.'

'That's because I forgot to tell her, as usual. You're busy, so I'll leave you to it. What are you doin' for lunch?'

'Going home.'

'No you're not. Pub – twelve thirty – good with you?'

'Lovely!'

'See you then,' Amy said, and was gone.

Cynthia MacBain, who had been getting her library book stamped out when Amy arrived, asked irritably, 'Who was that noisy woman with the dreadful blue hair?'

Stella beamed at her. 'That's Amy Rose, Mrs Ramsay's friend from America. She's been coming over to visit for a few years now. She's a very interesting lady.'

'Festivals and strangers with blue hair – this village is going to rack and ruin!' Cynthia muttered, snatching up her book.

'So how's life treatin' you, Stella?' Amy asked once Gracie and Joe Fisher had welcomed her back to the Neurotic Cuckoo and taken their orders.

'Very well. It's so nice to see you again, Amy, and have you back here in time for the festival. I think it's going to be really special this year.'

'I'm lookin' forward to it. I've been gettin' all the local news from Clarissa – she told me that your sister's been visitin', and stayed for quite a while. I didn't even know that you *had* a sister. You never mentioned her before.'

She noticed that Stella's smile dimmed a little. 'We're half-sisters, actually, and I'm quite a few years older than her. We haven't seen each other for years.'

'So you must have had a lot to catch up on, the two of you.'

Stella started to concentrate on reorganizing the salt and pepper holders. 'Not really. Elma was married, with two children, and that kept her fully occupied until recently.'

'So her kids are old enough now to be able to look after themselves and let Mom go visitin'?'

Stella left the condiments to their own devices and gave Amy a long, hard look. 'I imagine that Clarissa has told you the whole story – about Elma only coming to me because her husband had

left her and she didn't want to be alone. And about her being a
bully, and nobody here liking her and me being unable to find
the courage to tell her to go home.'

'She was worried about you. She told me about it on the
phone, and I was all set to try to help you when I came over.
Bullies are weaklings who try to make everyone else look small
so's they can feel big. It's hard to fight off a bully, 'specially hard
for a really nice person like you. I was goin' to get rid of her,
but Clarissa tells me you managed it on your own, so well done
you, girl!'

'I didn't. Dr Finlay—'

Suddenly, Amy noticed, Stella looked animated, her eyes
lighting up and a faint flush coming to her cheeks.

'—he's a very nice man who retired here and he uses the
library a lot, so we've got to know each other quite well – he
had a word with Elma and persuaded her to go back home.'

'Sounds like you've got a knight in shinin' armour to look out
for you, I'm lookin' forward to meetin' him,' Amy commented,
and then, as Stella's flush deepened, 'do I get the feelin' there's
romance in the air?'

'Not at all – he's never married and never wanted to. The same
goes for me, but I think that Elma was hoping to change his mind
now that she's on her own, and he lost his temper with her.'

'Whatever the reason, good for him,' Amy said as their meal
arrived.

Twenty-Seven

As Stella and Amy left the pub they spotted Muriel Jacobsen
standing by the library van. One hand rested on the handle of a
pram, and as soon as they left the pub they could hear its occu-
pant screaming.

'Oh dear, there's Mrs Jacobsen waiting for me –' Stella glanced
at her watch – 'and I'm late. The library should have been opened
ten minutes ago!'

As she showed signs of breaking into a run, Amy laid a

restraining hand on her arm. 'No need to rush, we're only yards away and it's a pleasant day, I'm sure she won't mind waitin' for a few more seconds.'

'I'm so sorry, Mrs Jacobsen,' Stella said as soon as they reached the van. She had to raise her voice slightly because of the furious roars coming from the pram. 'Amy and I had lunch together and I'm afraid that I forgot to check my watch.'

'That's all right, I've only just arrived. Amy, how lovely to see you back in Prior's Ford again.'

'Lovely to be back and I'm lookin' forward to bein' here for this festival that Clarissa's been talkin' about over the phone.' Amy gestured to the posters spread liberally around all the buildings. 'It looks like bein' somethin' special.'

'Oh, it will be!' While they were talking, Stella had gone up the steps and opened the library. As she disappeared inside Muriel glanced up at the open door and then back at the howling, red-faced baby.

'So who's this?'

'You remember the young couple who bought Ivy McGowan's house? This is their daughter Layla. Her mother's gone to Kirkcudbright to get her nails done – or something like that – and I'm babysitting. Layla's normally a very good baby but I can't do anything with her today. I think there's another tooth coming through.'

'Oh yes, Clarissa mentioned that there was a new baby at the almshouses. I'll keep an eye on her while you go into the library,' Amy offered.

Muriel looked doubtful. 'Are you sure? She doesn't know you, and with the mood she's in—'

'Oh, we'll be fine,' Amy assured her. 'I've never had any kids of my own, but I've helped hundreds of 'em into the world, and learned the knack of teachin' 'em a little bit about how to be decent kids before their parents take 'em home to be spoiled.'

'You started training newborn babies?' Muriel looked sceptical.

'Sure. Kids pop into the world hungry to learn – look at how much they have to find out before they even get to kindergarten. We all arrive with brains like little sponges, wantin' to suck up knowledge, and pretty well the first thing we learn is how to control our moms and dads 'cause sure as heck, they don't know how to control us. Go on with your books and leave me and this little lady to get acquainted.'

As Muriel went into the mobile library Amy plunged her hands into the pram and withdrew Layla, lifting her up so that they were face-to-face. Layla, in the middle of sucking in air to fuel another scream, stopped crying abruptly and stared at the bird-like face topped with blue hair only inches away.

'Hi, kid,' Amy said cheerfully, 'I'm Amy Rose – let's talk.'

When Muriel emerged from the mobile library carrying several books she saw Amy sitting on the bench outside the Neurotic Cuckoo, holding Layla on her knee so that the baby was facing her. Amy was talking and Layla, one fist stuffed into her mouth, appeared to be listening intently. The empty pram stood at the side of the bench.

'. . . and as soon as I walked down that gangplank between my parents and my little sandals hit American concrete I knew I was home,' Muriel heard Amy say as she approached. 'And boy, was I right!' Then as Muriel arrived Amy looked up. 'Hi, you got all the books you wanted?'

'I did, and I see that you've worked some kind of miracle while I was gone.'

'I was just tellin' her a bit about my history, since she's still too young to have any history of her own. You're a good listener, kid.'

Layla removed her wet fist from her mouth. 'Gumph,' she said.

Amy got to her feet and tucked the baby back into the pram. 'Well, we've all got places to go.'

'How long are you going to be here?' Muriel asked.

'I'm stayin' for the festival and then doin' a bit of travellin' before I start back home.'

'You must come and visit us at the almshouses – you remember that we usually have afternoon tea in the garden if the weather's decent?' Then, as Amy nodded, 'We'll look forward to seeing you one afternoon soon.'

'I'll be there,' Amy promised.

Over the next few days Amy reacquainted herself with the villagers. At Lynn Stacey's invitation she called in at the primary school in the last few days before they stopped for the summer break and spent half an hour teaching the oldest pupils how to create crosswords –. her own favourite, and lucrative, hobby since retiring. She looked in on the pupils rehearsing their Scottish Country Dance routine for the festival and the small art class that Alastair was teaching, and spent the best part of a day in the village hall, helping the members of the Women's Rural to decorate the place for the festival.

She had a cup of tea and a long talk with Naomi Hennessey in the church vestry and also spent an entire day visiting the Linn Hall estate, accompanied most of the time by Muffin the dog and Rowena Chloe, who made certain that Amy saw everything there was to be seen.

The little girl was delighted when Amy managed to climb up on to the top of the grotto, where the two of them enjoyed a long chat. By the time they returned to the Hall they had become firm friends, and Rowena Chloe insisted on taking Amy into the kitchen for a cup of tea.

'You've got a fine granddaughter there,' Amy told Fliss as they sat together at the table. 'She really knows every inch of your lovely gardens.'

Fliss beamed. 'We think the world of her. She's only recently come to live here permanently.'

'I heard all about that, and about her real mom living in Portugal with a man called Bob, and her dad gettin' married soon so that she can have two moms, one here and one in Portugal. She's a greatly loved and very practical little girl,' Amy said sincerely, and Fliss glowed with pride and invited her unexpected guest to visit any time.

Amy also went to Tarbethill Farm, where she spent an hour watching Stefan Krechevsky at work, and bought several pieces of his glassware to take back to America.

'We've hardly seen you since you arrived here,' Clarissa protested a week into the visit. 'We're both beginning to feel like poor hosts, leaving you to your own devices.'

'You're great hosts, both of you, and we'll be doing lots together before I go back home, but I don't want you to get tired of me too soon. In any case, I love goin' around on my own and meetin' people, and this is such an interestin', busy little village with such interestin' people in it.'

On a pleasant sunny afternoon she called in at the almshouses to find the residents gathered together in the garden, their chairs set in a circle around a rug where baby Layla was kicking her fat little legs.

Amy received a warm welcome, and Harold Cowan jumped to his feet. 'You sit there and I'll fetch another chair,' he said, and hurried off.

'Tea or coffee?' Cissie Kavanagh wanted to know, going to the folding table where everything was laid out.

'Coffee would be great – black, no sugar. I see you're all babysittin'.'

'Tricia's meeting some old school friends,' Cissie said as she brought Amy her coffee, 'It's no bother to look after the little one.'

'It may be no bother now,' her husband said as Harold returned with an extra chair, 'but wait until she's able to run around the place and we have to keep stopping her from hurting herself. Small children never worry about heading into danger – they seem to have a natural tendency towards suicide.'

'They're not as bad as all that, Robert,' Cissie said mildly. 'Our Rachel never got hurt when she was a toddler, apart from the occasional tumble.'

'That was because one of us was always there to keep an eye on her. I know that Derek's working in the butcher's shop six days a week, but where's Tricia most of the time? Out for coffee, out for lunch, shopping or getting her nails and hair and good-ness knows what else seen to.'

'Is it becomin' a bit too much for you people?' Amy asked.

They looked at each other for a moment before Hannah Gibbs said, 'To tell the truth, it is. Layla's a sweet little thing, but I'm sure that I'm not the only one beginning to think that Tricia's taking advantage of us.'

'P'rhaps someone needs to explain that to her,' Amy suggested, and again they all looked at each other uncomfortably.

'I know it's difficult for you folks, but it would be easier for me. I'm a visitor, not a neighbour.'

'Could you do that for us?' Robert asked eagerly.

'Sure, I'm used to talkin' to people and helpin' them to see things a bit differently. When's she likely to be back?'

'In about an hour,' Charlie Crandall ventured.

'Or two,' Robert Kavanagh added, and his wife shot him an irritated look.

'OK, you folks go back home in about forty-five minutes and I'll wait here with Layla until her mom comes. Then the two of us can have a nice little chat.'

Amy glanced down at Layla and was interested to see that the baby, lying on her back, had managed to turn herself almost in a circle by using her heels as leverage. Now she was looking up at Harold Cowan's long, rather sad face, and had suddenly become very animated, babbling away and reaching her little arms up towards him.

'She's certainly taken a shine to you.'

'She's always like that when she sees Harold,' Dolly Cowan explained. 'He seems to be her favourite person.'

'Babies often latch on to people who make 'em feel safe,' Amy said.

Just over an hour later, Tricia Borland arrived home and went round to the back of the row of houses in search of her daughter. To her surprise, instead of the usual group of neighbours there was only one woman in the garden, a blue-haired stranger talking animatedly to Layla, who was perched on her knee and apparently listening intently to what was being said.

'Excuse me—' Tricia hurried over to rescue her child.

'Oh, hi, you must be Tricia Borland, Layla's mom. I'm Amy Rose.' The stranger had an American accent.

'Where is everyone?'

'They all had things to do so I said I'd keep this pretty little lady company until you got back. Sit down for a minute and let's get to know each other; I'm a friend of Clarissa Ramsay's an' I usually visit Prior's Ford every year. I love this place an' I know all the folks livin' in these cute little old houses. They were tellin' me this afternoon what a great job you and your husband have made of modernizin' Ivy McGowan's place,' Amy went on as Tricia sank down on to a chair. 'Hey, Layla, your mommy's back home.' She handed the baby, who was still staring intently at her, to Tricia. Layla, startled, looked for a moment as though she was about to protest, but then, recognizing her mother, gave Tricia a wide smile that displayed her two little white teeth.

'Oh – well – thank you for looking after her,' Tricia stammered, once she had made sure that her baby was perfectly all right.

'It was a pleasure, honey. You've got a very clever little girl there. I've been tellin' her all about how I was born in England but then my folks took me to America when I was five and I grew up there.'

'She's just six months old,' said Tricia, puzzled. 'She doesn't understand what you're saying yet.'

'Oh, I know that, but I've always found that tiny little kids like to be talked to. They enjoy the sound of folks' voices; it makes 'em want to talk back and be able to communicate. They love eye contact too – it makes 'em feel that the person talkin' to 'em cares.'

Tricia was beginning to get interested. 'How many children do you have?'

'One answer is none, honey – but the other answer's hundreds. Me and my late husband were never blessed with kids, but I was a midwife, so I got to know all about newborns, and since I retired I've done a lot of babysittin' for neighbours. Can I say somethin' to you, Tricia?'

'What?' Tricia asked, while Layla happily played with the buttons on her mother's blouse.

'This afternoon, sittin' here talkin' to everyone, I noticed that your little girl had no trouble at all bein' among all those different people without you there to look out for her.'

'Oh, she spends a lot of time with our neighbours and she loves it. They all watch out for her, and it's good for children to get used to being among other people, isn't it?'

'Up to a point, but as they get older they need to know who they belong to. Like goslings.'

'Like what?'

'Baby geese – and ducklings. When they pop out of their eggs it's important that their moms are the first creatures they see because that's how they know who they belong to. If their mothers are out of sight and they first lay eyes on the farmer instead, then as far as these little newborns are concerned, he's their mother. It's called bondin', and it's very important.'

'Nobody said that to us in the maternity hospital or the ante-natal classes.'

'They don't always,' Amy agreed, 'but to my mind they should. Some of 'em seem to take it for granted that new parents already know everythin'. I myself always told new mothers about goslings and ducklings. Bondin' between babies and parents is necessary because although it's good for kids to know other adults like the nice people who live here, think of the poor little souls we some-times read about in the papers who get coaxed away by strangers.' Then, as Layla began to get restless, Amy got to her feet.

'Someone's beginnin' to sound hungry, so I'd better let you get her home. It was great to meet you, Tricia, I hope we meet up again while I'm still here.'

'What on earth did you say to Tricia Borland?' Cissie Kavanagh wanted to know when she and Amy met each other a week later. 'She's suddenly started spending more time at home, or taking Layla with her when she goes out.'

'Oh, I just talked about parental bonding. The ducklings and goslings,' Amy told her airily, 'rather than the birds and the bees – obviously she already knows all about *them*.'

Twenty-Eight

'This is just like the old days,' Dolly Cowan said happily as she applied clown make-up to Cam Gordon's face. 'Once Harold and I teamed up I often did his clown make-up for him. Sometimes I really miss the fun of the circus!'

'It must have been great,' Cam agreed. 'Certainly better than working for a building firm. I'm having the time of my life this week – I'm even beginning to wonder if I can get Harold to teach me how to be a real clown.'

It was the middle of Festival Week, and because the weather had more than played its part, with warm sunny days throughout, Prior's Ford had been thronged with visitors since the festival was officially opened on the village green by Stephanie McDonald.

Cam had been ducking and diving all around the village and the estate since the start, and Harold had finally and reluctantly agreed to don his clown costume for one last time, but only on condition that he had to appear for just one day.

He was getting ready in the bedroom while Cam had donned his hired costume in the spare room, and as he knew nothing about the intricate art of clown make-up, Dolly was doing it for him.

Cam, determined to make the most of the one-day appearance, had plastered posters all over the village with the picture of a clown below the heading, 'Look out for the Clowns!' It went on to inform locals and visitors that two well-known clowns would be in and around Prior's Ford during the festival. 'Try to spot the clowns!' it said at the bottom of the posters.

The idea, Cam explained to the Cowans, was that he and Harold were going to spend most of that morning in the Linn Hall estate, ending with lunch in the unused flower room, and then sneak around the village throughout the afternoon, appearing and disappearing but never staying in the same place for long.

'Ewan's going to pick us up from the almshouses in his flatbed truck at ten o'clock. The almshouses being near the edge of the village, not many people will be about in that area at that time. He's going to drive us through the village, past the pub and into the estate. I've cleared it with Lewis; he knows that I'm one of the clowns and I've told him that the other one is a genuine clown who hires himself out as an entertainer.'

At this point in the explanation, Harold, who had a horror of ever becoming a children's entertainer, shuddered. Dolly put a sympathetic hand on his arm when Cam made things worse by finishing with, 'He'll never know who you really are – I said your name was Coco. I've brought a massive box filled with jelly babies so that we can toss them out to the crowd while we're being driven through the village. Jelly babies won't hurt anybody.'

'It's not going to work,' Harold protested. 'For one thing, I'm not as young as I used to be – I don't think I'm going to be good at appearing and disappearing and rushing away from people, especially kids. My work was within a circus ring, with the audience kept at a distance.'

'We'll be fine,' Cam assured him blithely. 'Just make sure that you stay with me. We'll make some appearances here and there and when you've had enough I'll contact Ewan and he'll pick us up in the truck and drive us back to the village, where he'll slow down at one point to let me jump out of the truck. While all the kids chase me, Ewan will keep going and drive you to the farm. Nobody can follow him farther than the farm lane and he'll drive the truck right inside a barn where you can change into the clothes we've stored there and wander back into the village to meet Dolly.'

'It's going to end in disaster,' Harold told Dolly when they were alone. 'I like Cam, but I'm not sure that he's really thought this through.'

'It'll be fine,' she soothed. 'You'll look back on it when it's all over and be glad that you did it!'

But now that the day had arrived she found herself wondering if she had been wrong to coax Harold to become a clown for one last time. 'You will look after Harold, won't you?' she asked Cam anxiously.

'Of course I will. We're going to be the talk of the village for months to come. We're going to be the festival's main attraction!'

'I hope so.' She stepped back. 'That's your make-up finished.'

Cam rushed to the mirror, as he had done every morning that week. 'Wow! Is that me?' he said – as he had done every morning that week. And then, as the door opened to reveal Harold in full garb and make-up. 'Double Wow!'

Dolly took one look at her husband and fell in love with him all over again. As far as she was concerned, there was, and always would be, something about clowns . . .

'You look terrific, Harold,' she said, 'You're going to be a smash hit.'

His mouth was a wide crimson smile, but his voice, when he said, 'I don't know about that,' was gloomy.

Amy had thrown herself into Festival Week with great enthusiasm. 'I've never been involved in anything like this,' she told Clarissa and Alastair, 'and it's going to be a great thing to tell folks when I get back home! Patsy's gonna kick herself for not bein' here!'

So far, she had helped on various stalls, welcomed people to

the art and photography exhibitions in the Village Hall, and
now she and Hannah Gibbs were on their way to the Linn Hall
estate, where they had both volunteered to be on duty in the
tea tent.

The Main Street was packed with people and there were
balloons everywhere, some being held by children or tied to
prams, some floating overhead, globes of colour drifting up towards
the blue sky above. It was no surprise when the two women lost
contact with each other as they eased their way along. 'I'll see
you at Linn Hall if we don't meet up before then,' Hannah had
said as a family group pushing their way determinedly along the
street came between them.

'Fine,' Amy called, and kept going until she met up with Tricia
Borland.

'Hello, Amy, I was hoping we'd see you,' the young woman
beamed at her. 'I've told Derek all about how helpful you were,
and I wanted you to meet him – where is he?' She stretched
up on tiptoe to look around. 'Oh, there they are! Derek, over
here!'

A young man carrying Layla in a front-facing sling against his
chest eased his way towards them, one arm protecting the baby.
'Hi!'

'Derek, this is Amy, the lady I told you about – the one who
explained about ducklings,' Tricia said, and he grinned and shook
Amy's hand vigorously.

'I'm very pleased to meet you, Miss – Mrs—'

'Mrs Amy Rose, but I prefer to be known as Amy.'

'Amy – I wanted to thank you for your advice to Tricia. She
found it really interesting, and so did I – if you know what I
mean.'

Amy did know what he meant. As they struggled together
through the crowds Hannah had told her what an attentive mother
Tricia had become, no longer constantly expecting her neighbours
to keep an eye on her baby. 'I think that Derek is delighted,'
Hannah had added, 'now that Tricia's always home when he
finishes work instead of being off with friends.'

Now Amy told the young man, 'Oh, it was fun talkin' to your
lovely wife and daughter. Hi, Layla, are you havin' a good time?'

Layla had been peering around at all the people passing by; at the sound of her name she glanced at Amy, and suddenly her little face was wreathed in smiles. 'Ganga!'

'Look, Derek, she remembers Amy!' Tricia was delighted. 'She's really getting to know people now.'

Derek's attention was suddenly focused on a flatbed truck easing its way slowly along the busy road. 'We'd better get on to the pavement,' he said, and shepherded the two women before him. They reached the pavement just before the truck crept past. 'Look,' Derek said, pointing. 'It's carrying those two clowns we've heard about! Look, Layla.'

He eased the sling up to give the baby a better look while Tricia told him hurriedly, 'Derek, be careful! We don't want her to get bonded with clowns – it could mark her for life!'

But Layla had already seen the colourful figures in the back of the truck. One of the clowns, the one tossing handfuls of jelly babies out to the children in the crowd, waved at her and she frowned back, clearly unsure of this weird colourful being. Then as her gaze moved to the second clown, Amy noticed her eyes widen and the frown fade. She watched closely as the baby leaned forward as though struggling to get out of the sling. 'Da!' she cooed, and reached out both arms, a smile lighting up her little face.

Then the truck moved forward and Layla turned as far as she could to stare after it.

Amy found it all very interesting.

By noon the volunteer staff working in the tea tent on the Linn Hall lawn were being kept busy between keeping their customers happy and hurrying to and fro between the marquee and the Hall itself, where Fliss and Jinty were on duty in the dining room, dealing with requests for more food and more cutlery and dishes.

'Amy, would you mind taking this hamper to the flower room?' Alma Parr asked. 'It's some lunch for our two clowns – they're supposed to be on the estate at the moment and they'll be getting hungry.'

'No problem, if you can tell me where to find this flower room.'

'You'll find the door round the corner of the Hall, on the drive leading to the back of the house. The flower room has two doors, one opening on to the drive, the other into the house, both locked. It's got counters and cupboards and a big sink in it; in the good old days the gardeners used to deliver cut flowers to that room so that the lady of the house could come through the interior door to arrange vases of flowers for her maids to place around the house. Here's the key.' She handed over a large old-fashioned one. 'Make sure you lock the room again when you leave. One of the clowns has another key so that they can get in to have their lunch in peace and then lock the door behind them when they leave.'

Amy was hurrying along the front of the Hall when a clown suddenly appeared round the corner, running for his life and being pursued by some half-dozen children. 'I'll be glad when this festival's over,' he panted as he dashed past her. Then the children were flowing around her like a river around a boulder and she had to hold the hamper tightly as she was buffeted.

There were some more children at the side of the house, arguing with each other. 'The other one went that way,' one said, pointing towards the back of the house, while another said, 'I think he's in among the bushes!'

'You're both wrong, kids,' said Amy, who had caught sight of a flash of colour deep in the shrubbery at the side of the drive. 'I've just seen two clowns. One was running along the front of the house and the other one was heading across the lawns. If you're quick you might catch one of 'em at least.'

As they vanished round the side of the house she crossed the drive, put the hamper down and plunged into the shrubbery, pushing her way through until she found the missing clown, crouched beside some rhododendrons and trying to get deeper among them as she approached.

'Mornin', Harold, it's me, Amy Rose. I've brought your lunch an' if you're quick we can get across the drive and into hidin' before anyone else appears.'

As the clown rose slowly from the bushes she turned and fought her way back to the drive, looking to left and right. 'All quiet,' she reported. 'Let's go!'

By the time he reached her the key was out of her pocket and in the lock. She stepped aside to let him throw himself into the flower room, then followed him in and shut and locked the door while he collapsed on to one of the two wooden chairs, gasping for breath.

'Well now, this is a bit of history,' Amy observed, looking with interest around the room. 'Imagine havin' an entire room given up to just arrangin' flowers – talk about how the other half lived!'

'I'm going to strangle Cam Gordon,' wheezed the clown.

'Is that who it was? You don't want to hurt him, Harold – he was drawin' most of the kids away from you.' Amy had started unpacking the hamper. 'You'll feel better after you've had this nice lunch. Hey, there's even a bottle of wine here – just a small one, but enough for a glass each to cheer you up and ready you for the afternoon.'

'How did you know it was me?'

'A little bird told me – a cute little bird by the name of Layla.'

He groaned. 'I thought she recognized me when I was in the truck.'

'There's something about you, Harold, that that kid really loves. I've got to get back to the tea tent, but before I go, tell me what made you decide to dress up as a clown for the festival?'

'Cam – and Dolly.'

'Why did Dolly want you to do it?'

He had been slumped in the chair, but now he drew himself up. 'Because I *was* a clown. This is my outfit and my make-up; I was the great Mr Magnifico – but very few people know about Dolly and me being circus people, so I would appreciate it if you kept my secret.'

'If there's one thing I'm very good at – although I'm very good at others as well – it's keepin' a secret. How do you do, Mr Magnifico.' Amy held her hand out and Harold got to his feet and shook it. 'It's an honour to meet you. And now,' she said, making for the door, 'I'd better get back to the tea tent. Cam will be along any minute now. You'll be quite safe – I can lock the door on my way out because he's got a key. Enjoy your lunch.'

As she reached the door she turned, grinning. 'I love this village to bits,' she said. 'Every time I think I know it all, it throws another surprise at me!'

Prior's Ford's very first Festival Week ended on Friday, and on the following evening the entire village was invited to a festival party at Linn Hall. Of necessity, it had to be held in the two marquees as the house was not yet fit for a party, and also of necessity it had to be a 'bring-your-own-food-and-drink' occasion, but nobody minded that other than Cynthia McBain, who felt that it was 'rather demeaning to eat one's own food and drink one's own drink in a tent,' but attended nevertheless, having been told by her husband that she could stay home if she wanted, but he was definitely going to enjoy the party.

'This would be a great idea for our wedding,' Ginny said to Lewis as the two of them joined the people strolling about the lawns. 'We could hire the marquees again and use them for the reception.'

'I don't think your mother would like that.'

'I know she wouldn't, that's why I think it would be a great idea.'

'As that particular day is going to be the happiest day in my life, and hopefully in your life, and as we're about to spend a lot of money on getting the old place looking good again, let's make your mother happy too, and just go ahead with the planned reception in Linn Hall's magnificently restored public rooms.'

'Yes,' Ginny said contentedly as Rowena Chloe came running across the grass towards them, 'let's just do that!'